YESTERDAY CRUMB

AND THE STORM IN A TEACUP

YESTERDAY CRUMB

AND THE STORM IN A TEACUP

ANDY SAGAR

Orion

ORION CHILDREN'S BOOKS

First published in Great Britain in 2022
by Hodder & Stoughton

3 5 7 9 10 8 6 4

Text copyright © Andy Sagar, 2022
Illustrations © Marine Gosselin, 2022

A CIP catalogue record for this book
is available from the British Library.

ISBN 978 1 510 10948 3

Typeset in Sabon by Jouve (UK), Milton Keynes
Printed and bound in Great Britain by Clays Ltd, Elcograf S.p.A.

The paper and board used in this book
are made from wood from responsible sources.

Orion Children's Books
An imprint of
Hachette Children's Group
Part of Hodder & Stoughton Limited
Carmelite House
50 Victoria Embankment
London EC4Y 0DZ

An Hachette UK Company
www.hachette.co.uk

www.hachettechildrens.co.uk

For my mum and dad,
who taught me
that magic is priceless

Prologue

Upon a snowy winter's night, in an old Northern town called Sorrow-by-the-Moor, a door appeared where it had not been before.

Most doors have the courtesy to attach themselves to a house, or a school, or a museum, but this door was not nearly so well-mannered. It floated a few inches above the cobblestones, as if held there by strings, its wood coloured the warm brown of very strong tea.

The door slowly creaked open. A lady stepped out, wreathed in the aromas of cinnamon and gingerbread. She wore a dress like woven candyfloss. Her butterscotch-blonde hair tumbled from beneath a pointed hat around her rosy-pink cheeks. Her eyes were the colour of lavender. Upon her shoulder was a raven with sugar-white feathers.

'Over to you,' said the lady, hands on hips as she cast her gaze around the town square. The raven flapped on to a streetlamp. 'The shop needs me like a kitchen needs a kettle, and I've been away for long enough as it is.'

'This is all stuff and nonsense, Miss Dumpling,' said the raven, anxiously preening his feathers. 'Are you quite sure about this . . . *project* of yours?'

Miss Dumpling plucked a pink teacup from thin air, plumes of steam drifting from the amber liquid inside. 'It is a truth universally acknowledged that a witch in possession of great magic *must* be in want of an apprentice.'

While the raven muttered something under his breath, Miss Dumpling knelt upon a snow-covered flowerbed. She plunged her hand into the earth below, bringing up a pinch of soil. After sprinkling the soil into her tea, she drank it down in one go. For a moment, she blinked very rapidly. Then she smiled, feeling the magic at work. Her tongue had turned honey-gold in colour.

First, Miss Dumpling spoke to a sycamore tree (she was usually only fluent in oak and willow). Sadly, it was very old, and it no longer paid attention to the business of humans.

Second, she addressed the wind, but it was far too excitable and did not give her a straight answer.

Third, she consulted with a statue outside the church. It raised its stone top hat to her, and then pointed towards some circus tents on the edge of town.

Miss Dumpling beamed and thanked the statue. 'You're all set up with directions,' she said to the bird. 'Now, shall you do as I have asked, or must I find a new familiar who *will*?'

After a pause, the raven let out a prim sigh. 'I've never failed you before, and I don't plan to start today.'

With a wink, Miss Dumpling disappeared through the tea-coloured door, and left the raven grumbling and groaning as he set off towards the circus tents.

Meanwhile, curious little creatures were watching from the shadows. They nervously peered out from alleys and sewers, behind dustbins and under motorcars, all fur and feathers and horns and claws. They were whispering breathlessly amongst themselves.

'*By Oberon, don't you know who that was?*'

'*Of course I do! Does it mean what I think it means?*'

'*Oh, yes! It means Dwimmerly End is on its way. Dwimmerly End is coming to town!*'

Chapter One

Yesterday's Dreams

There was once a girl named Yesterday Crumb, and that was not even the most peculiar thing about her. For one, she lived and worked in a travelling circus, even though she was only twelve years old. For another, her hair was the colour of pumpkins, fiercer than any shade of ginger you have ever seen before, while her skin was so pale it was almost silver.

Oddest of all, instead of ordinary human ears, she had the pointed ears of a fox, reddish-brown and tipped at the end with the black of burnt toast. They poked out from her tangle of hair, and even though they were fairly small, any vixen worth her claws would tell you they promised to be marvellous in the future.

She spent her days curled in the corner of her iron cage, gawked at by circus patrons who paid good money to see the girl with the fox ears. She slept there, on a bed of straw; she ate there; she lived and played and dreamed there, with no friends save for the donkey who pulled her cage whenever the circus travelled to a new town.

'Would you look at those ears!' said a young lady in the crowd, tapping on her husband's shoulder.

Yesterday was bathed in the yellow light of a sign which read, *Yesterday Crumb, the Amazing Fox Girl!* Snow was starting to fall, but she was clad in a simple white dress. And, although it was against the rules, she had wrapped herself in a tattered brown blanket.

'You don't suppose they're real, do you?' the lady continued. 'Surely they're glued on or some such.'

The gentleman leaned in and studied her ears, as if Yesterday were a specimen in a museum gallery and not a girl with thoughts and feelings and a heart that could ache. 'Hm. Look pretty real to me.'

'What an odd little thing she is,' said the lady, barely suppressing a shudder.

I can hear you, you know! thought Yesterday. *I'm not called the Amazing Fox Girl for nothing, even if these ears do ruin just about everything else.*

She held her tongue, the constellation of bruises on her arm a reminder of what had happened the last time she had insulted a circus patron.

Instead, she tried to ignore the voices, and disappear into her one and only book. It was only small, no bigger than her palm, and was practically falling apart these days. The title on the front cover read *The Pocket Book of Faeries* and there was a picture of a man with dragonfly wings underneath.

It was a kind of storybook, written like a birdwatcher's guide, only for made-up creatures rather than real ones. Even so, every time Yesterday read it, she pretended that such creatures really existed. That there were river trolls who lived under bridges and feasted on moss and syrup for their supper. That there were pixies the size of toadstools who were born every time someone fell in love. That there were goblins who travelled the world with their markets, trading their wares in exchange for your earliest memories or the last years of your life.

Yesterday flipped open the cover, lingering briefly on the torn fragment of paper that should have been the book's first page. All that was left of it was a little scrap in the corner, on which her name, *Yesterday,* was written, and nothing more.

The book had been found by Yesterday's side, her only possession, when the ringmaster had discovered her as a baby outside his tent twelve years earlier. Yesterday often wondered who had left her the book and had written her name in it, and if it was the same person who had left her all alone at the circus, but finding out the answers to such questions was not a luxury afforded to the Amazing Fox Girl.

Yesterday sat and read all evening until finally a grumpy-looking man in a top hat and a dirty crimson jacket came over and slotted his key into the cage's lock.

'Grubs up, Crumb,' grunted Ringmaster Skelm, who was not well-known for his friendly manner.

Crumb was the surname he had given to Yesterday since, in Skelm's opinion, she was so small and obviously unwanted by whoever had left her behind.

'I'm not hungry,' said Yesterday, refusing to look up from her book.

'You'll do as you're told, girl,' the ringmaster said, baring his teeth. 'Or you'll have no dinner for three nights. Do you understand? Are you listening to me?'

Yesterday was not, in fact, listening in the slightest. She was completely lost in her book, as ever. Besides, she was sick of the same boring old turnip soup he fed them every day. It was hardly worth standing up for.

'Will you get your nose out of that thing for once!' Skelm bellowed.

'It's called a book, Ringmaster Skelm.' Yesterday sighed, turning a page. 'You might try reading one someday.'

Skelm's expression twisted into a sneer. 'You and that *book*. Forget your dreams and stories,' he said to her. 'Girls like you don't go on adventures. You don't end up with happily-ever-afters. You're no elegant princess, winning the heart of a prince . . .'

Yesterday tapped her chin thoughtfully. 'Fine by me. What would I do with the heart of a prince, anyway? Wear it on a necklace? If that's your idea of a happily-ever-after, you can keep it. Besides, this isn't that kind of book.'

Skelm gritted his teeth. 'I don't care what kind of book it is. You belong to this circus, and a circus attraction is all you'll ever be.'

Yesterday fixed him with one of her fiercest glares. 'And the ringmaster of a tacky circus, who picks on little girls just to feel important, is all *you'll* ever be. Now, would you mind disappearing?' she said airily, eyes returning to her book. 'You're eating into my reading time.'

There was a moment of agonising silence as Skelm's face contorted into a snarl. 'See what your attitude gets you, you little horror,' he growled at last. 'Nothing, that's what.'

And with that, he locked the door again and put the key in his pocket before storming off.

Yesterday gave another sigh, a prisoner once more. She looked out at the world beyond her cage. Paper lanterns twinkled among the circus tents, lanterns which she liked to imagine were jewels in a dragon's hoard. She watched as the remaining circus patrons lingered around the closing tents, snapping up their last toffee apples, marvelling at the acrobats' final performance, begging for their fortunes to be told by a yawning Madame Zufarru.

Soon they would return to their normal lives in the town of Sorrow-by-the-Moor. They'd go back to their normal homes and families, their hot dinners and warm, comfortable beds.

The light illuminating her cage was extinguished, making it difficult to read comfortably. Yesterday slumped back against the cage's bars. She glanced at *The Pocket Book of Faeries*. 'Maybe I would have had a normal life too,' she said to no one in particular, 'if I hadn't been born with these ridiculous ears.'

'Why do young people always think being *normal* would solve all their problems?' said a voice.

Yesterday sat bolt upright in her cage. She looked all around her, trying to work out where the voice was coming from.

'Then, the next minute, they're desperate to be *special*!' the voice went on. 'Being contradictory is a pitiful way to live one's life, if you ask me.'

Yesterday looked up. Perched on top of her cage was a raven, his white feathers shimmering in the moonlight.

'Don't you know it's polite to reply when one is spoken to?' the raven chided. 'Standards are slipping these days. They really are!'

Yesterday stared at the bird. *I must have fallen asleep at some point*, she thought. *I must be dreaming.* 'I beg your pardon,' she said, playing along with the dream, 'but I think you just *talked*.'

'What incredible powers of observation you command!' the raven squawked. 'I wonder what great discovery you'll make next. Perhaps you shall tell me that rain is wet, or that sphinxes riddle? Stand up straight, now, and remember your manners.'

Yesterday grudgingly got to her feet. 'Make out that I'm stupid all you like. But it's not exactly every day you meet a talking raven!'

'A raven, indeed!' the bird snapped. 'I may have been born a raven – we all have a past – but I am so much more than that now. I am a *familiar* and I must insist that you respect my title. I had to achieve all sorts of qualifications from the Royal College to get it. And I have a name, you know – a very fine one at that. It is Madrigal.'

'Oh, right. Well, I'm sorry, but there really was no way of me knowing,' Yesterday pointed out. She added, 'My name is Yesterday Crumb.'

Madrigal looked her up and down. 'Yesterday?' he echoed. 'How preposterous. A foolish name, if you want my opinion. A foolish name for a fool girl.'

Yesterday folded her arms. She was rapidly abandoning any desire to be civil. 'If you want *my* opinion—' She stopped abruptly. Her heart skittered as a thought came to her. 'Wait a minute, did you say you were a . . . *familiar*?'

She fumbled for *The Pocket Book of Faeries*. She had definitely seen that word before.

As she flipped frantically through the pages, Madrigal went on. 'Why of course I am a familiar! Anyone with a slightest bit of sense could have told you that. I am so very different from any ordinary raven that you might as well call me a *not*-raven, much as a "cat" familiar is a not-cat, and a "toad" familiar is a not-toad. There are conventions to these things, you see.'

Yesterday reached the right page of *The Pocket Book of Faeries*. '*Entry Sixty-Three: Familiar*,' she read out loud, squinting to read in the darkness. '*Animals who spend a great deal of time in the company of faeries often develop magical powers of their own, including speech and low-level bewitchments, making them excellent companions for witches . . .*'

She looked up at Madrigal, wide-eyed. 'You're a familiar,' she said. 'You're talking to me . . .' She glanced down at her book again, then back up at Madrigal. 'That's impossible. *This* is impossible. Completely and totally impossible!'

She truly hoped that he would prove her wrong.

'What a small mind you have,' squawked the not-raven, 'throwing around words like *impossible* as if they mean anything at all. Look at me, fool-girl, and listen. I am talking. I am a familiar. I am, you will agree, not simply possible – I am real.'

'If you *were* a familiar,' Yesterday argued, feeling as though her whole world was being turned inside out, 'that would make you a faerie, wouldn't it? Which would mean faeries exist. But faeries can't exist! Everyone knows that! This has to be a dream. It *has* to be.'

Madrigal tutted at her. 'This certainly isn't a dream, and faeries certainly exist. Who do you think ensures the seasons change when they should? Who do you think put the moon in the sky? Queen Victoria?'

The familiar chortled to himself, though Yesterday wasn't sure she got the joke. She wanted to tell him how peculiar he sounded. Then again, she was holding a conversation with a talking bird, so it was a little late to start calling things peculiar now.

Madrigal glanced around the circus and cawed disapprovingly. 'What a dismal place the world would be if it belonged only to humans. You know, it was *humans* who hunted down their most magical people and drove them into the realms of faeries all those years ago.'

'Our most magical?' Yesterday flicked through her book again, landing on a page with a picture of a man with horns sprouting from his head and a broomstick in his hand. 'You mean . . . *witches*?'

Madrigal peered at her book. 'Of course I mean witches! After they ran away from your ugly human cities and into the faerie kingdoms, witches soon became more faerie than human. Lucky them. Quite the improvement, I'd say. But why am I telling *you* all this? You should know it by heart. Every young witch learns this story in their crib . . .'

Yesterday blinked. 'What did you say?'

'I said, all young witches learn this in . . . wait. Surely you know you're a witch at least, don't you?'

Yesterday said nothing. She just stared. Madrigal groaned. 'For Oberon's sake,' he said. 'You have ears like that, and you couldn't figure it out? You even have *The Pocket Book of Faeries*! What does that volume say about witches, fool-girl?'

With trembling hands, Yesterday glanced down at the page. Her voice was shaking as she read out loud. '*After witches were forced out of human society, they reconnected with the magic of the wild. This soon evolved into a physical manifestation of certain animal features, like hooves, horns, pointed ears, snouts . . .*'

Madrigal cocked his head at her. 'You read that and never linked it to your own ears? A fool-girl, and how!'

Yesterday reached for her fox ears, touching their furry tips tentatively. 'I always thought my ears were only good for getting me the wrong sort of attention,' she muttered. 'If faeries are real, how come I've never seen one before? And how come I can't do magic? If I were a witch with magical powers, I would have broken out of this cage, for a start.'

'Everyone knows what happens if you spend too long in the human world, away from magic,' Madrigal said. 'Well, everyone except you, it seems. You *lose* it. You become a strangeling.'

'A . . . a what?' Yesterday asked. *That* word certainly wasn't in her book.

'I am not a librarian whom you can pester for answers to every little question,' said Madrigal. 'You want to know more? Ask Miss Dumpling yourself. We must hurry now.'

'Who's Miss Dumpling?' asked Yesterday.

Madrigal ignored the question. Instead, he swooped down and waved a weary wing over the padlock on Yesterday's cage. A second later, it melted. The metal trickled down the bars and on to the ground. It had been turned into golden honey, as one might drizzle into tea.

'Impossibler and impossibler,' said Yesterday, so startled that she forgot proper grammar.

Madrigal was already spreading his wings. 'Follow

closely, little fool-girl. Madrigal the familiar waits for no one!'

With a flourish of his white feathers, the not-raven flapped up into the air, and soared off towards the forest that grew beyond the circus's boundaries.

Carefully, Yesterday pushed open the cage door. Her heart was thundering against her ribs. She fetched her satchel from the corner and stowed her book inside. Then, slinging it over her shoulder and pulling her blanket more tightly around her like a cape, she took a deep, deep breath.

And she stepped out of her cage.

Yesterday felt electric as her first taste of freedom coursed through her veins. Quite without meaning to, she began to laugh.

But it was too early to celebrate her escape. She darted away from the cage, creeping between the tents as she headed towards the forest, keeping an eye out for Ringmaster Skelm.

At the edge of the circus grounds was a wrought-iron fence separating her from the forest beyond. As she placed a foot on to the first rung, she heard shouting. She peered back over her shoulder.

'Yesterday!' Skelm roared, charging after her, his voice bellowing through the whole circus. 'Yesterday

Crumb, come back here now, you wandering good-for-nothing!'

'Goodbye, Ringmaster Skelm,' said Yesterday defiantly. And without a second thought, she climbed over the fence and disappeared into the forest.

Chapter Two

A Splinter of Ice

'Madrigal?' Yesterday cried as she hurried deeper and deeper into the woods, her blanket billowing around her. If Skelm was trying to pursue her, she had long since lost him in the darkness. Shafts of moonlight speared through gaps in the trees and glistened upon fresh snow. Leafless branches gnarled overhead like spider legs, veiling the snow with deep blue shadows.

'Hurry up, fool-girl,' came the familiar's voice from somewhere up ahead, echoing through the trees. 'I have responsibilities to attend to. Important duties!'

'You have wings, I have legs – this isn't exactly *fair*,' said Yesterday, lumbering through ankle-deep snowfall. It was hard to work out exactly which direction his voice was coming from. 'Madrigal, slow down! This isn't funny!' she called into the forest. 'Madrigal, are you there?'

It seemed colder out here in the woods than it had done before. She buried her hands in her armpits to warm them up as she picked her way amongst the tangled, knotting roots.

Her blanket caught on a bramble bush and was ripped from her shoulders. 'Oh, great,' she mumbled, holding up the blanket, now torn in two clean pieces. She looked around at the crooked tree branches. Madrigal had almost certainly abandoned her. Now, she was going to freeze out here, lost and alone in the woods.

The frost gnawed at her arms and legs. 'I shouldn't have ever trusted that raven,' she said to herself, shivering. 'Or not-raven or whatever the right word is! How could I have been so gullible? Of course my fox ears don't make me a witch. He just thought he'd play a trick on me, didn't he?' She sighed and touched her ears. 'How long will it be until you two get me into trouble *again*?'

A sound crooned softly in the distance. Her skin bristled with goosebumps. A few steps closer and it grew louder: heartachingly beautiful music, coming from deep within the woodland. Yesterday paused for a moment, listening, her fox ears twitching, urging her towards it. With careful footsteps, she followed the sound of the melody.

Through branches waving in the breeze, she could make out a figure sitting on a tree stump, playing a white violin with purple-black strings. As she drew closer, the figure suddenly looked up, and she saw eyes of cold silver, like the edge of a dagger's blade.

Terror seized at her chest and she turned to retreat in the opposite direction.

Words came from behind. Her fox ears tingled.

'Going so soon?'

The music grew louder. Her legs seemed not to be obeying her any more. Her feet swivelled around and carried her back to the violin player, back to those eyes of glinting silver.

'Little cub, we must get you out of this frightful cold,' said the violin player, as he fixed his steely eyes on her. 'You might catch a deathly chill.'

The gentleman's long hair was as silver as his eyes and skin, glittering in the moon's pale glow. Framed by the lapels of his ghost-grey suit, a large iron key swung from a chain around his neck.

'Excuse me?' said Yesterday, with a frown. 'Who exactly are you?'

'I am Mr Weep,' the man said, inclining his head. 'A humble man of business. A man of contracts and deals and bringing wishful souls their heart's desires.' He smiled, and put down his violin. 'Perhaps there is something I can do for you?'

'Um, no, thanks,' said Yesterday, carefully hiding her ears beneath her hair. 'I'm actually looking for a white bird, have you seen him?'

'You mean the familiar? They are an ever-so quarrelsome bunch,' said Mr Weep. He tutted under his breath. 'Always full of mischief, like tricking lonely girls into thinking their fox ears make them special, just so they can leave them in the woods for a spot of fun.'

Yesterday winced. Had he heard her talking, just a moment ago? 'Everyone always makes fun of my ears,' she said. 'It was ridiculous of me to think he was any different.'

The silver-haired man's smile grew. 'You know,' said Mr Weep, 'a dear friend of mine had ears just like yours and I must say I find them quite remarkable.'

Yesterday blinked at him, then looked down at the ground. 'I'm not sure *remarkable* is the word I'd use.'

One of Mr Weep's eyebrows rose and curled like a serpent. 'Well, I am sorry to hear that. I know a place where ears like that are considered the height of fashion! You could come with me there, if you like.'

Yesterday felt a flicker of temptation. 'Really?'

'Oh, yes!' he said, standing and moving towards her. 'You could attend the most fabulous parties and brush shoulders with kings and gods and things greater than gods. You could have a dozen ladies-in-waiting, to braid ivy into your hair and bring you all the latest gossip; you could have two dozen hounds, to perform tricks for your amusement and gobble up your enemies; you could have three dozen knights, to defend your name and compose fine operas in your honour.'

Sounds a bit nicer than a cage, Yesterday thought.

Mr Weep's smile was only growing and growing, yet somehow it never reached his eyes.

Yesterday came to herself. 'I can't,' she said firmly. 'I don't mean to be rude, but strange men who hang around in dark forests at night are probably top of the list of people you're not meant to wander off with.'

Mr Weep laughed, took a step back, and bowed. 'Of course,' he said softly. He plucked a couple of strings on his violin. Yesterday suddenly felt dazed and drowsy. 'I understand entirely. But before you go off on your marvellous adventure, let me make another offer. While I find those ears of yours charming, it seems you find them bothersome. I could remove them very easily, if you'd like.'

Hope blossomed in Yesterday's soul, in spite of herself. If she had ordinary ears, it wouldn't matter that the not-raven had abandoned her. She could go and build a new life for herself anywhere she liked, free of people pointing and calling her names, full of possibility and promise.

'Could you really do that?' she found herself asking.

'Naturally. I am Mr Weep,' he said, checking his fingernails for dirt. 'I am capable of extraordinary things. Would you like to see?'

Mr Weep clapped his hands, and the bare branches of the forest bloomed in an eruption of flowers and leaves. Yesterday gasped as butterflies swirled around her and the air became fragrant with the scent of meadows in summer.

Then Mr Weep clapped again. The flowers crumpled and the butterflies struck the ground, wings shattering like glass. The leaves browned and fell to the earth. Tendrils of ice spread across the branches like frozen cobwebs.

Yesterday was speechless. Madrigal had turned her padlock to honey, but this man could play with the seasons as effortlessly as he played his violin. *Maybe he really could take away my ears,* she thought excitedly. Then, fear tangled with her excitement and turned it hollow.

'And what exactly do you want in exchange?' she asked.

Mr Weep looked thoughtful. 'In exchange? Oh, nothing much. Those pesky ears, first and foremost. Shall we put things in writing, to ease any concerns?'

He unfurled a roll of paper from nowhere, then handed her a quill.

'I really should read the terms before I sign,' Yesterday said, feeling very sensible. '*I, Yesterday Crumb, do hereby grant Mr Weep permission to remove the fox ears I find so very loathsome . . .*'

She started reading through the rest, although it was long and full of complicated legal words, and she struggled to make sense of it. She could hear Mr Weep tapping his foot impatiently next to her.

A moment later, he swiped the paper from her hands. 'Look, now, if you are going to waste my time by reading every single little detail, I think I should find someone more willing to take advantage of my generosity!'

'No, please,' said Yesterday, her stomach sinking. 'I'm more than happy to sign.'

'Hm, I suppose you can have another chance,' he

said, presenting her with the contract once more. 'But I don't have all day, you know.'

She signed her name quickly before he could change his mind again and the quill disappeared from her hand, along with the paper.

Mr Weep's smile twisted into a smirk. 'Very good, dear little Yesterday. Very good, indeed.'

A sudden pain stabbed at Yesterday's heart. She shrieked in agony and stumbled backwards, clutching her chest. 'What did you just *do* to me?' she gasped.

Mr Weep's voice echoed all around her. 'A curse,' he said languidly. 'To be precise, I have placed a splinter of ice in your heart. In one month's time, when the sun sets on the winter solstice, the longest night of the season, it will freeze your heart entirely, and you will die.'

'I'll *what*?' shouted Yesterday. 'But that isn't what we agreed! You were supposed to take my ears away!'

'And I will!' insisted Mr Weep. 'The Land of the Dead, as you will soon discover, is a place without difference. All those who live there lose what made them unique in life. Their features become blurred, their faces blank, their hair dull and grey. And you, dear Yesterday, shall lose your fox ears and finally look just like everyone else.'

'Why would you do something like that?' she demanded.

'The best games have the most dangerous stakes,' said Mr Weep calmly. 'You could always try to break the curse, of course. I *do* so like a challenge.' He chuckled viciously. 'What do you say, Yesterday? Are you up for my wicked old game?'

'Fool-girl! What are you doing?' a voice squawked. Madrigal swooped over to her, flapping in mid-air. 'Don't you know who you are speaking to? This man is a wicked, wretched crook! Get away from him right now!'

'Madrigal! Please, you have to help me,' said Yesterday. 'He tricked me and put a splinter of ice in my heart!'

The not-raven's eyes widened. 'You scoundrel!' he said to Mr Weep. 'Do you have no respect for the ancient laws? You have no right in this world, none at all – this girl is meant for Miss Dumpling, not for you!'

Mr Weep simply waved a hand dismissively. 'Take her, for all I care,' he said, smugness dripping from his words. 'I've made my gambit and the game is mine.'

'Be gone, demon!' Madrigal squawked, diving towards Mr Weep with his claws extended, but they found only air and falling snow.

Mr Weep had vanished, the sound of his laughter dancing amongst the trees.

Yesterday held her chest and winced hard. The pain seemed to be dying down a little, yet the shock was still immense.

'Come quickly, fool-girl,' said Madrigal, gesturing with his wing for her to follow him onwards. 'There's no time to waste. Miss Dumpling will know what to do with you. Oh, if only she hadn't wasted her last witching key . . .'

Yesterday froze. Could she trust him again? What choice did she have? She hurried after the not-raven, the shadows of the forest much darker now. Thistles pricked her ankles and branches blocked her path.

'Through here,' said Madrigal, disappearing into a gap between two trees.

Something glimmered up ahead. Yesterday hurried towards it, until she found herself in an open glade.

Standing before her was a tall, slender, somewhat wobbly-looking building.

Yesterday had to blink a few times. She wasn't sure if her eyes were up to no good.

Because the strange, wobbly building wasn't just hidden in the middle of the woods. It was also mounted on what looked like a pair of enormous flamingo legs, as if it might run away at any moment.

Buttery light spilled from the windows, promising warmth and life within. It was as if someone had draped a quilt of flowers over the pretty white walls – pink roses, blue hydrangeas, and yellow hyacinths climbed out of flower boxes, almost completely covering the place, getting into every nook and cranny.

Painted in gold upon a lavender, teapot-shaped sign swinging above the door were the words DWIMMERLY END – TEASHOP, EST 1756. MAGIC IS PRICELESS.

'Come along, now,' said Madrigal, beating his wings above her. 'No time to lose!'

He swooped in through an open window, leaving Yesterday outside alone.

For a moment, Yesterday stood, slack-jawed, unable to move.

Then, she stepped carefully towards the teashop.

All sorts of baked marvels were on display in the windows. Her gaze was drawn to an elaborate silver cake topped with flowers made of icing. *Dreamcake,* said the label in looping letters. *Sweet dreams in every slice!* Beside it was a small plate of caramel-coloured cubes, with a label that read, *Caramels for Courage – candied valour. One bite and you'll be brave as a bluecap!* Next to them were *Muffins of Merrymaking – guaranteed joy is but a chocolate chip away!*

Above the mouth-watering display of cakes and pastries and bread loaves, Yesterday noticed an old, somewhat faded sign in the window, written in elegant handwriting. It read: *Help wanted. Payment offered in cake, lodging, and as much tea as one can drink.* It was signed – *Miss D*.

The teashop's flamingo legs lowered as if to make it easier for Yesterday to climb the small flight of steps that led up to its front door.

'Thank you,' she said uncertainly, as she walked up the steps and went inside.

And, as the door closed shut behind her, the old sign in the window vanished, as if it had been waiting for her for quite some time.

Chapter Three

Miss Dumpling's Travelling Teashop

Yesterday's nostrils were flooded with the scents of cinnamon, chocolate, and gingerbread as she walked through the teashop's door. Then, she stood, stock-still, gawping at what met her on the other side.

She had stepped into a room crowded with tables dressed in tablecloths of every colour and pattern, all with mismatched chairs: velvet-lined armchairs and rickety rocking chairs; chaise longues, couches, and old wooden benches; stools, floor cushions, and even a throne or two. It was as if whoever owned the place had grabbed any old bit of furniture off the street, spruced it up a little, and given it a home in the teashop.

On the left side was a fireplace with flames glittering in every colour of the rainbow, like fiery rubies and emeralds and sapphires. Yesterday's eyes were drawn to the wallpaper, which depicted scenes of winter: pine tree forests dotted with cottages pumping out swirls of smoke; little ice skaters on frozen lakes, their images actually in motion as they spun and glided across the wallpaper; a blanket of snow, ever drifting from the cloudy sky.

Her eyes followed the scenes on the wallpaper to a chalkboard menu hanging from the opposite wall, behind a glass-fronted counter. It offered Hawthorn of Hopefulness (*for souls in need of a guiding star*), Oracular Oolong (*for glimpsing the mysteries of tomorrow*), and Mindful Mint (*for freshening dull perspectives*).

Something shot past, stealing her attention. She let out a gasp. 'Was that a . . .' she began.

And it *was*.

It was a flying teapot. Yesterday looked up to see all sorts of teapots hovering overhead: pink and yellow teapots; teapots decorated with flowers; teapots shaped like dragons; teapots shaped like boots; and even a teapot shaped like an octopus, each tentacle a spout. Now and again, they would whizz around the room, contents sloshing over the sides, topping up any empty teacups that could be found on the tables.

Yet, for all the action going on, there did not seem to be any customers.

Or at least, if there were any customers, Yesterday couldn't see them – but she could *hear* them. Her fox ears stood upright, picking up on snippets of chatter and conversation, laughter and gossip.

'Where is everyone?' Yesterday asked out loud. An orange teapot drifted past, floating lazily to a row of shelves at the back, full of other teapots that appeared to be snoring.

'Strangelings,' sighed Madrigal from a podium by the front door. 'Funny how you can have your eyes wide open, and yet see nothing important at all.' He gestured with his wing to a teacup, which was waiting patiently on a small table beside the podium. 'Drink up. Miss Dumpling prepared this specially.'

There was that word again, *strangeling*. Cautious yet curious, Yesterday reached for the teacup and gave the purple-coloured liquid a sniff. It smelt of violets and lavender. The smell was so strong she almost sneezed.

'How do I know it isn't poison?' she said, eyeing him warily.

The not-raven scoffed.

'Don't act like it's a stupid question,' said Yesterday. 'The last time I trusted someone with magic, they put a deadly ice splinter in my heart, in case you forgot.'

'Why would I bother rescuing you from Mr Weep if I was planning on poisoning your tea afterwards?' said Madrigal. 'Do whatever you wish. But if you want to live, I advise you to drink the tea.'

Yesterday couldn't really argue with that logic. She put the cup to her lips and took a sip. It tasted just like it smelt, fresh and floral, and Yesterday instinctively downed the whole cup.

Almost instantly, she felt so dizzy she nearly lost her footing. She steadied herself. 'What just happened?' she said, putting down the teacup.

'You received a gift,' said Madrigal. 'See for yourself.'

With his beak, he offered her a silver spoon from one of the tables and Yesterday took it from him, gazing upon her reflection in the metal. While her right eye was still its usual pale green, the left had turned a peculiar shade of violet.

She lowered the spoon and gasped. The tearoom had changed.

She could now see that the place was bustling with customers, who must have been there all along. The customers were as varied and mismatched as the décor: some had horns, some had tails. Some had feathers for hair or claws for fingernails.

At one table, four short gentlemen with pig snouts

and protruding tusks, dressed in smoking jackets, were sharing treats from a three-tiered cake stand. One popped some fudge into his mouth and said to the table, 'I hear the Goblin Market is projected to make very healthy profits this year, even if the teardrop *has* plummeted against the pound,' while the others nodded sagely.

At another table was a pair of creatures that resembled great big rocks with glinting eyes and beards made of shining moss. They sipped from teacups, which looked preposterously small in their enormous hands. 'Isn't Jollifying Ginseng a delight?' one said, rumbling with apparently uncontrollable laughter. 'Always makes me whoop till I wheeze!'

On a windowsill were three tiny women, the size of a handspan, with butterfly wings splaying from their backs like miniature stained-glass windows. They sat around the edge of a steaming mug, dipping their toes into what looked like hot chocolate.

'Faeries *are* real!' said Yesterday, gazing around the room with delight. 'Those little women are pixies, aren't they?'

She recalled their entry in *The Pocket Book of Faeries*. Most humans thought all faeries were small people with wings, but that only described *pixies*; pixies were just one type of faerie, like a magpie is one type of bird.

'And those must be trolls,' she said of the rock creatures, '. . . and those men in suits are goblins . . . and . . . and . . . I can't believe everything I've read about is actually real!'

Madrigal sighed. 'Enough gawking. On you go, through the tearoom and into the kitchen. Miss Dumpling's expecting you, and it wouldn't do to keep a witch waiting.'

Yesterday hardly heard him. Everything she'd known, all her troubles, the ice in her heart – they had all been swept away in the wonder of what now lay before her. She wandered through the tearoom in a daze, stealing quick glances at the customers, not wanting to stare. Gradually, she made her way between the tables, heading towards a glass-fronted counter, which teemed with colourful cakes and pastries like *Chimera Creampuffs* and *Wishfruit Tarts* and *Luckberry Jam Scones*.

Behind the counter, next to the shelves of teapots, was a door cracked ajar. Written upon it in looping gold was the word *Kitchen*.

''Scuse me, miss!' said a cheerful voice. Yesterday ducked out the way as a boy, maybe a little older than she, with curly hair and deep-brown skin, came charging past. He wore a smart waistcoat and a ridiculous purple jacket, which flourished and billowed behind him. Just when it looked like they might collide, the boy tossed a tray stacked with cake and cutlery over her head, then caught it on the other side.

He looked back at Yesterday with a wink and a smirk. Yesterday arched a disapproving eyebrow at him, then blinked. Where his nose ought to have been was the grey-furred snout of a wolf. What's more, while his right eye was hazel, the left was lilac.

He's like me, she realised with a start. But the boy was already off, so she hurried on through the doorway to the kitchen, hungry for more marvels.

Cupboards and counters and a very large oven lined three of the four walls. The flour-dusted countertops brimmed with chopping boards and mixing bowls, and with strangely labelled ingredients, like a carton of scarlet-shelled *Phoenix Eggs* and a block of smoke-black *Dragon Butter*. On the left side was an open door to a pantry, while on the right was a door to who-knew-what. Above them, rolling pins and whisks and graters and saucepans floated in the air, just like the flying teapots.

Yesterday wandered beneath them, staring up in awe. 'It's not a dream,' she had to keep reminding herself. The thunderous beat of her heart against her chest was all the proof she needed. '*It's not a dream . . .*'

The far kitchen wall had a large window to the forest beyond. In front of it was a cosy-looking table, set with tea for two.

Something rustled in the far corner. Yesterday's eyes snapped in its direction. There, lying in a nest of tealeaves, was a very strange creature indeed. It was about the size of a dinner plate and looked a bit like a turtle – if turtles had teapots for shells. The shell itself was made of white porcelain and was decorated with painted yellow flowers. Sticking out of the sides were a handle and a spout, from which trailed feathers of steam.

When the teapot-turtle caught sight of Yesterday, it leapt up from its nest with a flourishing spin and swam through the air as if it were water. It blew a cheerful string of bubbles at Yesterday, rubbing its shell against her fox ears, and she gave a light giggle that echoed through the room. With a swoop, it soared over a trio of lidless teapots waiting expectantly on a kitchen counter, tipped on to its side, and filled them with boiling water from its spout as it flew past.

'I see you've met Pascal,' said a voice from behind.

Standing by the oven was a lady who hadn't been

there a second ago, holding a tray of steaming, buttery croissants. She was impossibly beautiful, her hair the very gold of Yorkshire butterscotch. She wore a candy-pink dress and a pointed hat to match. She smelt distinctly of gingerbread.

Pascal swam past Yesterday and over to the lady, who tickled his chin.

'I've never seen anything like him before,' said Yesterday.

'He's a tea spirit,' the lady said, as Pascal gave a cooing sound and floated back to his nest, 'and a rather charming one at that.'

Yesterday looked up at the woman. She was almost completely speechless. What she managed to come out with was: 'I'm sorry for barging in . . .'

'Nonsense, darling. You are Yesterday, am I correct? Fabulous name. We love a touch of drama around here. Allow me to introduce myself.' The lady cleared her throat and gave a theatrical bow. 'I am Miss Victoria Dumpling, tea witch extraordinaire and proprietor of Dwimmerly End, humbly and gorgeously at your service.'

Yesterday had no idea how this woman knew her name, but she was pleased that she did. Somehow, she just knew she could trust her.

'Oh, Miss Dumpling,' said Yesterday, feeling all the emotions of the day rushing up to the surface, 'I feel like I've been turned upside down. This morning I was just a girl who lived in a cage in a circus. Now I'm free, and everything I've ever dreamed of is true . . . there are faeries, and teashops with flamingo legs, and talking birds, and . . . and I might be a . . . I can't even say it out loud. It's just too amazing to be true. But then that horrible, awful Mr Weep tricked me and now when the solstice comes in just one month's time . . .'

'Now, now,' said Miss Dumpling, smiling kindly at her, 'let's not get ahead of ourselves. First things first, let's have a nice cup of tea. Call me biased, but to my mind, there's nothing that can't be solved with a pot of tea, a slice of cake, and a very dear friend.' She went and took a seat at the table by the window, beckoning for Yesterday to follow her.

Yesterday joined the witch, and two plates of chocolate cake miraculously appeared next to the two pink teacups and teapot that had been waiting there.

At a nod from Miss Dumpling, Pascal drifted over and filled the teapot with hot water, then swam back to his nest again.

Yesterday gazed greedily at the cake and tea. 'It

looks delicious,' she said. 'But I can't pay. I don't have any money.'

Miss Dumpling frowned, as if the remark had puzzled her. 'Don't worry about that,' she said, blowing on her tea. 'Magic is priceless, haven't you heard?'

Yesterday looked up at her, and smiled. She took a tentative bite of chocolate cake. The taste was rich and creamy and delicious enough to make all her worries feel like they were ten thousand miles away.

'Gorgeous teacups, aren't they?' Miss Dumpling went on, taking a sip from her own. 'Made from coral – a gift from the mermaid duchess of the River Thames herself. Oh, there I go, name-dropping. You must have endless questions for me, darling, so ask away!'

Yesterday indeed had a lot of questions to sort through. For some reason, the first one she asked was: 'What's a tea witch? I mean, I know what witches are and I know what tea is, but I've never heard of the two being put together.'

'Oh, bless my crumpets, you've never heard of a tea witch!' said Miss Dumpling. 'We tea witches can brew a whole menu of fabulous concoctions. Teas that let you turn you into beasts, or read the thoughts of others, or heal from any hurt. I'm sure we can sort out whatever Mr Weep did to you. In Dwimmerly End, we do it all, you see: we go where the wind takes us, picking up lost strangelings along the way and opening our doors to any faeries in need of a good, strong brew, whether it be a Chamomile of Confidence or something to mend a broken heart.'

'What's a strangeling? Madrigal called me one but I haven't a clue what it is.'

'Ah,' said Miss Dumpling, leaning back in her chair. 'A strangeling is someone from the faerie world who's been left in the hands of humans for too long. We magical folk lose our gifts the longer we're around humans, until, soon enough, we can't even see faeries any more – other than the ones who *want* to be seen.'

'So that tea Madrigal gave me . . .'

'Gave you your faerie-sight back,' Miss Dumpling finished. 'You are witch-kind, Yesterday. Those ears give you away in a heartbeat.' A pair of faintly glowing stalks popped out from beneath the tea witch's hair. 'Just like my antennae! We witches were all humans once. After they chased us away, the faeries embraced us, and now we've been close to them for so long that we are faeries ourselves.'

'And what about Mr Weep?' Yesterday asked, glancing nervously out of the window, as though she might catch him peering nosily into the teashop. 'Is he a faerie too?'

Miss Dumpling's smile vanished. 'Mr Weep is something different altogether. He isn't a faerie, nor is he a human. He's a king, if titles are your bag.'

Yesterday blinked. 'A *king*? What's he a king of?'

Miss Dumpling took in a deep breath. 'He is the Demon King, who rules over the Land of the Dead, a kingdom of ice and shadows, a place of ghosts and demons. A tea witch's natural enemy, now that I think about it.'

Yesterday shuddered, fear thrilling along her spine. 'I don't know if Madrigal told you . . . Mr Weep put a splinter of ice in my heart. He kept acting as if it was some kind of game, but why would anyone like that take an interest in me?'

'It is a mystery, indeed,' Miss Dumpling admitted. 'I can only guess his dark magic is not all that it seems. Nothing a cup of tea can't take care of, mind! Demons like him can't enter Dwimmerly End without an invitation, so you are safe here. But we had better see to that splinter before it causes any more issues, don't you agree?'

She clapped her hands together and one of the cupboards swung open. A book shot out and landed on the table. It had a leather cover with a teapot decorating the front. Embossed upon the spine was the title, *The*

Tome of Terrific Tea Witchery by Camellia Culpepper and Zuo Mei. Miss Dumpling flicked through the pages.

'Here we are!' the tea witch declared. 'The Perfect Panacea – a tea that can cure any illness, cleanse any poison, break any curse. Its magic will thaw the ice in your heart, no doubt about it! Says here that all we need is some unicorn milk and a ... hm ... and a mournful rose. Ah.'

'Is everything all right?' asked Yesterday.

'Well, I know for certain that we do not have any mournful roses in our pantry. Not to worry. I'm sure Mr Wormwood, our gardener, will find us one in his tea garden faster than you can say *oolong*!'

Miss Dumpling closed the book with a heavy thud.

'But what if we can't find one?' said Yesterday. 'And you can't make this Perfect Panacea of yours by sunset on the winter solstice? That's only a month away! Then my heart will freeze and I'll ...'

She swallowed nervously.

'... and I'll die.'

Miss Dumpling gave Yesterday a serious look. 'Darling, this isn't over until the kettle's boiled. We came here tonight because the tealeaves told me there was a lost strangeling in need of our help, and we shall not let you down.'

'You came here just for me?' said Yesterday.

Miss Dumpling smiled mischievously. 'Why, darling, of course! Rescuing lost strangelings is what Dwimmerly End is all about.'

Yesterday felt like she was glowing. For the first time in her life, she mattered to someone.

'And while you're here, darling, we have unicorns that need milking, plants that need pruning, and cakes that need baking. You could be just the ticket. Indeed, I have been looking for an apprentice for some time. How would you like to do some magic of your own?'

Yesterday could not believe what she was hearing. 'You want me to be your apprentice? Aren't you supposed to . . . I don't know . . . *interview* me first for a job like that?'

'What do you suppose I'm doing right now?' Miss Dumpling said, arching an eyebrow. 'You are a witch, which means *possibilities*. You could be a storm witch, raising tempests to do your bidding, or a beast witch, who rallies monsters to your cause. But if you ask my opinion, you really ought to consider being a *tea* witch. We really do have the most fun.'

Yesterday shook her head quickly. 'I would love to – really, I'm so flattered that you would ask – but I'm afraid I don't have an ounce of magic in me. I know you think I'm a witch, and I know I have the ears of a fox, but I'm pretty ordinary in all the ways that count.'

'Ordinary is as ordinary does, darling,' said Miss Dumpling with a shrug. 'The finest tea can brew in the humblest of teapots, and don't you let anyone tell you otherwise.'

'I hope I wouldn't disappoint you,' said Yesterday, looking at the floor. 'Or put you in any danger from that monster, Mr Weep.'

'Saucers and silliness! My grandmother used to say that even the fiercest monsters can be slain. That goes for fear, sorrow, and loneliness as much as any demon or dragon. I notice you haven't touched your tea.'

She pushed the cup towards Yesterday.

'This tea is Dreamer's Dandelion, flavoured with sweet dreams and wild wishes,' Miss Dumpling went on. 'One of my favourite witch-brews. Have a sip, and may it inspire you to do mad, marvellous things.'

Yesterday took a sip and found it tasted like sweet honey and citrus. A heartbeat passed and the tea took effect.

Her fox ears tingled. Sounds seemed to be coming from nowhere and everywhere, or maybe even from her own head: the sound of pages rustling in a library;

of a piano playing; of a quill scratching across paper; of chisel upon stone as it was chipped and sculpted into a masterpiece. She had no idea how she knew what all those sounds were. She just knew.

Yesterday overflowed with a wondrous sense that the world was made just for her, that everything was possible and nothing would cause her pain.

Maybe I really do have magic. Maybe I could work here, she thought. *I could live a life of magic and tea and cake.*

I could belong.

'I'll take the job,' she said at last. She burst into a wide grin. 'And I promise I'll be the best apprentice ever.'

'Oh, what a grand day!' cried Miss Dumpling, leaping from her chair. 'We must celebrate at once! Tea and jam sandwiches for all!'

Chapter Four

The Confectionary Laboratory

Yesterday gobbled down a dozen of the jam sand-wiches Miss Dumpling made for her. Once finished, she was so exhausted, she could hardly stop yawning.

'I say, Madrigal! Jack!' Miss Dumpling called, cupping a hand around her mouth to project her voice through to the tearoom. 'Would you both come here a moment, darlings?'

The door swung open. The boy with the wolf snout entered, Madrigal upon his shoulder. 'You called?' said the not-raven stiffly.

'Would one of you be a gentleman and show my new apprentice Yesterday to her bedroom? The poor thing is exhausted.'

'Isn't it enough that I spent my evening chasing after her through the woods?' Madrigal muttered.

'I'll do it, Miss Dumpling,' interrupted the boy. 'Is it bedtime already?' He fished into his pocket and produced a pocket watch. As he flipped it open, the watch barked at him, 'You're very late, you know!'

'I guess it *is* bedtime!' he said, with such a big smile that Yesterday couldn't help smiling too.

'Miss Dumpling, while you're here,' he went on, 'any thoughts on us finally getting that wish-fuelled hot air balloon I've been going on about? They're all the rage in the Seelie Court.'

'We've been over this before, darling,' sighed Miss Dumpling. 'We're a teashop – we don't *need* a wish-fuelled hot air balloon. Yesterday, this is Jack Cadogan, confectioner and inventor of very clever things, like that bossy-watch of his.'

'It's definitely an improvement on the bossy-toilet I built last week,' Jack said. He gave Yesterday a light nudge with his elbow. 'So, you're the girl who's got Madrigal all grumbly?'

'I guess I must be,' said Yesterday. She noticed a scar on his neck, shaped like the numerals *XIX*, dull and grey.

Jack's smile became a grin and he bit into a muffin. 'Is your name really *Yesterday*?' he asked, in a muffin-muffled voice. Yesterday nodded warily. 'I think I'll call you . . . Yester . . . Yessie . . . *Essie*! That'll work – Essie!'

Miss Dumpling gave a clap. 'I think Essie sounds splendid!'

Yesterday went a bit pink. No one had ever given her a nickname before, or not a nice one, anyway. 'You can call me Essie, I suppose,' she said, trying not to show how wonderful it felt to be called something other than 'Crumb' for once.

Madrigal flapped away, muttering to himself, 'Nicknames! Such stuff and nonsense!'

'Don't mind him, Essie,' said Jack. 'He can be a bit of a grump, even at the best of times.'

'A *bit* of a grump?' said Yesterday. 'I've met puddles more cheerful.'

Jack chuckled. 'He warms up to you eventually.' He paused. 'Well, sort of. In his own Madrigal way.'

Miss Dumpling handed them each a mug, rich with the scents of chocolate and fresh mint. 'Here you go, dears. Two cups of Pearlescent Peppermint – strictly speaking a hot chocolate, not a tea, but a witch-brew nevertheless. Forget dentists and toothbrushes: one cup of this, and you'll have perfectly pristine teeth for a year! Now, time for bed. I suspect we've all had quite enough excitement for one day.'

Yesterday took her mug gratefully and drained the thick, creamy contents in one go. Then she followed

Jack out of the kitchen, heading through the door on the right-hand side. It led to a small hallway, where there was a spiral staircase and two more doors, one with a sign in gold writing that read *Unicorn Stable* and the other *Tea Garden*.

Yesterday could hear huffs and grunts coming from the other side of the stable door as they made their way up the stairs. 'Do you really have unicorns here?'

'Sure do,' said Jack, with a yawn. 'Our customers expect fresh unicorn milk with their tea, and I don't blame them! We have the gryphon roost upstairs too – gryphon eggs make the best cakes, everyone knows that. What we need now is a kraken tank. Kraken ink goes great in Liquorice for Laughter. I practically begged Miss Dumpling to get me one for my birthday, but she told me krakens belong in the ocean. *So* boring, don't you think?'

As they climbed up and up the stairs, they passed portraits of twinkly eyed ladies in pointed hats with teapots in hand, and names written underneath: *Mrs Rose Dwimmerly . . . Mrs Merriment Dumpling . . . Miss Victoria Dumpling . . .*

Yesterday paused a moment at the last painting, which depicted Miss Dumpling in an armchair, Madrigal on her shoulder and Pascal in her lap.

'You coming, Essie?' asked Jack from the top of the stairs.

Yesterday smiled at the painting – even in her portrait, Miss Dumpling seemed welcoming and wise – and then hurried after her new friend.

On the next floor were a number of doors, each adorned with the same golden writing – *Library, Confectionary Laboratory, Storm-Catching Chamber,* and *Tealeaf Reading Room.* Yesterday wondered how they managed to fit so many rooms into the teashop.

'Want to see my lab?' Jack asked. 'It's where I make Dwimmerly End's world-famous sweets . . .' He paused. 'Well, they're not world-famous yet. But they will be someday!'

'Yes, please!' said Yesterday, her mouth already watering. 'As long as I can have a sample?'

Jack led her into the confectionary laboratory, crowded with machines and strange experiments. In one corner, a metal sphere crackled with electricity. Underneath were three tubs, one bright pink, one yellow, and one creamy white, labelled as *Birthday Cake, Summer's Day,* and *Old Books.*

'My take on ice cream,' said Jack, hands on his hips as he struck a proud pose.

In another corner, cobalt-blue and acid-green

chemicals fizzled in beakers beside a plate of faintly glowing yellow candies marked *Shining Sherbets (warning: may cause temporary blindness)*. On the far side of the room, lengths of a stringy pink candy were holding up an entire bed that was hanging from the ceiling. A label read *Elasti-Taffy (maximum load: two unicorns and a bouquet of violets)*.

'Are you a witch too?' Yesterday asked, gazing around.

'Sure am,' Jack said. He pulled a lever on a boxy-looking machine, and it started whirring and grumbling. 'I'm the teashop's confectionary witch – think chocolatier meets magician.'

'And science professor, by the looks of it,' Yesterday murmured, casting her eyes around the peculiar contraptions.

A tray shot out the side of the box-shaped machine. 'Try this,' said Jack, plucking a squidgy white cube from it.

Yesterday narrowed her eyes and studied it carefully. 'What is it?'

'A Marshmallow of Memories,' said Jack. Sniffing at it, he added, 'Experimental batch, of my own devising. Quite pleased with it, truth be told.'

Yesterday popped it into her mouth and chewed. It suddenly felt like her skin was being warmed by glorious sunlight. Her fox ears stood on end, and she could have sworn she heard the sloshing of waves against rocks and the cries of seagulls. She could even smell and taste the saltiness of the sea.

It was a bit too much to swallow, but she tried to be polite. 'Was that a *memory* I just tasted?' she asked, suppressing a wince.

Jack beamed. 'Got it in one!' he said, with a finger snap. 'One of my memories, to be exact. A trip to the beach with my mum when I was little. I wish the memory would be a *bit* more vivid. But I'm getting there!'

The Marshmallow of Memories had left an odd aftertaste, as though the salt of the seawater had given way to the salt of tears. 'Is Miss Dumpling your mother, then?' Yesterday asked.

Jack shook his head. 'Not in the strictest sense,' he said. He scampered over to one of the machines, fiddling with the gauges and valves. 'My mum's gone. Lost both my parents during the Unseelie War, back when I was small. The Seelie Court crushed the Unseelie rebels, but innocents got caught in the crossfire.'

Yesterday didn't know what the Unseelie War was, but now wasn't the time to request a history lesson. 'I'm sorry. I shouldn't have asked.'

'That's OK,' said Jack. 'Barely remember them. Plus, I was lucky. I found a new family. Lost my magic for a while, but now it's all around me, and I guess that makes things all right.'

'So that means you're a . . . a strangeling, like me?'

'That's right. Welcome to the club,' he said, giving an elegant bow. He straightened up again and said, 'You won't believe how Miss Dumpling found me.'

Yesterday's curiosity was thoroughly piqued. 'How'd she find you?'

'Well, after the war I was on my own for ages, living on the streets. Then, some humans caught me trying to steal apples from their orchard. They thought I'd lost my marbles, going on about trolls and elves, and didn't know what to make of my funny old wolf nose.'

He went cross-eyed as he tried to look at his own snout. It made Yesterday giggle, even though the story was getting quite serious.

'They ended up sending me to a hospital, full of boys and girls like us.'

Yesterday blinked at him. 'You mean . . .'

'Strangelings,' Jack confirmed. 'Kids with animal parts who didn't know they were actually faeries. This mark –' he pulled down his collar to point at the *XIX* she'd noticed earlier on his neck – 'tells you I was Patient Nineteen. Not a person. A number. Trust humans to make things as boring as possible, right? But I broke out of there with nothing but a hairpin and a pair of frozen fishfingers. Then, I stumbled across Dwimmerly End when I was running for freedom. Turns out, Miss Dumpling was planning to get all of us out anyway. So, I helped her set the other strangelings free, and we found new homes for everyone.'

'Wait a second, did you say fishfingers?' said Yesterday, totally bewildered. 'That can't be true.'

'It *is* true! Swear it on my finest caramels,' said Jack, laughing as he placed a hand over his heart. 'How about you? What's your story?'

Yesterday shifted. 'An awful lot more boring than all that, for a start,' she said. 'Let's see. I lived in a cage in a circus, then, one day, along came the grumpiest bird in existence and next thing I knew, I was in a teashop with flamingo legs. Not a human in sight.' She let out a sigh. 'Don't you think it's just horrible how they treated us? Humans, I mean?'

There was something uneasy yet liberating about calling humans *humans*. As if Yesterday wasn't one of them any more. As if she had escaped and was running free in a new world – a world where she belonged, where she was meant to be.

'Well, at least now we never have to worry about them ever again,' said Jack. 'Dwimmerly End welcomes pretty much everyone, but Miss Dumpling doesn't suffer bullies.' Then, with a smile, he motioned towards the door. 'Shall we get back to the tour?'

Yesterday had almost forgotten where they had been going. 'Sounds good to me,' she said. They headed out of the laboratory, and up yet another flight of stairs.

'Bedrooms and bathrooms are along here,' Jack said, when they reached the next floor. 'Wendy the water spirit lives in the boiler. All you've got to do is ask politely, and you'll get all the hot water your heart desires.'

Yesterday noticed the stairs went higher still, but she could see only shadows and cobwebs at the top.

'What's up there?' she asked.

'The gryphon roost. And the sunlight suite,' said Jack. 'Your bedroom should be right this way.'

'*Should* be?'

'This is Dwimmerly End,' Jack explained, as he led her down the corridor. 'You can't always trust it not to get bored and switch all the rooms around. Here we go!'

To Yesterday's surprise, the door had *Yesterday* imprinted on it in the same gold lettering as the other doors, as though the teashop had wanted to give her a warm welcome.

She opened the door and inside, she saw a

comfortable-looking bed covered with pink linen, a white desk with pens and sheaves of paper, and pretty wallpaper depicting slender cherry blossom trees, with sparrows dancing along the branches. As Yesterday stepped inside, however, the wallpaper changed, as if the room were putting on fresh clothes for its new occupant. The blossoms shifted and rearranged themselves into a field of stars, nebula dust swirling all around, planets spinning across the ceiling overhead.

She walked over to an immense wardrobe and opened it. Inside were dresses and aprons and trousers and shirts and boots and shoes – all, quite impossibly and miraculously, her size.

'I can't believe this is happening,' said Yesterday, gazing at the starlight that danced across her walls. 'I can't believe magic is real, and has been just around the corner all this time – and most people never realise it!'

'Thank goodness for those fox ears of yours, eh?' said Jack, giving her another nudge. 'Otherwise Madrigal might never have spotted you. Anyway, goodnight, Essie. This is only the beginning, you know. The *boring* part, before the real magic gets started.'

'Goodnight, Jack,' said Yesterday, as he closed the door behind him, although she really wanted him to stick around a while longer. She needed to know *everything* about her new world, her new home. But as she clambered into her warm, comfy bed – a world apart from the bed of straw she was used to sleeping on – it was so soft and lovely that she felt sleep dragging her under almost immediately.

As she began to drift off, a thought nagged at the back of her mind: *how did Mr Weep know my name? How did he find me in the forest?*

And why would someone like him go out of his way to put ice in my heart?

But soon even that thought faded away, and Yesterday fell into a deep sleep, dreaming of faeries and ravens, of teapots and tealeaves.

*

Meanwhile, just beyond the glowing windows of Dwimmerly End, skulking back between the trees and into the snowy forest, were three little creatures.

You might have said they looked like giant rats, if rats had fur of pure shadow and walked around on two legs like humans. They grumbled like humans too, muddy whiskers twitching around mouths full of sharp teeth as they passed a flask of dwarven whisky between them and bemoaned their fate.

'The boss isn't going to be happy about this,' Lachrimus chittered.

'Meddling tea witch,' snarled Bread-and-Slug. 'He should have just let us kill the girl. Imagine asking a trio so versed in the art of murder as ourselves to *hold back*. It's an insult, is what it is.'

'I should like to see you say that to his face, Bread-and-Slug,' Lachrimus replied, taking a sip of whisky. 'I wish the boss would at least tell us why he needs the girl so badly. What do you make of all this, Pyewacket?'

Pyewacket was the eldest and wisest of the three (though she was still prone to petty acts of violence now and again).

'It's odd. I won't dress it up in no finery,' Pyewacket said, stroking her shadowy, ratty chin with her shadowy, ratty claws. A robin chirruped at her from a branch above. She frowned, pointed a claw at the creature, and it froze into solid ice. 'I haven't seen him this interested in someone from the Land of the Living since . . .'

A voice interrupted her. 'Since what, I wonder?'

The words came from the shadow of the trees.

The three imps froze. Pyewacket trembled with fear. 'N-nothing, oh, glorious Demon King!'

Mr Weep emerged from the darkness, a silver umbrella held over his head, an eyebrow arched in mild amusement. 'You seem dreadfully afraid, my dear imps,' he said. 'Tell me, what has you so on edge?'

The imps looked at one another. Pyewacket fidgeted nervously. 'We followed the girl, just like you told us to,' she said. 'She's ended up with the tea witch.'

'Has she now? Fascinating.'

The imps looked at each other nervously.

Pyewacket cleared her throat. 'Mr Weep,' she said. 'Pardon our intrusion, it's just . . . we thought . . . that is, you acted as if the girl was quite important for your plans.'

'Oh, she is,' said Mr Weep. 'She is critical to my grand scheme.'

'I think what sister Pyewacket means,' said Lachrimus, 'is that we thought you'd be a bit, you know, frustrated?'

'Frustrated?' said Mr Weep. 'Why should I be frustrated, dear Lachrimus? The little cub is cursed. Our game has begun, and the opening move is in my favour. Oh, this shall be a good time. A devilishly good time, indeed.'

Pyewacket was starting to feel annoyed, despite herself. Their master was often prideful and arrogant, but this was too much.

'Lord and master,' she said, 'I don't mean to suggest that you haven't seen things from all angles –' she saw his grim glee trickling away and hurried to get to her point – 'but isn't there the smallest, slightest possibility that the tea witch might have some brew that could break your spell?'

Mr Weep gave a slow nod. 'Doubtful,' he murmured. 'But I suppose we could make Yesterday's challenge more interesting.'

Lachrimus tapped his feet excitedly. 'Does this mean, your lugubrious lordship, that you will assemble your legions and lay waste to the teashop?'

Mr Weep thought about it for a few moments, then he thought about it for a couple more.

'It is true that crushing one's enemy beneath one's boot can be enjoyable, but to let her destroy herself – that is the truest delight. My imps, you will follow the teashop. Keep an eye out that they don't meddle too much. And in the meantime . . .'

There was a pause. All was silence and moonlight and snowfall.

'I am going to compose a letter,' Mr Weep announced triumphantly. 'One of you will deliver it this evening to the Royal College of Witches. I'm sure they will be very interested to know that there is an unlicensed strangeling practising magic in Miss Dumpling's teashop.'

Mr Weep grinned his wicked grin, and the imps all grinned along with him.

Chapter Five

How to Brew a Miracle

Upon her first morning at Dwimmerly End, Yesterday put on a pale blue dress from her wardrobe, tied an orange apron over the top, and bounded down the stairs two at a time, bursting to begin her new life.

When she reached the kitchen, she heard muffled voices coming from behind the closed door. It was a conversation between Miss Dumpling and Madrigal. Her fox ears flicked to attention.

'If you want my opinion on the matter, your strangeling "hobby" is not respectable,' Madrigal was saying. 'We should have stopped doing it years ago! Imagine if the College found out.'

'You can't expect me to turn her away, darling. Besides, no witch worth her broomstick cares about being respectable! So what if choosing a strangeling as one's apprentice is a little, dare I say, unconventional? The finest tea parties have cakes of all shapes and sizes, and life is much the same.'

There was a pause. Then, 'You'll give her everything and then she'll walk out on us, just like the others . . .'

Yesterday's stomach knotted. They were talking about her. But how could Madrigal ever think she would turn her back on Dwimmerly End? And what was so *unrespectable* about strangelings that meant making her an apprentice was such a questionable idea?

She cleared her throat loudly to announce her presence, then opened the door. 'Good morning,' she murmured.

Miss Dumpling was whisking up some batter in a mixing bowl, with Madrigal sitting upon her shoulder. A knife was chopping up a banana on to a plate, while a pair of oven mitts pulled a tray of steaming hot croissants from the oven, all by themselves.

Miss Dumpling set her mixing bowl aside and smiled. 'Morning, darling!' she said, thrusting a croissant into Yesterday's hands. 'I shan't hear any of that *no-breakfast-for-me* nonsense young folk come out with these days. A life that is too quick for breakfast is too quick for its own good.'

'How do you make them do that?' Yesterday asked, glancing at the knife and the oven mitts.

Miss Dumpling put one hand on her hip. 'My, my, aren't we curious for eight o'clock in the morning?'

'If I'm going to be a witch's apprentice,' said Yesterday, shooting Madrigal a quick, sharp look, 'I want to know everything.'

Miss Dumpling's smile doubled in size. 'Just as a tea witch must know her customers and her ingredients, so too must she know her kitchen. Everything in here answers to me.'

She clapped her hands and all the cutlery jaunted over to the sink and started washing themselves up. The kitchen counter remained littered with strange ingredients: a glass bottle containing a frothy white liquid labelled *Unicorn Milk*; a box of six golden-brown *Gryphon Eggs*, each one the size of a fist; and a jar of thick, pale blue *Will-o'-the-wisp Honey*.

'I suggest we go and see our gardener Mr Wormwood right away,' Miss Dumpling said, once Yesterday had finished her breakfast. 'If anyone knows about getting hold of a mournful rose, it's him. Once he finds us one, I can use it to brew the Perfect Panacea, melt the ice in your heart, and all will be right as rooibos by supper.'

She led Yesterday out of the kitchen and into the hallway with the spiral staircase. They passed the door to the unicorn stable and instead went through the door marked *Tea Garden*.

Yesterday gasped as they stepped into a vast greenhouse brimming with a jungle of leafy emerald. Orchids and lilies and pansies bloomed in old teapots repurposed as planters, alongside flowers of stranger kinds: flowers that changed colour as you walked by; flowers that seemed to sing quietly as their leaves rustled and their petals fluttered; flowers that sparked and crackled like molten rock.

Tiny creatures like floating blue flames drifted between the flowers, without setting them alight. One came and rested on the back of Yesterday's hand for a moment, leaving no burn or mark, before drifting away into the tea garden. 'Are they will-o'-the-wisps?' she asked, delighted, remembering an entry in *The Pocket Book of Faeries*.

Miss Dumpling nodded. 'Rather charming, aren't they? When they sleep, they leave behind a substance rather like candlewax.'

'And then you turn the wax into honey?' Yesterday suggested.

Miss Dumpling raised an eyebrow, looking both

curious and proud. 'Precisely,' she said. 'And sugar, as the case may be.'

Yesterday gazed up and noticed a slanted glass ceiling. It was just hidden behind a steely grey cloud, which had somehow been captured and brought indoors. With a rumble, rain began to fall, pitter-pattering against leaves and petals. Miss Dumpling took an umbrella from a basket and held it over their heads.

'Mr Wormwood prefers freshly caught rainstorms over plain old watering cans,' Miss Dumpling said, as they wove their way between the plants. 'A word of warning: he's a dryad, a kind of woodland faerie, and he's a few trees short of an orchard, let's say.'

In the centre of the tea garden, a pair of glass jars sat upon a white-iron table. In one, labelled *Bottled Rainstorms*, lightning crackled and dark clouds gathered. In the other, little golden orbs bobbed around cheerfully. Its label read *Bottled Sunlight – Use Sparingly*.

'Ah! Here comes Mr Wormwood now!' Miss Dumpling announced.

A green-skinned gentleman in overalls, whose hair was all autumn leaves dappled orange and gold, was walking in their direction, stopping to chat to the flowers on his way.

'Miss Hyacinth, you've done quite a commendable job with those new petals of yours,' he was saying, stroking a moustache of pine tree needles. 'And Mr Orchid, I don't care what the pansies say, your stem is looking as healthy as ever!'

'Mr Wormwood, darling?' said Miss Dumpling. 'So sorry to barge in like this, but some introductions are in order.'

The dryad stood upright. 'Oh, Victoria, you look fresh as a foxglove!' he said. He reached into an empty flowerbed and snapped his fingers. A lily grew from the soil in a matter of seconds. He plucked the flower and put it behind Miss Dumpling's ear.

Miss Dumpling blushed pink and chuckled, her antennae briefly poking out from her golden curls. 'Ranunculus, you are too much a gentleman for your own good!' she said. 'This is Yesterday Crumb, my new apprentice.'

'I like your garden,' said Yesterday, who was not precisely an expert on pleasantries. 'It's . . . um. Very green.'

Mr Wormwood leaned in and inspected her with big, bright eyes. 'New apprentice, eh? Ask politely and you may plunder my tea garden all you like. But if I catch you stealing, I'll turn you into a slug. Or maybe a watering can. Or a watering-can-shaped slug! Your choice, sapling.'

He started chuckling to himself as he saw the horrified look on Yesterday's face.

'Don't worry, darling,' said Miss Dumpling reassuringly. 'Mr Wormwood has only turned people into slugs on a handful of occasions.'

The dryad narrowed his eyes at Yesterday. 'There's dark magic in this one, Miss Dumpling. The flowers told me so.'

Yesterday's chest tensed around the icy splinter, and she felt a shiver go through her.

'We were rather hoping you might help with that,' said Miss Dumpling.

'Hmmm,' said Mr Wormwood, scratching his moustache pines. 'Follow, follow, follow! Got plenty to do, but we can walk and talk.'

Mr Wormwood led them into a small grove. The leaves of the trees were all different colours: plum pinks, goldenrod yellows, dragonfly blues, and marmalade oranges. From the branches dangled apples, seemingly wrought from glittering gold.

'These apples!' Yesterday gasped. 'I've never seen anything like them.'

'Wishfruits,' Mr Wormwood corrected her. 'This is

my wish orchard,' he explained proudly. 'Grown from seeds given to me by a djinni, no less.'

'They're perfect for my Wishfruit Tarts,' Miss Dumpling told Yesterday. 'No need for shooting stars or wishing wells round here!'

Yesterday blinked. 'These trees grow *wishes*? But then why don't I just eat one and wish the ice out of my heart?'

'Oh, if only it were that simple,' said Miss Dumpling, as Mr Wormwood hammered a small tap into the trunk of a wishfruit tree. 'We are not djinnis, darling. When one eats a wishfruit, the ensuing miracle could be anything from turning your eyes a different colour to granting you the power of flight. In any case, back to this *dark magic* business. You haven't got any mournful roses lying about, have you, Ranunculus?'

Mr Wormwood burst out laughing. Then he stopped. 'Oh!' he said. 'You're being serious. The mournful rose is one of the rarest flowers known to man or faerie. No one knows where it grows, not even the bumblebees. The mournful rose cannot be tracked – even reading your tealeaves wouldn't work, Victoria. '

Yesterday paled.

'Ah,' said Miss Dumpling.

'You *could* try the Goblin Market,' suggested Mr Wormwood. He turned the tap's nozzle, and began collecting drips of shimmering wishtree sap in a vial. 'Though you know what they say about goblins and their poisoned roots.'

Miss Dumpling grimaced. 'It would be a start. We'll get going as soon as possible. The market can't be too far ... A good session in the tealeaf reading room should be enough to track it down. Ranunculus, could I pinch some toothweed?'

The dryad nodded, and led them to a plant with fang-like thorns that snapped when fingers got too close. Then they said farewell to Mr Wormwood and headed back to the kitchen.

Yesterday slumped down at the kitchen table and put her head in her hands. 'What happens if we never find a mournful rose?'

'Darling,' said Miss Dumpling, hastily bringing her a fork and a plate of emergency apple strudel, 'in this teashop we nibble cakes, we sip tea, but we never, ever feed our fears. Once you've learned a spell or two, you'll see that we can overcome any obstacle. And no time like the present, don't you think? We can't have you heading off to the Goblin Market without a trick or two up your sleeve. Besides, if you're going to be working in Dwimmerly End, you'll need to do tea witchery of your own.'

Yesterday's gloomy mood evaporated immediately. 'Could you teach me how to make teapots fly?' she asked, her forkful of strudel left uneaten. 'Or how to make that dreaming tea you gave me last night?'

'Aren't we putting the milk before the teabag?' chuckled Miss Dumpling. 'I will show you how to brew a miracle in good time. But first things first, you can help Jack in the tearoom.'

Yesterday frowned. 'I don't mean to be rude, but what does waiting tables have to do with magic?'

'Tea witchery is all about patience, compassion, and, most importantly, *listening* – to ourselves, to others, to the world around us. Understanding the needs of our customers is the perfect start to your teaching, don't you think?'

Yesterday didn't have much choice but to agree. 'But what if I make a mistake?'

'Then you should be grateful,' Miss Dumpling said firmly. 'Did you know the inventor of gingerbread added ginger and cinnamon to his dough entirely by accident? If it hadn't been for that mistake, we wouldn't have our dear friend the gingerbread man, and I suspect the world would have been much sorrier without him.'

Yesterday nodded doubtfully. *I'll try my best*, she thought. Even if that meant talking to a tearoom full of strange faeries, while being courteous and charming, and remembering what people had asked for, and making no mistakes, and bringing their orders quickly without spilling anything, and . . .

'Ready?' asked Miss Dumpling brightly, holding open the tearoom door for Yesterday.

You can do this, Yesterday told herself with absolutely zero conviction, as she stepped through the doorway, heading to whatever trials awaited beyond.

Chapter Six

Jumbling Jasmine

The door shut behind Yesterday, leaving Miss Dumpling and the kitchen on the other side. She took a deep, steadying breath. *No going back now.*

In the tearoom, Jack was standing on a chair, busily writing the specials on a chalkboard behind the cake-counter, next to the shelves of teapots. Through the counter's glass, Yesterday could see a belly-rumbling assortment of cakes and pastries: spiced phoenix-egg meringues; faintly glowing birthday cakes; a gingerbread house, shaped like Dwimmerly End, trotting around the other baked delights; and much, much more.

She pulled her attention to Jack and his chalkboard. The first tea on offer promised to mend broken hearts (*made with locally sourced teardrops*). Others on the board included the Dreamer's Dandelion that Miss Dumpling had made for Yesterday the night before (*to inspire creativity and a touch of madness*) and Jumbling Jasmine (*for all your creature comforts*).

Even though it was early, the tearoom was packed with customers. Yesterday tried to identify them in her head, based on the entries in *The Pocket Book of Faeries*.

There was a faun – a goat-horned, goat-hoofed gentleman, with a cinnamon-brown moustache – who was reading a newspaper and drinking a cup of tea. On closer inspection, he seemed to be cross-referencing the horoscopes with his tealeaves.

There was a finely dressed elf lady with antlers and sharply pointed ears, who was sitting very still with her teacup while a levitating paintbrush painted her portrait all by itself. A dryad with hair made from orchids was blowing on a steaming hot cup of tea, while a pair of hairy dwarves with tumbling black beards argued loudly over who got the last cinderspice roll.

The noise of them all laughing and gossiping and slurping their tea was deafening for Yesterday's sensitive fox ears, and her heart began to race.

Jack turned, and his face lit up at the sight of her. 'Morning!' he said, jumping down from his chair. 'Miss

Dumpling mentioned she might have you work with me for a bit. Looking forward to it?'

'I guess,' said Yesterday, swallowing down her terror. 'I'm not much of a customer service kind of person, to be honest. Back in the circus, the ringmaster used to say he couldn't tell what was more off-putting about me: my ears or my attitude.'

'What a . . . pleasant man,' said Jack.

'Yep. A real charmer.'

'I'll be wrapping presents while you do the serving,' said Jack, gesturing to the counter. 'We really should have automatons to do this sort of thing, don't you think? Now *there*'s a good idea, I reckon. Let me write it down. I'll have to tell Miss Dumpling.'

'Did you say *presents*?' said Yesterday.

Jack nodded, snipping a length of blue ribbon with some scissors. 'We get tons of Christmas orders round about now. Mr Wormwood told me it used to be even busier, back when the paths to the Land of the Dead were open. Ghosts used to get special tourist visas to do their Christmas shopping, and we'd be packed. Ghosts love their afternoon tea.'

'Why don't they come around any more?' asked Yesterday, a little disappointed to have missed out on such a sight.

'Mr Weep closed the borders between the Land of the Dead and the Land of the Living ages ago. Now you have to go through Immigration.' Jack shuddered. 'No one really knows why he shut the gates. On a cheerier note, do you think you could go and take that lady's order? She's been waiting for ages.'

Yesterday froze. The prospect of speaking to a customer filled her with dread. There was just so much that could go wrong. Miss Dumpling and Jack were kind, but what if other faeries were like humans, and said something cruel when they caught sight of her fox ears?

But that was ridiculous. She had seen faeries with horns and feathers and claws. Surely fox ears weren't so strange in a place like Dwimmerly End.

Surely . . .

Either way, if she wanted to make the tearoom her home, she had to do this.

'Right,' she said. 'Yes. Take an order. I can do that. Which customer was it again?'

'Over there.'

Yesterday turned to look and nearly yelped out loud. The customer was a lady with two heads. One of her heads had bright red hair streaked with black, while the other had black hair shot through with red. They were dressed, improbably, in a sumptuous white wedding dress. *A gemini,* Yesterday thought, recognising the two-headed creature from *The Pocket Book of Faeries.*

She hurried over, almost tripping on the way. 'About time,' snorted the mostly dark-haired head. 'We've been waiting for *eight – whole – minutes.*'

'Impatient shrew,' mumbled the mostly red head.

'What did you call me?' growled the other.

The red-head gave a shrug with her shoulder. 'You warty-mouthed toad!'

'Bossy-bellied fruit bat!'

'Insolent, slime-dragging slug!'

Yesterday decided it was time to interrupt. 'Um . . . sorry about the wait. I'm new. What can I get you today?'

'Aren't *you* supposed to figure that out?' said the dark-haired head, her attention snapping from the red-head to Yesterday.

Yesterday blinked. Suddenly, she felt as if she had forgotten how to talk. 'Of course. Er – maybe a tea that dyes your hair, so you both match?'

'Don't be *absurd.*'

'Right. What about a tea that makes you grow a third head?'

The dark-haired one's lips drew back into a snarl.

'Can't you see I have enough on my plate sharing a body with *this* idiot?'

The red-head chuckled to herself. 'You're lucky to have me. I keep you grounded. Stuck-up cockatoo.'

Yesterday sighed, her fear giving way to frustration. 'Will you stop bickering for a second? I've seen circus acts less dramatic than you two.' The pair of heads looked at her, startled. 'Are you always this vicious to one another?'

The dark-haired one's face scrunched up, her expression sour. 'We're late for my wedding,' she explained. 'My sister here refused to come until we'd had our morning tea. And now we won't make it in time for the ceremony!'

'I never thought you should marry him anyway,' muttered the red-head. 'Gold-digging gecko.'

The dark-haired one glared at her. As she opened her mouth to hiss something back, Yesterday cut in. 'Maybe we can make everyone happy here. What about a tea that'll get you to your wedding on time?'

The heads looked at each other. 'That would do,' said the red-head.

Yesterday beamed. Had she actually figured out an order correctly? 'Coming right up,' she said, and she spun around and headed back to the counter.

'Well, that was traumatic,' she said to Jack, who was tying a pink bow on a box of macarons.

'Mmm, thought they might be. Geminis can be nasty pieces of work.'

She shot him a look. 'You knew they were going to be like that and sent me there anyway? For my first go?'

Jack gave her a playful bump with his elbow. 'Well, yeah. But in my defence, you *do* take yourself too seriously. You should've seen your face!'

Yesterday let out a chuckle, but she still vowed to get revenge. Maybe she could use whatever magic Miss Dumpling taught her to turn him into something unpleasant. *Maybe a frog,* she resolved. That seemed traditional.

Wings flapped from behind Yesterday. She whirled to see Madrigal landing on the cake-counter. 'I see you're serving customers, fool-girl?' said the familiar, hopping over to them. 'Let me guess. You've already forgotten their order.'

'Well, it's complicated,' Yesterday admitted. 'They need a tea that'll get them to their wedding on time. Maybe something that could give them wings?'

'Like a Jumbling Jasmine?' Jack suggested. 'They also call it a Zoo in a Brew.'

'I'm sorry, a *Zoo in a what*?' said Yesterday.

'A Zoo in a Brew,' Jack repeated. 'The Jumbling Jasmine lets you turn into animals. Miss Dumpling makes it all the time.'

Yesterday grinned at Madrigal. 'Looks like the customers want a Jumbling Jasmine, then,' she said to him, all smugness. 'Not a bad first try for a fool-girl, wouldn't you say?'

Madrigal turned up his beak and flew off to his podium by the front door, mumbling, 'Young people today! No manners. None whatsoever!'

'All right then,' said Yesterday, making for the door to the kitchen. 'I'll just go and give Miss Dumpling the order.'

She pushed open the door. Pascal was floating merrily through the air, but Miss Dumpling was nowhere to be seen.

'Oh, I forgot,' said Jack, appearing by her side. 'Miss Dumpling's up in the tealeaf reading room, looking for the Goblin Market.'

'I'd better fetch her,' said Yesterday, starting for the other door.

Jack seized her hand. 'No!' he said quickly. 'You *never* interrupt a tea witch when she's reading her tealeaves. It can throw her predictions into all sorts of chaos. We don't want to risk that.' He headed back through the door to the tearoom. 'She'll probably be back down in a minute.'

Yesterday winced. Through the closing doorway, she saw the two heads of the gemini going red-faced as their argument grew in ferocity. *Those don't look like satisfied customers to me,* she thought, and they were bound to only get more and more frustrated the longer they had to wait.

She chewed her lip, thinking carefully. Why couldn't *she* make the Jumbling Jasmine? *Surely, all I have to do*, she thought, *is follow a recipe. How hard could it really be?*

First, Yesterday crept back into the tearoom, sneaking past Jack, who was now busy cutting a slice of unicorn-milk cheesecake on the counter. On her tiptoes, she reached for one of the teapots from their shelves. She didn't have time to pick carefully, so she grabbed a simple white one before anyone noticed what she was up to.

Teapot in hand, she returned to the kitchen. She went to the cupboard from which she had seen *The Tome of Terrific Tea Witchery* shoot out the night before and carried the book over to the table by the window. She turned to the contents page and scanned it until she found *Jumbling Jasmine*.

'It's only tea,' she said to herself, flicking to the right page. 'What could be so tricky about *tea*?'

She reached the recipe and read it through.

Jumbling Jasmine, or
the Zoo in a Brew
Difficulty Level: Considerably Tricky

Ingredients

One tsp ground cinderspice
One tsp finely chopped toothweed
A pinch of jasmine petals
One teapot's worth of unicorn milk (boiled, preferably
by tea spirit, salamander, or dragon)
Optional: pickled starlight, to extend the
magic's longevity.

'Toothweed!' Yesterday said, recognising it as the plant Miss Dumpling had plucked in the tea garden. She peered into the pantry and traced her finger along the shelves. '*Sphinx Spit . . . Hydra Oil . . . Leprechaun Moustache Bristles . . .*' She grimaced, wondering how those things could ever be used to make something delicious. 'Here it is! Toothweed.'

She took one of the leaves from a little tin and fished some white jasmine petals from a glass jar. As she left the pantry, she grabbed a pint of white unicorn milk.

She brought the ingredients back to the table by the window. She longed to have the kitchen respond to her needs and commands as it did for Miss Dumpling. But it seemed that a kitchen only answered to its witch, and the very idea of Yesterday having one of her own was as distant and wishful as a falling star.

Pascal glided over to her. 'May I help you?' said Yesterday. He started tapping his nose on the pint of unicorn milk. 'You want some milk, do you?'

She removed the stopper from the milk and let Pascal gulp some down. Moments passed, and steam tendrils curled out of the spout of his shell. Then, he floated over to her white teapot and tipped on to his side, filling it with warmed milk.

'Oh!' said Yesterday. 'You were trying to help me!' The tea spirit spiralled up to her and she scratched him under the chin gratefully.

Next, she chopped up the toothweed and sprinkled it in with the jasmine petals. 'So,' she told herself, 'according to the recipe, all I have to do now is say the words of the spell.'

She placed her hands around the teapot. After

taking a moment to calm her nerves, she whispered, *'Tea before me, change my shape, from bird to beast, from fish to ape . . .'*

A bolt of energy zapped through Yesterday's core. She gasped sharply. It felt like the air had been knocked from her lungs. It didn't feel right. It didn't feel right at all. Had she made a mistake somewhere?

Her eyes fell on the recipe. Above the toothweed were the words *One tsp ground cinderspice.* 'I missed an ingredient,' she said, horrified. 'That *cannot* be good.'

Almost immediately, the teapot's porcelain fractured, one sharp ravine cleaving across its body. The lid of the teapot fired off and shattered against the ceiling. A greenish fluid began bubbling over the top of the teapot and oozing down the sides. More and more kept pouring out, even though Pascal had only put a few glugs of milk into the pot. It was more like a thick sludge than actual tea, and it just kept coming. The air filled with a sharp scent, like raw garlic.

'I thought I smelt something weird,' said a voice from the door to the kitchen. It was Jack, his wolf snout wrinkling at the odour. 'Is that . . . burnt toothweed? Bitter, isn't it?'

'Get in! Close the door!' Yesterday said to him,

dashing over and pulling him inside before anyone in the tearoom – namely, Madrigal – found out what was happening. 'I tried to make the Jumbling Jasmine by myself, and . . . and . . .'

A mixture of curiosity and delight and worry crossed Jack's face. He stepped over to the bubbling teapot. 'Well,' he said, examining it. 'You probably shouldn't have been doing magic by yourself. Not as a strangeling.'

'What does that mean?' said Yesterday, glancing from Jack to the spurting fountain of green sludge coming from the teapot.

Jack looked at her with a devilish grin. 'It means things are about to get very interesting.'

The pool of green sludge expanded across the table. It reached a mustard pot that had been left there. As it seeped around the pot's edges, something rather strange happened. The mustard pot began sprouting fur. And whiskers. And two little cat ears.

'Oh, no!' cried Yesterday. Jack was laughing maniacally. 'Won't you be serious for a minute? This is all going wrong!'

The green tea sludge was pumping out of the teapot at an ever-increasing rate. It touched a spoon, and, a second later, the spoon grew wings and began flapping around the place. The sludge pooled around a teacup that had been innocently waiting to be washed. Spider legs sprang from its sides, and the teacup began skittering up the wall.

Then, the sludge oozed off the edge of the table and began dripping down on to the floor.

'Well, this is a pickle,' Jack observed, scratching his chin.

Yesterday glared at him as they retreated from the encroaching sludge. 'A *pickle*?' she said. 'Jack, this is not a pickle – it's a nightmare! What's going to happen when it starts seeping into the tearoom and turns all of our customers into . . . into . . . *things*?'

Jack waved his hand. 'You worry too much, Essie,' he said, strolling over to a cupboard and taking out a mop.

'Be careful, Jack!' said Yesterday, watching as the green tide crept in his direction.

'All we need is to get this mop and . . .' Jack gave a little cry as his feet slipped out from beneath him. 'Sweetmeats!' he cursed, as he fell into the lake of green sludge, which promptly swallowed him up.

'J-Jack?' Yesterday said to the spot where Jack had been. 'Jack, are you all right?'

A moment passed. Then, two little white ears popped out of the sludge. A twitching nose and set of whiskers followed. Next thing Yesterday knew, a white rabbit sprang out of the green sludge and landed on the counter beside her, looking up at her expectantly.

'Great,' said Yesterday, her shoulders drooping. 'Now you're a rabbit. And I'm on my own with . . . with *this*.'

Yesterday edged away from the spreading slime. She was aware she was getting backed into a corner, between the kitchen counter and the tearoom door, but there was nowhere else to go.

She had to think, and fast. There had to be a way of solving this.

She remembered Miss Dumpling's words.

Listen.

I have to learn how to listen.

That was it. That was the solution. She took a deep breath and closed her eyes.

Her fox ears stood to attention, and she listened carefully, just as Miss Dumpling had told her to. She focused hard, clearing her mind of everything – everything other than the grumbling, rumbling sound of the sludge creeping ever closer.

'It sounds almost like it's complaining,' Yesterday realised out loud. 'Like it's . . . bitter? Wait, that's right – Jack said burnt toothweed gets bitter. What makes things *less* bitter?' She thought for a moment. 'Sugar!'

The only trouble was, the sludge was now between

her and the pantry. 'Pascal!' she called, and the little tea spirit leapt up from his nest. 'Pascal, I need you to bring me some sugar from the pantry. Please can you do that?'

The tea spirit made a cooing sound, then swam off through the air to the pantry shelves. The sludge was getting closer and closer to Yesterday, to the door to the tearoom, to all the customers.

Come on … come on … Yesterday thought desperately. *Please, Pascal, hurry.* Then, the tea spirit returned, drifting leisurely over to her. He had a jar of will-o'-the-wisp sugar clutched between his legs, glittering like diamond dust. He dropped it into Yesterday's outstretched hand.

'Thank you, Pascal!'

There was no time to debate whether her plan was ridiculous or not. She opened the jar of sugar and flung a pinch at the sludge. She watched, hoping against hope that it would work. Sure enough, where the sugar landed, the sludge slowed, and gradually dissolved into the ground.

Yesterday grinned.

She ran around the kitchen, throwing the sugar over the encroaching flood, until she had stemmed the tide. Finally, she reached the teapot itself, still pouring out gallons and gallons of wicked green sludge. She tossed a whole dollop of will-o'-the-wisp sugar at it. The teapot stopped rattling, and the sludge stopped oozing.

Yesterday staggered backwards, putting the jar of sugar down on the counter. All around her were strange animal-cutlery hybrids. She slumped down on to the floor, her back against a cabinet. Pascal floated down and landed on her lap, mewing gently as she stroked his shell.

'Well, Pascal,' she said, watching as rabbit-Jack hopped around her, 'be honest. Have you ever seen an apprentice get fired quite as quickly as me?'

'Fired?' asked a bright voice from the back door. 'Why would anybody be getting fired?'

Yesterday paled. She scrambled to her feet, still holding Pascal. 'Miss Dumpling,' she said. 'I'm so sorry. A customer wanted a Jumbling Jasmine, and they had a wedding to get to, and you were so busy and I wasn't meant to disturb you, and I didn't want to mess up my first lesson, and—'

The tea witch came into the kitchen, looking around curiously. 'Fascinating,' she said, leaning down to the mustard pot, which meowed back at her. She tapped it, and its fur and ears disappeared, and it became an ordinary mustard pot again. 'Oh, aren't strangelings such a delight to have in the kitchen?'

'You're being sarcastic,' said Yesterday glumly.

Miss Dumpling looked at her, astonished. 'Sarcastic? Darling, do you truly think so little of me? By the looks of things, I'm guessing you didn't add cinderspice.'

Yesterday nodded.

'Cinderspice balances out the toothweed. For most tea witches, the recipe wouldn't have worked at all. So, I'd take this dramatic display as a good sign of things to come, if I were you! And besides, I can clean up this mess in no time.'

She bent down and scratched rabbit-Jack between his ears. He grew and grew and grew, until he was a boy with a wolf snout again. 'Wh-what happened?' he said, looking rather dazed.

'Just a touch of magical mayhem,' said Miss Dumpling with a chuckle.

'But Miss Dumpling, I broke the rules,' said Yesterday. 'I caused chaos! And that customer is *still* waiting for their order.'

'Darling, this is Dwimmerly End. You are a witch. Rule-breaking is practically encouraged. And don't you worry, we have our solutions for angry customers – don't we, Jack?'

'If anyone gets cross,' said Jack, straightening up and raising a finger, like a professor giving a lecture, 'just bring them a slice of cake for free. Nobody can be angry with someone who brings them cake.'

'The important thing,' Miss Dumpling went on, 'is that you slowed down, and stopped, and *listened*. You couldn't have got that magic under control without doing so.' Her smile twinkled. 'I think we ought to put on a feast this evening.'

'You do?' Yesterday said.

'But of course,' said Miss Dumpling. 'This calls for a celebration. Because you're ready for step two of tea witchery: brewing the tea itself. Properly, this time, mind. We'll get started first thing in the morning. And it would never do to perform magic on an empty stomach.'

Chapter Seven

Three Wondrous Thoughts

When Yesterday came down to the kitchen for dinner, she found Miss Dumpling, Jack, and Mr Wormwood waiting for her at the table by the window, with Madrigal perched on the windowsill.

The table was overflowing with buttered pumpkins and baked cheeses, with salted pastries and the sweetest jams, with toasted sandwiches and bowls of rice, with honey-glazed carrots and gleaming roast potatoes. The gravy boat sailed through the air, pouring little dollops on to particularly thirsty-looking plates, while the salt and pepper grinders wandered around the table, politely offering some extra seasoning to those who wanted it.

'Try the gryphon egg omelettes, darling,' said Miss Dumpling, while Yesterday greedily devoured everything she could manage. 'Usually it's a breakfast delicacy, but any rules that tell you what you can eat at which meal are a load of rubbish, if you want my opinion.'

The tea witch swirled a deep red liquid around a bronze goblet. 'This wine comes from the vineyard of Bacchus,' said Mr Wormwood, sipping at his own. 'Am I right, Miss Dumpling?'

'Yes, Ranunculus,' Miss Dumpling replied. 'He's a much friendlier chap than his brother. That Mars is a quarrelsome fellow – a god he may be, but a gentleman he is not.'

Yesterday went to bed stuffed with food and absolutely exhausted. Even so, she was too busy daydreaming to get any sleep, her mind sifting through all the possibilities of what the next day might bring.

In the morning, she threw her dress and apron on before hurrying downstairs. 'Essie! Is that you?' called a voice from the library as she thundered past. She retraced her steps, and poked her head around the door to find Jack, sitting cross-legged amongst the bookshelves as if he were a bumblebee in the petals of a flower.

The teashop lurched suddenly, presumably shifting from one flamingo leg to another, causing a book to fall off its shelf. Jack caught it without even looking and placed it back where it had been.

'Morning, Essie,' he said. 'I've got something for you. Be careful in here, by the way. The books do tend to get themselves into mischief.'

Yesterday opened the door fully. 'What does *that* mean?'

Jack gave a sly grin. 'There's very little out there more dangerous than a book,' he said, ducking as a book flapped right past him like a bird and landed on top of a bookcase. 'Just last week, we had to stop the fiction section invading the unnatural history shelf. We were picking paper out of the carpet for weeks.'

Yesterday looked along the spines of the books. They had strange titles, like *Cooking with Manticore Venom*, and *One Thousand Uses for Luckberry Jam*, and *Mastering the Art of Elven Baking*.

'Miss Dumpling wanted me to give you your own copy of *The Tome of Terrific Tea Witchery*,' Jack went on. '*The Tome* has all the recipes a tea witch could ever need. You already have your own *Pocket Book of Faeries*, right?'

Yesterday nodded. 'Whoever ditched me at the circus as a baby was generous enough to leave me one,' she said. 'I have no idea why.'

'Every faerie child gets given a *Pocket Book* when

they're little, witches included,' said Jack. 'Whoever left you there obviously wanted you to know who you were. Maybe they didn't really want to give you up at all.'

Yesterday's belly squirmed – thinking about why she had been left at the circus often left her queasy. To change the subject, she asked, 'Does the *Pocket Book* help with tea witchery?'

'Of course,' said Jack. 'If you know about different types of faeries and what they like, then you'll be one step ahead when it comes to figuring out what tea they should order.'

He handed over the enormous copy of *The Tome of Terrific Tea Witchery*.

'Thank you,' said Yesterday, hugging the book close to her chest. She resolved to study it every night before bed.

They headed down to the kitchen together. There they found Miss Dumpling waiting with yet another plate of croissants. After Yesterday had gobbled down a couple, and Jack had scampered off to his lab, the tea witch sat Yesterday down at the kitchen table and put a mint-green teapot in between them.

'Now,' Miss Dumpling said. 'Are you ready for your lesson?'

Yesterday nodded, straightening up and trying to look serious and clever.

'The first principle of practical tea witchery is that everything is alive – everything, everything, everything. Think of magic as holding a conversation with a universe that happens to be on the shy side. As tea witches, we must listen to each ingredient's story, to every flower petal and every sprinkle of sugar, to find out where it came from, how it got here, and precisely what manner of magic it has on offer.'

Yesterday sat patiently, and waited for more.

'There are many more principles,' said Miss Dumpling, reaching for a plate of brownies that had, at some point, materialised on the windowsill, 'but I should say we've earned ourselves a break, don't you agree?'

'I could manage a *bit* more,' said Yesterday.

Miss Dumpling beamed, plucking up a brownie and popping a chunk into her mouth. 'You are the very picture of a good student, darling! Very well, then. On with the show! Tea witchery is all about drawing on an emotion, a thought, or a memory, and mixing it with magic. The ingredients speed the reaction up, while the tea you brew carries the spell's effects to whoever drinks it. Still with me, Essie?'

Yesterday blinked up at her teacher. 'Um ... not exactly.'

Miss Dumpling swallowed her mouthful and tutted. 'Silly me. I fear I've gone too far the other way! I've made things too dull and *classroomy* now. Theory's all jolly well and good for scholars, but we are ladies of action! I invite you to declare war on boredom from this moment until your last. Go on! Declare it!'

Yesterday smiled. 'I declare war on boredom!'

'Fabulous,' said Miss Dumpling, giving her a polite clap. 'We learn by doing, isn't that right? How about we start with the Jumbling Jasmine – so I can show you how it should *actually* be made.'

Yesterday paid close attention as Miss Dumpling pursed her lips and whistled brightly. A moment later, a jar of toothweed, a tin of cinderspice, a few jasmine petals, and a pint glass of white unicorn milk trotted out of the pantry and vaulted on to the table.

The cinderspice had a black stem and warm, orange petals. Miss Dumpling sliced the stem and prised out its crimson seeds, crushing them in a mortar and pestle. Once Pascal had warmed some unicorn milk in his shell, he floated over and poured it into the mint-green teapot. Miss Dumpling threw in the toothweed and the jasmine, sprinkled in a pinch of the ground-up cinderspice, and replaced the lid.

Then, she clasped her hands around the teapot, and began to murmur an incantation.

'*Tea before me, change my shape, from bird to beast, from fish to ape . . .*'

Trails of steam drifted from the teapot's lid, filling the room with smells, one after another: first a muskiness, then a fiery spice like cinnamon or ginger, then the freshness of wildflowers.

Miss Dumpling poured herself a cup of thick, brown liquid and took a sip.

She winked, then changed.

First she became a gold-feathered falcon and soared around the kitchen. She landed upon the counter and became a mouse, scurrying past the plates and cutlery and teacups. Then she leapt off the counter and became an orangutan. She leapt on to one of the baskets hanging from the ceiling, and swung from one to the next.

Finally, she landed and became Miss Dumpling again. Yesterday stood up and applauded.

'Your flattery will go straight to my head!' the tea witch said (though she still took a bow). 'Now, the Jumbling Jasmine is a Considerably Tricky brew, so why don't we start with something easier?'

She turned to a different page.

Hair-Changing Hibiscus
Difficulty Level: Piece of Cake

Ingredients

One tsp hibiscus petals
Dollop of wishtree sap
One teapot's worth of unicorn milk (boiled, preferably
by tea spirit, salamander, or dragon)

'A simple tea that lets one change hair colour at will,' said Miss Dumpling cheerfully. 'Much cheaper than getting it done at a salon, I think you'll agree.'

They went through to the tearoom so Yesterday could pick a teapot to work with. 'Once you complete your training and become a tea witch proper,' Miss Dumpling said, as Yesterday reached for a cheerful pink teapot, 'you shall forge a teapot of your own in the smithies of the brewhammer dwarves. That pink one, so it happens, was my first, and it is very dear to me indeed.'

The next job was to gather the ingredients. 'Remember how the wishtrees in Mr Wormwood's orchard had leaves of every colour?' said Miss Dumpling. 'Well, we're channelling that multicoloured marvel right into the tea. Head to the pantry and see if you can find some wishtree sap.'

Yesterday dashed through to the pantry and scanned the shelves. She found a small vial of pearlescent liquid that changed colours whichever way you tilted it, labelled *Wishtree Sap*.

On her way back, she noticed some of the kitchen utensils – the sugar pot, the pans floating overhead, a few spoons lying here and there – clink and scramble uneasily away from her, as if they remembered what had happened the last time she'd attempted magic. Yesterday sighed: it was one thing to doubt your own abilities, and quite another for the kitchen itself to do so.

Pushing her anxious thoughts to the back of her mind, she popped what she hoped was more or less a dollop of the sap into the teapot, tossed in the hibiscus petals which Miss Dumpling had found for her, and had Pascal fill the teapot with some freshly warmed unicorn milk.

'Splendid ingredient preparation, darling – I couldn't have done it better myself,' said Miss Dumpling, bending down to examine the mixture over Yesterday's shoulder. 'Now, clear your mind – purge it of all nasty thoughts and chittering distractions – and brew me a spot of magic!'

Yesterday took in a deep, slow breath, pausing for a moment to let her fox ears tune in to all the sounds of the room: the echoing pipes, Miss Dumpling's gentle breathing, and, eventually, the swishing of the liquid inside the teapot.

And then, she heard something else. A voice, deep inside her head, one that sounded mostly like Ringmaster Skelm, with a hiss of Mr Weep's icy whispering.

What are you thinking? it said. *Trying to do magic? Spare me! You don't belong in this kitchen. A circus is the only place for you. Those ears of yours are only good for gawking at . . .*

She winced and tried to push the thoughts aside. Heart thrumming away, she placed her hands around the teapot and read the words of the spell from *The Tome of Terrific Tea Witchery.*

'Colours of sky, colours of land, shift and yield at my command.'

Energy jolted through Yesterday's arm, right down to her fingertips and into the teapot. Moments passed, stretching into little eternities.

The teapot began to wobble on the spot.

Then a blast of multicoloured tea shot out of the spout. Madrigal let out a yelp as it splattered all over his feathers. Yesterday clapped a hand over her mouth. Where the tea had landed, Madrigal's feathers had turned blue, green, and bright, eye-catching pink.

'Fool-girl!' the familiar squawked, squirming as he examined his multicoloured wings. A smell of rotting flowers filled the air. At that moment, Jack came in through the kitchen door, and fell apart laughing.

'You've made me look like a clown!' Madrigal went on. 'This is not at *all* respectable! And would you stop laughing, Mr Cadogan?'

'Sorry, sorry, you're right,' said Jack, stifling a giggle. 'There's nothing funny about this.'

Miss Dumpling wiped a gleeful tear from her eye. 'Yes, nothing at all!' she said, biting her lip to keep back a grin. 'Sorry, Madrigal, we'll get you fixed in no time. The brewing was a *little* wild, darling,' she said to Yesterday, 'but let's see how the magic is now the tea has settled down.'

Carefully, Yesterday poured herself a teacup. Then, she took a small sip. It didn't taste of the sweetness promised by the aroma of the wishfruits. In fact, it didn't really taste of anything.

She looked up at the others. 'Well, has anything changed? I don't *feel* any different.'

Miss Dumpling and Jack were both giving her sympathetic smiles. 'You're still delightfully ginger, darling, I am afraid to say,' said Miss Dumpling.

Yesterday gave an enormous sigh.

'Never mind, Essie,' said Jack, giving her a light squeeze on the arm. 'It was only your first try.'

'Yes, not to worry, dear,' added the tea witch. 'Magic, like all things worth their while, takes patience and practice.'

Yesterday felt like a popped balloon. She remembered the nasty voice – the one that had gone on about her ears, about how she belonged in Ringmaster Skelm's circus. 'Just before I said the spell, I heard this voice. It was saying such horrible, horrible things, and I . . . well, it ruined everything.'

Miss Dumpling was nodding, full of understanding. 'Sometimes, magic requires us to be so open to the world that it exposes us to the lowest parts of ourselves,' she said. 'It stops you doing anything marvellous. So, when I have a serious case of the miserables, I try to think of three wondrous thoughts.'

Yesterday glanced up at her. 'Like what?' she asked.

Miss Dumpling looked out of the window, a dreamy

expression crossing her face. 'Oh, lots of things. Like the moon at night, or the first bluebells of spring, or having a cup of hot chocolate with my friends. I find that always does the trick.'

Yesterday smiled, and was about to suggest they try again, when the whole teashop moved dramatically.

'What was that?' she gasped, nearly losing her footing as the dirty plates scuttled over to the sink to clean themselves up.

'I told Dwimmerly End to get moving as soon as she was awake,' said Miss Dumpling. 'The Goblin Market has a habit of moving about, so we have to give chase if we want to buy a mournful rose and melt the pesky ice in your heart.'

Yesterday dashed to the window. The teashop was bounding through the woods on its enormous flamingo legs, picking up pace as it emerged from the trees and out into open ground on the other side.

Yesterday watched from the window in awe, marvelling at the snow-covered hills as they rolled past. 'I wonder why people bother with horses and motorcars when they could just strap a pair of legs to the bottom of their homes!'

Just then, something came sailing through the open window and swept past Yesterday's face.

She jumped back with a gasp.

Jack tried to grab the zipping thing but it fluttered straight past him and landed delicately in Miss Dumpling's hand.

It was an elegant paper swan.

With a puzzled frown, the tea witch opened it up and read the message scrawled upon it. 'Oh dear,' she said, her face darkening. 'Oh dear, oh dear.'

'What *now*?' Yesterday said.

Miss Dumpling sighed. 'Somebody has reported us to the Royal College of Witches.' She glanced at Jack and Madrigal. 'They want to test Essie's witchery.'

Yesterday frowned. 'The Royal College of Witches? Who are they?'

'They come up with all the rules of witchcraft and make sure nobody has any fun,' grumbled Jack. 'Everyone is supposed to get a licence before they practise magic – I remember getting the letter announcing my test a few months back. With strangelings, the College is really, really strict . . . which is why Miss Dumpling doesn't let them know she's taken one in until they've settled in first.'

Sickness churned in Yesterday's stomach. 'How am I supposed to pass a witchery test when I've barely started my training? And what's so bad about strangelings, anyway?'

'The College thinks we're dangerous because we didn't grow up with magic around us,' muttered Jack. 'I mean, they're not *totally* wrong. Our magic can be a bit . . . messy to begin with.'

The incident with the Jumbling Jasmine popped into Yesterday's thoughts.

Miss Dumpling handed the letter to Madrigal to read. 'It seems the College will come and test you for your witch's licence in a fortnight, Essie. If they decide you're *too* dangerous, they may take away your magic and send you back to the human world.'

Yesterday felt light-headed and needed to steady herself against a counter. 'Send me back?' she repeated. 'But what about Mr Weep? What about the ice in my chest? Surely they can't do that. *Surely.*'

To be kicked out of the faerie world so soon, before she'd even had her first adventure, before she'd thawed the ice in her heart and broken Mr Weep's curse – it was beyond cruel.

'My guess is Mr Weep's behind all this,' said Jack, curling his hands into fists so tight his knuckles blazed. 'I bet he told the College you were here. He's trying to stop you from finding the mournful rose.'

'I imagine so,' Miss Dumpling agreed. 'We may only have two weeks until your test, and just under a month until the solstice – but where there's a witch, there's a way! We'll keep pursuing the Goblin Market, we'll track down that rose, and we'll train you for the test, all at the same time.'

'But I haven't managed to get a single tea right yet,' Yesterday pointed out. 'The two I've tried to make ended up awful. Look at Madrigal! He looks ridiculous!'

The not-raven tutted, but restrained himself from saying more.

Yesterday's fox ears drooped. 'What if there really is something wrong with these silly old ears, and I can't listen as well as you hoped after all, Miss Dumpling?'

Miss Dumpling looked at Yesterday with a very serious glint in her eye. 'Saucers and silliness, darling,' she said. 'Tea brews best when brought to the boil! All this means is that we're going to have to take your training to the next level.'

'You think I actually have a chance of passing their test?' said Yesterday. 'You don't think they'll send me away?'

Miss Dumpling gave a wink. 'Not if I have anything to do with it, they won't.'

Yesterday, despite herself, began to feel calmer. 'Maybe I'm being silly. I'll keep trying until I get the hang of it. You watch me, I'll do it! And I'll show that horrible Royal College of Witches how wrong they are about strangelings.'

Miss Dumpling's smile was warm and wise. 'Glorious news, darling. Now, Jack, Madrigal – fetch us some unicorn milk, would you? We have tea to brew.'

Chapter Eight

Unicorn Milking

Over the next two weeks, Yesterday prepared furiously for the College's arrival, studying every element of Dwimmerly End's business – from the tearoom to the kitchen, from the pantry to the library.

With Jack's help, she learned to always shave extra chocolate on to a pixie's coffee, to always bring a faun a saucer of unicorn milk with his tea, and to make sure any gnome who came into Dwimmerly End was well-supplied with luckberry jam for his scones. All the while, Miss Dumpling burrowed herself in the tealeaf reading room, tracking down the Goblin Market. But since it was a *travelling* market, finding it was rather a challenge, even for someone as skilled as Miss Dumpling.

Yesterday refused to forget it was Mr Weep who'd

almost certainly tipped off the College about her joining Dwimmerly End. He was trying to throw obstacles in her way, trying to make it all the more difficult for her to break his curse.

She didn't know what game Mr Weep was playing, but she intended to show him just what kind of an opponent he was dealing with.

Each night, Yesterday pored over *The Tome of Terrific Tea Witchery* and *The Pocket Book of Faeries*, memorising every word, and each morning, she got up and did it all again.

Sometimes she would need fresh ingredients for her brews, and when she went to fetch them from Mr Wormwood's tea garden, he would test her on the different flowers and herbs.

'Tell me, sapling! What's this one called?' he asked one day, pointing to a flower with deep purple leaves.

Yesterday hesitated. She wasn't sure about that one. 'A – a cupidsroot?' she guessed. 'Used in Heartbreaker's Bane?'

Mr Wormwood tilted his head sidelong at her. 'All flowers bloom in their own time,' said the dryad. 'Don't rush into your answer because you're trying to impress me! Your tea witchery lessons apply here as in the kitchen – listen. Listen to the garden, to the trees and the bushes. They care for you, and they will give you the answers you need.'

Yesterday sighed, searching through her knowledge of *The Tome of Terrific Tea Witchery*'s appendix, which listed all the plants used in the book's recipes. Then, she stopped.

She listened, her fox ears standing up tall. She could hear *something* in the tea garden – a whispering, a great murmuring. Something ancient and new at the same time.

And, soon enough, the answer came to her.

'It's . . . I know! It's a dreambloom. The petals are used in Dreamer's Dandelion, to give inspiration or sweet dreams to the drinker. The seeds are used in Dream*walker*'s Dandelion, which lets you wander into other people's dreams.'

'Correct!' cried Mr Wormwood, clapping his hands. A thousand cherry blossom petals popped out of thin air and fell down gently, like confetti. 'You know, little sapling, if this tea witchery business doesn't work out, you might consider becoming a gardener. The flowers certainly like you well enough!' He leaned in and whispered conspiratorially, 'They told me so themselves.'

Yet, no matter how hard she tried, every witch-brew

Yesterday attempted ended up in mayhem. Her Pearlescent Peppermint erupted in a frothy fountain of chocolatey-minty milk. Her Chamomile of Confidence tasted like soil, and the flavour was so sharp it was like being pricked in the mouth with thorns. And she had tried the Hair-Changing Hibiscus so many times, she had lost count.

'Ugh, I just can't do it!' she said one evening after everyone had gone to bed, as the teapot launched a jet of tea across the kitchen, turning the wall opposite into a kaleidoscope of pinks and blues and greens. 'I give up,' she muttered.

'So soon?' snapped a voice from behind.

Yesterday's ears shot to attention. She turned. Madrigal was perched on the edge of a kitchen counter.

'Have you been watching me this whole time?' Yesterday asked.

The not-raven snorted. 'Someone needs to keep an eye on you.'

Yesterday scowled. 'Why, because I'm a strangeling?'

'I am *trying* to help, fool-girl.'

Yesterday glared at him. 'Oh, really? Well, I'm quite capable of figuring this all out by myself, thanks.'

Madrigal let out a scoff. 'That isn't what it looks like to me.'

Yesterday took a deep breath, trying not to let the familiar's words get to her. 'Why bother helping me?' she said. 'You'd be delighted if I got kicked out.'

Madrigal fixed her with a sharp look. 'Do you know what it will do to Miss Dumpling if you fail the College's test? You are not the only one who may face punishment. Contrary to what you might think, it's not *all* about you.'

'And you putting extra pressure on me is meant to help, is it?' Yesterday snapped.

'You clearly need all the help you can get.'

Yesterday felt her temper slipping, but she didn't much care. 'Why do you always have to be so nasty to me? Any chance you get, that's what you do. What, exactly, don't you like about me, Madrigal?'

Madrigal sneered, flapping up on to a higher shelf. 'Do you want a list?'

Yesterday folded her arms. 'Yes, actually, I would.'

'Where to begin? Always thinking only about yourself – selfish. Practising tea witchery without your teacher present – reckless. Always bothering with your ears – vain.'

'That's not vanity!' Yesterday shouted, feeling hot tears prick her eyes. 'Have you ever been locked in a cage on your own, with no friends and no family, strangers gawping at you all hours of the day? If you had, you might have a bit of a complex about it too. You think so very highly of yourself and so very lowly of others, but at the end of the day, you're just a hateful little bird with no friends other than Miss Dumpling, and you don't even deserve her.'

The not-raven was quiet.

'What? Giving me the silent treatment now?' said Yesterday. 'Oh, how will I survive without being insulted every five minutes for my selfishness, for my vanity, for my—'

'*I won't fail her again!*'

Yesterday stared at the not-raven. 'What did you say?'

'You think you're the first apprentice to come Miss Dumpling's way? There's been a dozen before you, fool-girl. Every time I bring them back for her, and every time they up and leave again, taking a piece of her heart with them. One way or another, you're just going to disappoint her like the rest.'

Yesterday glared at him in silence, her lips twitching as she bit back a torrent of spite. Moments passed between them. Neither said a word. Then Madrigal straightened up. 'I . . . I should not have said that,' he said quietly. 'I was not myself.'

Yesterday turned her back on him, collecting up all the dirty, cracked, and spoiled teapots from the day's failed magic and piling them up by the sink. 'I'm going to bed. I'll sort all this out in the morning. I'm sure you'll think I'm a lazy layabout either way.'

She stormed past him and headed up to her room. As she lay there in bed, wide awake and furious, she realised that she could go one of two ways.

She could fall to pieces, accept that she was never going to be a good tea witch, and give up now, before she let Miss Dumpling down.

Or she could prove Madrigal just how wrong he and the entire Royal College of Witches were about her – about *all* strangelings.

Yesterday Crumb gritted her teeth, and determined to go with the second option.

*

The next day didn't go any better.

It was the day before the representative from the College was due to arrive, and nothing was going right for Yesterday.

If anything, her magic was getting worse, her tea fizzing angrily over the teapot's edge or splattering as high as the ceiling. *We're wasting time,* thought Yesterday bitterly. *I'm spending all my energy on trying to pass this test when I should be finding a way to thaw the splinter of ice in my heart.*

It seemed Mr Weep's plan – telling the College about Yesterday to derail her quest to break his curse – was working. And Miss Dumpling still hadn't tracked down the Goblin Market.

'I am starting to worry they may not be in England at all,' the tea witch said that evening. 'Or even our world, for that matter. Goblins are notorious for travelling to . . . unusual places in search of the best deals. Lands Dwimmerly End cannot go and the tealeaves cannot see. Quite extraordinary, really.'

'So, what if they don't come back before the winter solstice?' said Yesterday, barely able to stomach her dinner.

'Then I will go wherever they have gone,' the tea witch replied, 'and I will drag them back myself.' There was a heavy pause. 'Now, I think an early night is in order. We'll all need our spirits at their brightest tomorrow to celebrate when Essie passes her witch's licence test!'

Yesterday couldn't help smiling, even if her success was anything but guaranteed.

It was the day of her test.

Yesterday was exhausted. She had slept badly and every muscle in her body was begging her to crawl back into bed and take a long nap. She had woken extra early, determined to master just one spell, determined to show the College and Mr Weep and every single person who had ever doubted her just what she was made of.

She must have ground up a hundred cinderspice seeds and poured a dozen pints of unicorn milk already that morning, but the magic just . . . wouldn't come.

When Jack came into the kitchen, he found her with her sleeves rolled up, her hair wild and frizzy, shouting at the teapots. 'Why won't you just work like you're supposed to!'

'Maybe you need to take a break,' he said, coming over to her side. 'I reckon we should go and milk the unicorns together.'

'A break?' said Yesterday. 'The College's representative is coming *today*, Jack. I have to crack this spell!'

'You also need more unicorn milk,' Jack pointed out, gesturing to the empty pint glasses.

Yesterday hesitated. She wanted dearly to master

just one brew, but maybe Jack was right. Maybe she did need a break. Her fingers were so sore that she didn't think she could slice open another cinderspice stem for all the tiffin in Scotland.

'Promise we'll come back right after?'

'Deal,' said Jack, leading her out of the kitchen.

Despite the wintry cold outside, the walls of the unicorn stable were painted in springtime shades of yellow and green, and a carpet of grass and clover and snowdrops bloomed from the floor, the air filled with their meadow-like aroma. There were three pens – one to the left, one to the right, and one straight ahead.

'Afternoon, ladies!' Jack called, his voice echoing through the rafters. 'I've brought a guest.'

Immediately, three heads appeared over the pen gates. One was bright white, the second was golden brown, while the third was a rich, silky black. Their manes were curling coils of silver and gold, braided with flowers from the tea garden. They might have looked just like horses, if it wasn't for the fact that each one had a spiralling horn protruding from their foreheads.

'Meet Bonnie, Connie, and Lonnie,' said Jack, proudly, gesturing to each in turn. 'Scottish glen unicorns. Former steeds in the Faerie Queen's war cavalry, in fact – until they hurt their hooves back in the Unseelie War.'

Jack pushed open the wooden gate to Bonnie's pen and picked up a stool in the corner, and a metal bucket. The white unicorn, Bonnie, nuzzled him gently with her nose, then let him sit by her and start milking.

Jack looked up at Yesterday. 'Want to have a go? It's super easy.'

'Not particularly,' said Yesterday, eyeing Bonnie warily.

'I thought you'd love the unicorns,' Jack said, a little disheartened.

'I do,' said Yesterday, her fox ears standing tall and cautious. 'It just seems like good practice to keep your distance from creatures with razor-sharp horns that could skewer you like a marshmallow.'

Jack chuckled, patting the unicorn's flank. 'Are these the first monsters you've ever met?'

'Monsters!' said Yesterday. 'Don't they mind you calling them that?'

'We call all magical creatures monsters,' Jack said. 'Being a monster isn't always a bad thing.'

'Oh, I see. And, yes. They're the first,' Yesterday confirmed. 'Back in the circus, Ringmaster Skelm would stick a pair of fake wings on one of the donkeys and tell customers he was a pegasus, but I don't think that counts.'

Jack smiled. 'You sure you don't want a go? I'll show you how. You'd be amazed how much milking a unicorn can teach you about magic.'

A moment passed between them. Yesterday finally swallowed hard and said, 'OK. I can spare a few more minutes. I'll give it a try.'

With her heart thumping in her chest, Yesterday opened the pen's gate, hesitating for just a second.

Bonnie reared up, brandishing her front hooves, and gave a loud and terrifying whinny. Yesterday immediately backed out again.

'You can't let her know you're scared!' said Jack, leaping to his feet to stroke the unicorn soothingly.

'But I *am* scared!' Yesterday pointed out.

'Use your ears,' Jack suggested, as the unicorn began to settle again. 'Listen to how scared *she* is. Unicorns are super shy, but if she knows you're in charge, it'll settle her right down.'

Yesterday nodded and closed her eyes, letting her ears twitch and listen. She heard the unicorn's heavy breathing and the anxious stamping of her hooves. Jack was right. What did she have to fear from this lovely, timid thing? She took a deep breath, and walked in again, this time with her shoulders straight and her eyes firmly fixed on the unicorn.

Bonnie stayed very still, watching carefully as Yesterday entered. A moment passed. She took a small, uncertain step towards Yesterday. Then, the unicorn sniffed at her, and began to lick at Yesterday's face with her hot, sticky tongue. '*Gross!*' Yesterday cried, but she laughed all the same.

'Well done,' said Jack, motioning to the stool. 'Now, sit here.'

The unicorn stood quite happily and peacefully as Yesterday sat down. Jack guided her thumb and forefinger gently around the unicorn's udders.

'That's it,' he said. 'Squeeze down then bring your hand back to the top. Listen to the unicorn, and slow down if she sounds grumpy.'

'Nothing's happening,' said Yesterday, after a few minutes. 'What am I doing wrong?'

'If you ask me,' Jack said thoughtfully, taking a step back, 'I reckon you've got magic front to back. Topsy-turvy. You're thinking too much and feeling too little. Listening to the nasty thoughts in your brain when it's your heart that's got to do the talking. So, stop listening to your mind,' he said, tapping on his temple, 'and listen to your instincts.'

And how, exactly, am I meant to just stop listening to my mind? thought Yesterday. Then she remembered Miss Dumpling's words.

Think of three wondrous thoughts.

Yesterday closed her eyes again.

One: unicorns are real, and their milk goes perfectly in hot chocolate.

Two: I live in a travelling teashop with flamingo legs.

Three: I finally have people I can call friends.

She breathed in slowly and squeezed downwards until she heard something – the sound of milk, trickling into the bucket.

She opened her eyes.

'There you go!' said Jack. 'You're milking like a pro!'

'Shh!' Yesterday giggled, her fox ears lowering as she relaxed. 'I'm supposed to be *listening*, remember?'

Soon enough, Yesterday fell right into the rhythm of unicorn milking. One by one, they visited all three unicorns, filling up six whole buckets of milk before carrying them back into the kitchen.

'As much as it pains me to admit it,' she told Jack as they poured the buckets into pint bottles on the kitchen counter, 'this was very helpful, thank you. And thank goodness I've still got some time left to—'

A voice rumbled through Dwimmerly End, echoing off the kitchen walls, unnaturally loud. 'Stop this teashop in the name of the Royal College of Witches!' it said. 'I *mean* it, Miss Dumpling.'

The teashop juddered to a halt. Pots and cutlery tumbled off the counters and clattered to the floor.

Jack looked at Yesterday, his eyes full of fear. 'Oh, *sweetmeats*,' he said. 'The College has arrived!'

Chapter Nine

The Witch's Licence

Miss Dumpling hurried in from the tearoom. She looked at Yesterday but said nothing, instead racing to the window to gaze outside.

Yesterday joined her, peering out nervously. Hovering in the air was a lady on a broomstick with a black cat perched in her lap. She had storm-grey hair down to her shoulders, and a pointed hat and cloak the same colour.

'That's the same witch who tested me,' Jack said. 'They call her the Owl Witch – all-knowing, with talons like knives. Her familiar helps her hunt down small birds for her magical research.'

Yesterday grimaced, her stomach churning with a sickening fear.

'Mr Cadogan, I don't think you are being as helpful as you think,' said Madrigal from the windowsill.

The witch zipped around to the front of Dwimmerly End and, moments later, they could hear her barging through the tearoom door.

'Is the fool-girl ready?' said Madrigal. 'Has she managed to brew a single tea without making a mess?'

'Now who isn't being helpful?' muttered Yesterday. She paused, listening to her breath flowing in and out of her lungs. *You're thinking too much and feeling too little* . . . 'I can do this. I know I can.'

'That's the spirit,' said Miss Dumpling. 'Wait here just a moment and I'll go and butter her up. Remember everything I've taught you and you'll be as fabulous as a florentine.'

With that, the tea witch had gone. The College was here. There was nothing anyone could do about it.

'You've got this, Essie,' Jack murmured in her ear. 'You've got more magic in your toenails than most people have in their whole bodies. All you have to do is relax and show them what you can do!'

Yesterday nodded, though her mouth had gone dry. She tucked her fox ears under her hair, nerves rising as she prepared to face the Royal College of Witches.

The kitchen door burst open, and Miss Dumpling entered, followed by the Owl Witch, her broomstick in hand. Her cloak, Yesterday now realised, was made of the feathers of many different birds, woven together: falcon feathers, chicken feathers, gull feathers, partridge feathers, and who-knew-what else. She had a pinched face and an upturned nose, like a beak turned upside down, and two bright purple eyes, like Miss Dumpling's. Instead of feet, she had bird-like talons, and she stalked along like a predator.

The witch's cat familiar (or rather, 'not-cat') prowled after her. *Hello, lunch,* it mouthed to Madrigal, eyeing him hungrily. Madrigal turned away with a slight shudder.

'And who, might I ask, raised these concerns with you?' Miss Dumpling was saying.

'An old and well-respected friend of the College,' said the Owl Witch, in a high and haughty voice.

With her cloak of feathers draped around her frame and her feet that curled into claws, she did indeed look rather like an owl, Yesterday thought. As the witch's eyes settled on Yesterday, she felt as though the owl was trying to decide whether she was a mouse to be set free or gobbled alive.

'Oh, just go ahead and say who it was – *Mr Weep,*' said Madrigal, rolling his eyes. 'We all know it was him, getting the College to do his dirty work.'

'Watch your tone, familiar,' the Owl Witch snapped. 'Miss Dumpling, this is precisely why I advised you to pluck his feathers more often. Otherwise, one's familiar can develop quite the rebellious streak.' She looked at Yesterday again, with eyes so cold and clinical they would have made a surgeon jealous. 'This is the girl, I presume?'

'You presume correctly,' said Miss Dumpling. She turned to Yesterday with a comforting smile. 'Essie, this is Lady Iris Saturnine from the Royal College of Witches. She is here to test you.'

'The College's rules are simple,' said Lady Saturnine, not taking her eyes off Yesterday. 'Strangeling magic is unpredictable by nature. Unless you can prove yourself to be safe and trustworthy by passing our test, you will be forbidden from studying tea witchery. Why *do* you want to be a tea witch, young lady?'

Everyone in the room turned to look at Yesterday.

'Why?' she said, her voice quivering. How could she even begin to respond to a question like that, one with an answer so obvious, yet so hard to explain? She collected herself. 'I grew up living in a cage, and I won't ever go back to that life. I just *won't*. I want to do wonderful things and go on adventures and see the world. The world that was always hidden from me, I mean. *This* world. *Our* world.'

Lady Saturnine glanced at the not-cat, who shrugged

back at her. She cocked her head at Yesterday. 'A satisfactory answer, if a bit melodramatic,' she said. 'Now, let's see, what sort of test should I set? Perhaps, this evening, you could steal the moon from the sky and place it in a teapot?'

Yesterday blinked a few times.

'Iris, I think that may be rather unreasonable,' Miss Dumpling said. 'Why doesn't Yesterday simply perform some tea witchery for you instead?'

Lady Saturnine gave a slightly disappointed sigh. 'I suppose that will do. Succeed, child, and you will be awarded a witch's licence. Fail, and I will be forced to take your magic away for ever, and expel you from our world.'

Yesterday nodded. She was relieved she didn't have to pinch any moons. But now she had to actually perform magic safely, for once.

'You will make for me a Chamomile of Confidence,' said Lady Saturnine primly.

A Chamomile of Confidence? thought Yesterday, prickling with panic. *But I've never even tried to brew one of those before . . .*

But what choice did she have? She had to block out the voice telling her she couldn't do it, and just listen to her instincts, like Jack had said.

'Certainly,' she said, through a slightly clenched jaw, reminding herself to be polite. 'Coming right up.'

She thought hard and remembered the recipe from *The Tome of Terrific Tea Witchery.*

Chamomile of Confidence
Difficulty Level: Considerably Tricky

Ingredients

One tsp cinderspice
One tsp chamomile petals
One teapot's worth of water (boiled, preferably by tea spirit, salamander, or dragon)

I can do this, Yesterday told herself. *I can do this. I know I'm a tea witch. I just . . . have to prove it.*

She took a deep breath, then went and fetched the cinderspice from the pantry. Lady Saturnine scrutinised her every single action. It was almost impossible to concentrate on the tea witchery with those sharp eyes on her. But Yesterday focused on the ingredients, and got to work.

She ground the cinderspice and chopped up the chamomile petals while Pascal boiled some water.

Then, Yesterday combined the lot in a teapot decorated with curling green ferns.

Nervousness twisted inside her like a knife. She closed her eyes. She breathed. She thought of three wondrous thoughts.

One: the glitter of the moon on freshly fallen snow.

Two: Miss Dumpling's croissants for breakfast.

Three: I finally have something like a home, and something like a family.

She stretched her shaking fingers out and placed them around the teapot. She could hear Jack whispering to Madrigal on his shoulder, saying, 'She's got this, Mad.'

After a moment's pause, she whispered the incantation. *'Heart of tiger, fire's glimmer, may courage boil and valour simmer.'*

A marvellous energy rose up within her. The universe was not her foe; it was her friend, and she had nothing to fear – not today, not ever.

Then the darkness crept in. And so did the voice.

No one here cares about you. They're just being polite.

You're a circus act. A girl with fox ears.

You'll never be a real witch.

It coiled around her three wondrous thoughts,

squeezing out all the joy and replacing it with fear and doubt and shame.

She remembered herself in her cage in the circus, being laughed at and called cruel names.

She thought, *What if I have to go back there? What if this is all taken away from me? What if Mr Weep . . .*

She opened her eyes suddenly and gasped as a jolt of energy lanced through her body. The magic was pouring through her and into the teapot – the delight and the despair, tangled into one. The milk started to bubble, tendrils of black vapour trailing from the spout.

'Did it . . . did it work?' Yesterday said. Miss Dumpling was backing away slowly, eyes fixed on the now rattling, rumbling teapot. 'What's wrong?'

Cracks snaked across the porcelain. 'You were technically perfect, darling,' said Miss Dumpling. 'But the tea seems a bit, well, *disturbed*.'

And with that, the teapot exploded.

Chapter Ten

Inflammable Witches

Fire roiled over the kitchen table. Shards of charred teapot blasted out like bullets, striking pots and pans.

Lady Saturnine squawked an incantation. The shards of porcelain froze in the air, and reassembled back into a teapot. Miss Dumpling murmured a spell and the flames politely extinguished themselves with a crackle.

There was a silence.

'That's not supposed to happen, I take it?' said Yesterday.

'No,' said Lady Saturnine severely. 'I have seen quite enough. You are incapable of performing magic safely, Miss Crumb. The College will not be awarding you a witch's licence. You shall be stripped of your magic and your memories, and then you shall be sent back to the human world without further ado.'

'You're going to take my magic *and* my memories?' Yesterday said. She felt as though she were free-falling through empty air. 'I'm going to forget faeries, forget Dwimmerly End . . . forget all of you?'

'Well, how else did you think it would work?' said Lady Saturnine. 'We can hardly send you back knowing everything you know. And it would make it harder for you to settle back in, if you knew our world was right here, just out of reach. No, that wouldn't do. There's only one thing for it . . .'

'Iris,' Miss Dumpling said, stepping between Yesterday and Lady Saturnine. 'I have put up with a great deal from the College for years now. I've paid my dues, I've let you examine my students. But I will simply *not* put up with this. I will not allow you to squander Yesterday's potential!'

Lady Saturnine sneered at Miss Dumpling. 'Victoria, Victoria, Victoria,' she said. 'Sometimes I forget how reckless you can be. But you are a witch of the College and you will obey my authority on this matter. This girl must be expelled from the faerie world at once!'

'Iris Saturnine,' said a voice from behind them. 'You

will stop and you will think for one moment about what you are asking Miss Dumpling to do.'

Yesterday turned. To her surprise, it was Madrigal who had cut in, perched atop one of the counters.

The grey-haired witch glared at the bird. 'What did you say, familiar?'

'Have you forgotten your own history?' Madrigal continued. 'Witches used to carve their own solitary paths through the world. It is perhaps because they did not work together that they were defenceless when the humans turned on them with fire and hate. That is why your kind fled the human world to join the world of the faeries, is it not? Your College was set up for a very simple reason: because when witches stand as one, they are inflammable.'

For a moment, Lady Saturnine looked shame-faced.

'This girl may have spent more time with humans than faeries,' said Madrigal, gesturing at her with his wing, 'and she may be ill-mannered and coarse . . .'

'Thanks,' muttered Yesterday.

Madrigal ignored her and went on: 'But she has been through more than you can imagine in her very short lifetime. If Miss Dumpling thinks she has promise, and if you believe Miss Dumpling to be an astute and honest witch, then you ought to trust her opinion and give her a chance to guide her apprentice along the right path. Is not being part of a coven precisely what it means to be a witch?'

Lady Saturnine pursed her lips. She seemed to be very deep in thought. She thought and she thought and she thought and Yesterday was almost dying for her to stop thinking and say something.

'Very well,' said the witch at last. 'The girl will have one more chance. I will return with the new moon to test her again and see if she has improved. Until then, she is not permitted to do any magic outside the walls of this teashop. That is my final word.'

'Oh, Iris, darling,' said Miss Dumpling, bursting with delight. 'You are most wise and elegant and absolutely *not* the officious harpy everyone says you are.'

'Hmph,' said Lady Saturnine, quite literally looking down her nose at Yesterday. And with that, before Yesterday could get out a single word, the Owl Witch swept out of the teashop, her familiar following behind her.

Once they were gone, the whole room breathed a sigh of relief. Jack and Yesterday collapsed at the table.

'Um, Madrigal?' said Yesterday, looking over at the not-raven. 'That was . . . a surprisingly nice thing you just did for me.'

Madrigal turned his back on her, hopping off the

kitchen counter and up on to Miss Dumpling's shoulder. 'I didn't do it for you.'

'Well,' said Jack, leaning back in his chair. 'Glad that's over. Anyone up for custard tarts?'

But Yesterday was too distracted for tarts. 'Until the new moon,' she said. 'When is that?'

'A few days after the winter solstice,' said Miss Dumpling, taking the cracked teapot over to the sink. 'Plenty of time to iron out those creases, I dare say!'

'But, isn't the winter solstice only two weeks away?' said Jack.

'And that's when this stupid splinter is going to turn my heart to ice,' said Yesterday. She put her head down on the table. 'So now I have to try not to die *and* pass Lady Saturnine's next test? Lucky me.'

'One step at a time, dear,' said Miss Dumpling, returning to Yesterday's side and patting her on the shoulder. 'Now, first things first. What's for breakfast, and why isn't it cake?'

*

A couple of days later, Miss Dumpling thundered into

the kitchen, where Jack and Yesterday were busy rolling out croissant dough.

'Miss Dumpling,' said Madrigal, wearily, from the windowsill. 'Why do I get the impression you are about to propose mischief?'

Miss Dumpling smiled wryly at him. 'Mischief, darling? From me? Where on earth did you get that idea?'

'You have that look on your face. Your mischief-making look.'

Miss Dumpling chuckled. Jack and Yesterday dusted the flour off their hands and came over to listen. 'I have fabulous news. The Goblin Market has reappeared! The tealeaves say it'll be in York by tomorrow.'

'York's not far away at all!' said Jack, turning to Yesterday. She was so stunned she couldn't say a word; she really had started to lose hope. 'We're going to do it, Essie. We're going to find the mournful rose and break your curse after all!'

The teashop marched onwards, all through the day and well into the night, in pursuit of the Goblin Market. By the following morning, Dwimmerly End had nearly reached its destination.

'We'll arrive this evening!' said Miss Dumpling triumphantly, beckoning Yesterday to the kitchen window and pointing at a city in the distance. 'The human city of York. Now all that remains is to find the Goblin Market, buy a mournful rose, brew a Perfect Panacea, and Mr Weep's wickedness will be thoroughly thwarted!'

'Then you'll be able to focus on the College's next test,' Jack said cheerfully.

Something told Yesterday things were not going to be as simple as that.

Though they still had just under two weeks left until the winter solstice, Yesterday could already feel Mr Weep's ice beginning to work its wicked magic. At night, she would sometimes lie awake and shiver and tremble as she felt the splinter burrowing deeper and deeper and deeper.

'Don't worry,' said Miss Dumpling, as though she knew what was on Yesterday's mind. 'This evening, you and Jack and Madrigal will go to the Market together, and find that rose.'

'You want the girl to go to the Goblin Market?' said Madrigal, from his perch on one of the kitchen shelves. 'With all due respect, Miss Dumpling, have you lost your mind?'

'I lost my mind a long time ago, darling,' said Miss Dumpling, sitting down at the kitchen table, blowing on a teacup which had not been in her hands a few seconds ago, 'and I have no intention of ever finding it again. Yesterday has faced Mr Weep and the Royal College of Witches. I am sure she can more than keep up with the hustle and bustle.'

Jack came to Yesterday's side and hoisted himself on to the kitchen counter, his legs dangling over the edge. 'Yeah, Mad,' he said, grinning smugly at Madrigal, 'Essie's *Essie*. I reckon she can wheel and deal with the best of them.'

Yesterday's cheeks went a bit pink. She hopped up on to the counter alongside Jack. Madrigal let out a sigh. 'A fool-boy *and* a fool-girl,' he muttered. 'Just when I was starting to like you, Mr Cadogan. Have you forgotten Mr Weep and his demons? Will they not be out there, waiting for her?'

Miss Dumpling shook her head and set her teacup on a saucer. 'He wouldn't dare strike at the Goblin Market,' she said. 'The goblins have very strict rules about decorum amongst customers. And if you and Jack go with Essie, she shall be in more than safe hands.' She turned to Yesterday. 'Now, darling, you know I would come myself if I could, but the teashop is bound to me, to my soul. If I leave it for too long, it begins to lose its magic, and that won't do at all.'

Since Mr Wormwood was similarly bound to the tea garden, he couldn't go along either. Instead, he had shown them a picture of what they were looking for in the appendix of *The Tome of Terrific Tea Witchery*. 'The mournful rose's petals are radiant silver,' he'd explained. 'Think of moonlight turned into a flower, scented like graveyard soil. That is what you must seek.'

'We'll need something to give the goblins in exchange,' Jack said. He leaped off the counter and began rifling through the cupboards. He eventually produced a small, pink tin of Caramels for Courage for bartering, on the logic that treats from Dwimmerly End could be resisted by no man, woman, or faerie.

Miss Dumpling beckoned Yesterday over to the kitchen table. Lying beside her teacup were some ground-up coffee beans and a tiny vial labelled *Sphinx Spit*. 'These are the ingredients for a Clairvoyant Coffee, aren't they?' said Yesterday, frowning.

Miss Dumpling nodded. 'This coffee lets one read the minds of others – and protect one's own from scoundrels and ne'er-do-wells. If you bring a flask of it with you, you can take a sip of the coffee if and when the need arises. The Goblin Market is marvellous fun, but it's always better to be safe than sizzled.'

'Need I remind you,' said Madrigal, flapping on to

the windowsill, 'that Lady Saturnine ordered the girl not to do magic outside Dwimmerly End?'

'What the College doesn't know won't hurt them,' Miss Dumpling said, a slight edge to her voice. 'Besides, I think this is an excellent opportunity for some practice – both at making a witch-brew *and* putting it to use.'

Yesterday's frown deepened. 'You want *me* to brew it?' she said, fidgeting nervously. 'Even though my last tea exploded?'

'Indeed, I do. Practice makes perfect, darling!'

Yesterday sighed. Miss Dumpling was a formidable foe, and difficult to argue against. Rolling up her sleeves, she got straight to work.

Following the recipe in *The Tome of Terrific Tea Witchery*, she popped the ground coffee and the sphinx spit into the teapot. Once Pascal had boiled up a pot's worth of water, he poured it in for her, and Yesterday placed her hands around the teapot's body.

The Clairvoyant Coffee required its brewer to be grounded and firm, rooted in the earth. She steadied herself, trying to stay in the moment rather than being snagged away by anxious musings. Lady Saturnine had come, and she had survived. She was still in Dwimmerly End, still amongst her new friends, still amongst magic.

There was nothing to be worried about, nothing to fear. There was only the kitchen, the teapot, and the magic, just waiting to be unleashed.

Come on, Yesterday, she told herself, closing her eyes. *Think of three wondrous thoughts.*

One: the beauty of the flowers growing in the tea garden.

Two: the aroma of freshly baked gingerbread.

Three: magic exists, and I was born to do it.

Her mind now clear and calm, she said the words of the spell.

'*Coffee, coffee, roast and rise, may none hide from my all-seeing eyes.*'

Yesterday felt the usual surge of power building within her but, this time, there was no jolt, no overwhelming kick. It was sharper, certainly, but it cut through her quickly and cleanly. The teapot started to whistle as the air filled with the earthy aroma of roasted coffee beans.

'Please tell me it worked for once?' Yesterday asked, opening one eye uncertainly.

Everyone leaned over, scrutinising the teapot, watching out for any signs of explosions. Jack sniffed with his wolf snout, and gave her a gleeful smile. 'Smells pretty good to me.'

Miss Dumpling matched Jack's smile. 'We won't know for certain until you try out the magic for yourself,' she said, her antennae popping out from her hair and having a little wiggle. 'But, if my instincts are to be trusted, this feels like a jolly good pot of Clairvoyant Coffee!'

'At least it didn't explode this time,' said Jack cheerfully.

Yesterday chuckled. 'I suppose that *is* something,' she said, watching as Miss Dumpling poured the fragrant coffee into a flask and handed it to her to store in her satchel. 'Are you sure you don't want to brew a spare, Miss Dumpling? In case mine doesn't work when we're, you know, *dealing with mind-stealing goblins*?'

'Darling,' said the tea witch, flashing her a knowing look, 'there is no *in case*. There is no *what if*. There is only magic.'

Yesterday was looking at her teacher, trying to figure out exactly what that might mean, when Madrigal interrupted. 'Shoes on, children,' he said, as the teashop slowed to a halt. 'We have arrived in York. It would be quite inadvisable to miss the Goblin Market and have to start our chase all over again.'

Then, he flapped up on to Yesterday's shoulder, his

claws gripping firmly. Until now, Madrigal had only perched on the shoulders of Miss Dumpling or Jack. This was the first time he had opted for hers.

'Come now, fool-girl,' said Madrigal. 'The Goblin Market awaits.'

*

Outside the teashop's window, three little creatures were watching and listening.

'Send word to Mr Weep,' said the one named Pyewacket. 'They're trying the Goblin Market, as expected.'

'And what if they *do* buy a mournful rose?' said Lachrimus.

Pyewacket leaned back. 'They aren't going to buy any mournful roses, brother,' she said. 'Arrangements have been made. Plans have been put into motion. Poor little Yesterday Crumb is about to have a very bad day.'

Chapter Eleven

The Goblin Market

Madrigal led Yesterday and Jack through the snaking roads and alleyways of York. Narrow streets meandered between rows of muddled houses, dusty bookstores, and charming fudge kitchens. Oil lamps glimmered in the grey evening haze like tiny stars. Above it all loomed the cathedral of York Minster, its spires glinting, its gargoyles sneering down upon the city-folk below.

Eventually, they reached a square full of fashionable boutiques and coffee-houses, all closed for the night.

In the middle of the square stood a huge train. There was no station that Yesterday could see, nor rails, and it went unnoticed by the handful of humans hurrying home by twilight, who somehow knew to walk around it.

Faeries were bustling around the train, lugging their

shopping. Lumbering trolls brandished parasols against the moonlight. Slender elves with pointed ears and antlers cheerfully carried away their shopping bags. Pixies fluttered hither and thither.

Everyone held whatever they had bought that evening: glittering swords and spears, magic mirrors, dresses woven from moonlight, perfume bottles filled with sweetened manticore venom. A goat-horned busker played his pipe while a legion of mice tap-danced all around him for coins. Two boys with cornflower-blue scaly skin were laughing and flinging handfuls of colourful fire at each other from pouches tied at their waists.

'Behold, fool-girl,' said Madrigal from Yesterday's shoulder. 'This is no train of the sort that might carry you from London to Bath in an afternoon. You stand in the presence of the Goblin Market.'

'Loads of famous confectioners were goblins, you know,' said Jack, bouncing on his heels in excitement. 'I bet we'll find tons of new ingredients I can use.'

'Remember why we are here, won't you, Mr Cadogan?' Madrigal sighed.

Yesterday had been poring through the entry for goblins in *The Pocket Book of Faeries* every night since she learned they would be visiting the Market, so she knew that each carriage of the train was a self-contained shop. Lanterns hung over their doors, their pale light glowing invitingly. There were clever devices at the front and back carriages for the train to lie down and collect up its own tracks, so the Goblin Market could go wherever it pleased.

'A word of warning,' Madrigal continued. 'The Goblin Market is a casket of wonders and treasures, but it is in the nature of treasure to dazzle, and even the most magical of markets have their crooks. Some might wish to buy your true name, your teardrops, your memories, anything. Have that coffee of yours at the ready.'

Just as Madrigal had said, all kinds of fabulous things were on offer, and Yesterday wanted to see utterly everything. One shop sold shadows, harvested fresh that morning. Another listed lost spell books from a long-forgotten city amongst its wares.

They wandered along the length of the train, looking for something promising. They passed an alchemical brewery, where elixirs of youth and draughts of true love's kiss could be bought at the cheapest rates this side of Atlantis, but they didn't have any mournful roses in stock. There was a haberdashery shop, in the window of which sat a pair of Wellington boots with little wings labelled *Seven-league Boots*. Yesterday dearly wanted to pop into the cursesmith, where one could pay good money to have one's stars uncrossed or to set hexes upon one's foes, but Madrigal urged them on.

About halfway down the train's length, Jack's wolf snout wrinkled. He sniffed at the air. 'I'm getting something,' he said. 'Smells like ... graveyards and bones, mixed with something flowery. That seems mournful rose-esque, right?'

'How do you know what graveyards and bones smell like?' Yesterday asked, but he didn't answer.

Jack's nose led them to a fruit and vegetable shop named Goblin Gobbles. Next door was a tattoo parlour, where the artist was using wasp stingers as tattooing needles; in the window were a dozen wasp nests, their inhabitants buzzing sleepily.

Yesterday headed into Goblin Gobbles and found it teeming with boxes of the most delicious, juicy-looking fruits. There were plump mangos and fat cherries. Pineapples shone gold and honeydew melons released their sweetness into the air. There were gooseberries and damsons, pears and quinces, apples and grapes, fresh from the vine.

But what lured Yesterday most was a single glittering plum, lying alone in a basket, deep purple and heavy with sweetness.

'Welcome to Goblin Gobbles!' said a gentleman behind the shop's counter. He was made entirely of metal, with cogs where his eyes should have been, little brass digits for fingers, and a grandfather clock ticking in his chest. 'We have raspberries richer than rubies and pears more precious than pearls. How may I be of service?'

'That's an automaton!' Jack said to Yesterday.

'What's an automaton?' asked Yesterday, pulling her eyes away from the plum.

'*I* am an automaton!' the clockwork man announced cheerfully. Yesterday noticed the word *breathe* was scrawled across his brass forehead in gleaming green letters. 'My master made me, then brought me to life. My name is Widdershins. I run the shop for my master. It's a very important role. Lots of responsibility.'

'Nice to meet you, Widdershins,' said Yesterday, smiling at the friendly automaton. 'I'm Yesterday, and this is Jack and Madrigal. We're looking for a—'

'What's all this then?' snorted a voice from the back of the shop. It belonged to a goblin. He had the face of a pig, with little tusks protruding from his lips, and a wet brown snout. He stood only as tall as a breakfast table, and wore a jacket stitched together from handkerchiefs and napkins. He had emerged from a door behind the shop counter, which connected to the neighbouring carriage.

'Oh! Mr R-Rottenpockets, sir,' exclaimed Widdershins. He straightened up. 'Th-this is Miss Yesterday, Mr Jack, and Mr Madrigal. They seem very nice indeed. I think you'll like them a lot.'

The goblin, Mr Rottenpockets, gave the automaton a withering look and said, 'Enough yammering, you unsightly bunch of scrap metal.'

In a flash, the goblin produced an iridescent feather with an inky nib, shimmering like the Northern Lights. He scratched out the word *breathe* on Widdershins' forehead, which vanished at once. The automaton fell completely still, his head lolling towards his chest.

Yesterday stared in horror.

'Sorry about that,' said Mr Rottenpockets, tucking away the feather. 'Hard to find an automaton who can keep his thoughts to himself, you know. Now, what can I interest you in? We have pomegranates from Proserpina's orchards and apples from Idun's grove. Everyone can find something to whet their appetite at Goblin Gobbles.'

'You killed him!' said Yesterday, standing slack-jawed.

The goblin rolled his eyes. 'He's an *automaton*. Who cares? I'll bring him to life again once he's learned to bolt his mouth shut.'

'Isn't that a Quirky Quill?' said Jack, squinting at the feather. He added to Yesterday, 'It's a really rare magical device. Anything you write *breathe* on will come to life and be your servant. How much for the Quill, my good goblin?'

Madrigal tutted from Yesterday's shoulder. 'Behave yourself, Mr Cadogan.'

'It's not for sale,' said the goblin, eyes narrowing at Jack.

'Ignore him. We're not here for the quill,' said Yesterday, still feeling very uncomfortable about the poor, slumped automaton.

'We're looking to buy a mournful rose,' said Madrigal, turning his attention back to the goblin. 'Are we right in thinking that you might have one in stock?'

A smirk slithered across the goblin's mouth. 'That is a most rare flower, you know. The rarest, even. You would not believe what I had to do to get my hands on one. I'll sell it to you, but it will cost you dearly. An arm and a leg at the very least! Your voice would cover the cost handsomely.' He glanced at Yesterday. 'Or perhaps your soul?'

Yesterday shuddered. 'My soul isn't for sale,' she said curtly.

'No trouble, no trouble,' said Mr Rottenpockets. 'The

soul is a weak currency these days, anyway. No one's buying, everyone's selling. Simple supply and demand.'

'We've got Caramels for Courage!' said Jack enthusiastically, producing the small tin from his pocket. 'Made them myself.'

The goblin blinked at him. 'Is that it? Is that all you have to trade with?'

'Um. Yes?' said Jack. 'They're quite delicious. And we could all use some courage now and again, wouldn't you say?'

The goblin pursed his lips as he watched Yesterday thoughtfully. He reached out to the plum she had been eyeing since she entered, and snapped his fingers. The plum lifted into the air and glided into his hand. 'You say you only came for the rose, but I see other desires in your heart, strangeling.'

Madrigal interrupted promptly: 'Just the rose, thank you very much.'

Yesterday's gaze locked on the plum and its promise of sugary juices.

'Do you not see how the girl longs to taste goblin fruit?' said Mr Rottenpockets softly, like a mother to a child. 'You are missing something, aren't you, strangeling? Goblin fruit can fill the void.'

'It can?' Yesterday said dreamily. She shook her head

to clear a sudden dizziness from her mind. 'No, thank you, sir. We'll take the mournful rose and that's it.'

'Just imagine how sweet that goblin fruit tastes,' said Mr Rottenpockets. 'Don't we all deserve our indulgences, now and again?'

'Fool-girl, the Clairvoyant Coffee – drink it now,' whispered Madrigal, but she could barely hear him. 'We have a job to do! Need I remind you of the ice Mr Weep lodged in your heart?'

'Who's Mr Weep?' said Jack languidly. His eyes had glazed over, and his wolf snout was sniffing curiously at a bushel of apples.

Madrigal turned to the goblin and said, 'I see what you are doing. This whole Market should be shut down because of scoundrels like you!'

'Me, a scoundrel? That's rich!' said Mr Rottenpockets. 'There's only one reason why a faerie would have mismatched eyes like theirs – they're neither-nors.' He spat the words out like they were poison.

Yesterday did not know what *neither-nor* meant, nor did she care. Right now, she only wanted one thing.

The goblin turned to her and said sweetly, 'Why not eat, scrumptious? Why not soothe your broken soul?' His grin stretched from ear to ear. 'Why not give in to temptation? Submit to your hunger. Slake your thirst.'

Yesterday was entranced. 'Just a nibble couldn't hurt, I'm sure.'

'Just a nibble,' Jack agreed, as he reached for an apple.

Yesterday took the plum and split it apart with her hands. *Submit to your hunger. Slake your thirst.* She took a bite, caring little for the scarlet juices dribbling down her chin like blood. 'Madrigal!' she cried through her mouthful. 'Madrigal, it's so utterly delicious, you have no idea. You just *have* to try some.'

Madrigal stared at her, twitching slightly. His eyes were growing wide, dark, intoxicated. 'But we do not know where he grew his fruits. The Market plays on your wants, then swallows you whole. Or so I have heard. Where did I hear that?'

Mr Rottenpockets only smirked. 'You're a smart familiar. You shouldn't listen to such gossip.'

'No, I suppose I shouldn't.'

'Madrigal,' said Yesterday, pleading. She could have sobbed. The juices were so sweet, and she was only getting hungrier and hungrier. 'You must give this a try!'

'You're missing out, Mad!' Jack said. 'This is the most delicious thing I've ever eaten in my life!'

'D-delicious, you say?' the not-raven said. 'I must

say, I am feeling rather ravenous. I think I must try one of these fruits. Yes, just one taste ... just a little taste ...'

He flapped off Yesterday's shoulder and plucked a grape with his beak, before swallowing it whole.

Almost instantly, his eyes rolled back in his head, and he collapsed, a heap of feathers on the floor. Heartbeats later, Jack slumped down next to him.

'Jack? Madrigal?' Yesterday said, still chewing the same mouthful of plum. It had turned into foul-tasting soil in her mouth and she spat it out. She glowered at the goblin. 'What have you—'

But she crumpled to the ground beside Madrigal and Jack before she could finish her sentence.

Chapter Twelve

Yesterday-Flavoured Jam

The moment Yesterday awoke, she became aware of a stabbing pain in her head. Groaning, she forced herself to sit up and take in her surroundings, only to bang her forehead on something – a ceiling. A very low ceiling.

Her eyes snapped open. To her horror, she realised she was squashed in a tiny, enclosed space. In front of her was a glass door. She peered through the glass to try and get a sense of where she was and saw . . . a kitchen?

That's when she realised – *I'm in an oven.*

With increasing desperation, she pushed and yanked at the door, but it would not open. It would not budge even an inch.

She looked through the glass again. The kitchen

beyond was not at all like the one in Dwimmerly End. There were ovens and counters hewn from scrap metal. A pantry was sealed off behind a steel door. Mismatched pots and pans dangled from racks on the ceiling. A pot of crimson sludge bubbled and boiled on a stove on the other side of the room. The shelves were stacked with jars – she could make out the labels: *Mermaid Scales* and *Pickled Dragon Hearts*.

Her friends were nowhere to be seen.

Just then, Mr Rottenpockets entered the kitchen, a meat cleaver glittering in his hand and a shadowy rat-like creature at his side.

'Oh, I was *extremely* happy to receive your letter, Miss Pyewacket,' said Mr Rottenpockets to the rat-creature. Yesterday pressed her fox ears against the glass to listen. 'It is a great honour to do business with Mr Weep. Quite a shame he couldn't come to collect his order himself.'

Mr Weep! thought Yesterday, her heart sinking. *Of course he's behind this.*

'I don't mean to be rude,' said Pyewacket, sneering as she cast her eyes around the room, 'but Mr Weep wouldn't be caught dead in a place like this. Sorry, mate, that's just how High Society is these days. It's all about where you're seen, and who you're seen with.'

Mr Rottenpockets made an attempt at a thin smile. 'The important thing, of course, is the payment . . .'

'You'll get your payment,' snapped Pyewacket. 'Two dozen harpy livers, as agreed in advance – a vast improvement on whatever *she* offered you, I'm sure. Where is the girl now?'

Mr Rottenpockets paused. 'Oh, she, ah . . . escaped,' he said vaguely.

Pyewacket shot him a look. 'You'd better not have done anything to her, Rottenpockets.'

Rottenpockets froze. 'Hm?' His eyes drifted to Yesterday in the oven. 'Like I said, she ran off. If any harm comes to her, it's nothing to do with me.'

Pyewacket made a small clicking sound, her rat teeth chittering. 'Let's just hope for your sake it doesn't,' she said. 'Fetch us the rose, then. This conversation's boring me.'

Rottenpockets disappeared into the pantry for a few moments, then returned with a single flowerpot. Growing from the soil was a flower. Just like Mr Wormwood said, its petals gleamed like sheaths of moonlight. The sight of it gave Yesterday chilling tingles.

The mournful rose, she thought. *And he's going to hand it over to that thing working for Mr Weep!*

She banged ferociously on the oven door, trying to force it open, but it was no good. The rat-creature seemed not to hear her. She shook hands with the goblin, and walked out of the shop, taking the mournful rose with her.

Yesterday clenched her jaw. *I can't lose that rose,* she thought. *The winter solstice is less than two weeks away!*

The goblin put on a chef's hat and headed over to the stove across the room to give the pot a stir. Then he turned suddenly, as if remembering something. His eyes met Yesterday's as he came and peered into the oven.

'Good evening, my treat,' the goblin said, his mouth contorting into a fanged smile. He unbolted the oven door and cracked it open just an inch. 'Did you sleep well? I'm afraid I had already promised that mournful rose of yours to Mr Weep's secretary.'

'What am I doing in an oven?' Yesterday demanded.

'Why, what does it look like?' He leaned in, his breath clouding the oven's glass. 'I am going to roast you, then mix your soul with my berries. Then we shall all enjoy Yesterday-flavoured jam on toast.' His eyes narrowed at her. 'Would you like that, neither-nor? Would you like to be scrumptious goblin jam?'

'Not particularly,' Yesterday said. 'I'd quite like to remain alive, if I'm honest. There's not much one can do from the belly of a goblin.'

'But your soul will give my jam the most amazing flavour,' Mr Rottenpockets reasoned.

'What about Mr Weep?' she said. 'Didn't you hear that Pyewacket creature? If he finds out you've *eaten* me, you have no idea what he'll do to you!'

The goblin smiled almost pitifully at her. 'But, little neither-nor,' he said, 'you are quite valuable to someone very important. And all that greed, all that coveting – they are the perfect seasonings for a merchant like me! You are an unmissable delicacy, I assure you.' With that he closed the oven door and straightened up again.

Yesterday felt terror rising in her. She knew she had to think, and think fast. She hammered on the door again. 'How do you *know* I'll be so delicious?' she shouted.

Mr Rottenpockets crouched down. He raised a long, bushy eyebrow and re-opened the door. 'What did you say?'

'I might taste disgusting, for all you know! I'm almost certainly poisonous. I think if you're going to add an untested ingredient to your culinary masterpiece, you should at least have a taste first.'

161

With a furrowed brow, the goblin stared at her.

'Just think!' Yesterday urged. 'I could spoil the whole thing. Just a finger. That's all it would take. So you can taste and know if it's a good idea.'

The goblin frowned as he weighed up her suggestion in his mind. At last, he said, 'Oh, all right. Might as well, I suppose.'

He pulled open the oven door and reached inside with clawed hands, clasping Yesterday's wrist like an iron vice. He yanked her out and dragged her to a counter. Sweeping aside a few dirty plates and a fork encrusted with unpleasant-looking gunk, he pressed her arm against the counter, splaying out her fingers. Then he reached for a glinting cleaver.

'Right,' he said, raising the blade into the air, 'I shall just take a finger . . . or perhaps one of your lovely ears. Ooh, imagine, salted fox ears on toast, my favourite . . .'

While he was deliberating, Yesterday was frantically eyeing up the crusty fork, wondering if she might just be able to reach it with her other hand. While the goblin's eyes were on her ears, she took her chance. With her free hand, she lunged for the fork, grasped it, and drove it swiftly into the goblin's arm. The goblin shrieked in agony, dropping his cleaver on to the counter with a clang.

'You worthless morsel!' he roared, as he plucked the fork from his flesh. Fumbling for the cleaver, he fixed his foul eyes upon Yesterday. 'Forget roasting you first. You'll just have to boil in the jam!'

'Oh, *please*,' Yesterday snapped. 'I've met pixies more intimidating than you.'

Mr Rottenpockets seized the cleaver and charged. He swung madly, his blade a flash of deadly silver. Yesterday ducked instinctively and the blade spun through the air, cutting off a tuft of her hair, which fell into the pot of jam with a sizzle.

Yesterday grinned. 'Missed me.'

With a frenzied shriek, the goblin pounced at her. He seized her neck, his claws digging in as he squeezed tighter and tighter. He pressed her against the side of the pot, her hair spilling down into the jam, singeing the ends.

Yesterday scrabbled all around, searching for something, anything, to use as a weapon. Her fingers found the handle of a pan hanging above the pot of jam and she swung it as hard as she could at the goblin's head.

The blow struck Mr Rottenpockets right in the temple. He staggered backwards, and she swiped her foot at his ankles to help him on his fall. With all her strength, Yesterday thrust him towards the open oven, slamming the door shut as he tumbled in.

The goblin pounded his fists against the glass. 'Sorry?' said Yesterday, lowering herself to his eye level and cupping a hand around her fox ear. 'Can't quite hear you. Glass is too thick, I think.'

She gave a shrug, and a grin, and turned her back on the oven-trapped goblin.

On the ground, she spotted something gleaming. It was the Quirky Quill. It must have fallen from the goblin's pocket. She picked it up and put it in her own pocket, before scanning the kitchen, searching for any sign of where Jack and Madrigal might be.

An idea came to her. She pushed through the kitchen door, returning to the fruit and vegetable shop. There, she found the automaton Widdershins, still as motionless as when she had seen him last.

With the Quirky Quill, she wrote *breathe* upon his brow and he shuddered back to life.

'Oh!' gasped the clockwork automaton. 'What happened to me? I felt as though I were dreaming, but all there was in my mind was darkness and despair.'

'Mr Rottenpockets shut you down,' Yesterday explained. 'I know he built you, Widdershins, but he's a horrible goblin and I won't apologise for saying so. If you help me find my friends, I reckon you'd be more than welcome to stay with us for a while.'

Widdershins steepled his brass fingers nervously. 'But . . . but I belong here.'

'No, you don't. You were *made* here, but I don't for one second believe this is your home. Home is something you choose for yourself. Would you choose to stay with someone who turns you on and off whenever he pleases?'

The automaton looked at the ground. 'No, I suppose not,' he said sadly. Then he looked up at her and smiled. 'I choose to come with you – if you're sure that's all right with you?'

'I'm sure,' said Yesterday, smiling. 'So, Widdershins, will you help me find my friends?'

The automaton's cogs and gears wheeled around cheerfully. 'Well, of course I will!' he said, leading her back through to the kitchen. 'Now, let's see . . . Oh! I know where they'll be.'

He went to one of the kitchen cupboards, doing his best to ignore Rottenpockets, who was still hammering his fists on the oven door. He pulled hard on the cupboard's handle, but it appeared to be locked. He carried on pulling until, with a sharp jerk, he ripped the door clean off its hinges. As he placed it neatly on the counter, Jack, Madrigal, and Yesterday's satchel tumbled out of the cupboard and on to the floor. Jack and Madrigal appeared to be sleeping.

'What is going on here?' said Madrigal, waking with a start. 'Where are we?'

'We ate goblin fruit,' explained Yesterday, shouldering her satchel, 'and then the goblin nearly ate us. But I defeated him, stole his Quirky Quill, and freed his automaton.'

Madrigal blinked at her. 'Ah,' he said, fluttering up on to her shoulder. 'Business as usual, then. Give Mr Cadogan a kick, will you?'

'Five more minutes,' Jack murmured, turning over to face the other way.

At last, after Yesterday had poked him in the ribs, Jack groggily picked himself up.

'Some rat-creature who works for Mr Weep ran off with the rose,' said Yesterday. 'We have to find her before it's too late!'

'Sounds like a galtzagorriak imp,' groaned Madrigal. 'She is probably back in the Underneath by now.'

'There must be *something* we can do!' Yesterday said, leading everyone through to the main shop.

'Have some faith, won't you, Mad?' said Jack, peeking out of the front door. 'If we let them escape with our mournful rose, we might never find another!'

Yesterday refused to accept they had lost. Then, she remembered what was in her satchel. She reached in and pulled out the flask. As she removed the lid, the place filled with the all-encompassing aroma of coffee.

'The Clairvoyant Coffee!' said Jack, his wolf snout wiggling with delight. 'Better late than never, eh?'

'Time for some emergency magic,' agreed Yesterday, bringing the flask up to her lips. 'Let's just hope I brewed it properly.'

She took a deep breath and drank down every last bitter drop.

Then, she looked up, and everyone in the room started to scream.

Chapter Thirteen

Clairvoyant Coffee

'What?' said Yesterday with a frown. 'Why are you all screaming at me?'

'Sorry,' said Jack. His shocked expression had changed to a delighted grin. 'See for yourself,' he told her, gesturing to Widdershins.

Yesterday looked at her reflection in Widdershins' brass chest and saw what everyone was screaming at. A third eye had wriggled out of her skin and established itself upon her forehead. It blinked curiously back at her. 'Gosh,' she said, observing it from different angles. 'The brew actually *worked*!'

She couldn't believe it. She had done real tea witchery for the very first time. It was almost overwhelming. Despite their circumstances, her smile was radiant.

'Hm. It seems it did,' said Madrigal, a faint trace of surprise in his voice. 'Congratulations, I suppose.'

'Go on, then!' said Jack, bouncing from foot to foot with excitement. 'Give it a try!'

Yesterday swallowed nervously. 'Well, OK. Here goes nothing.'

A little unsure of what exactly she was meant to be doing, Yesterday closed her eyes and did her best to concentrate.

She reached out with her mind and, to her surprise, she felt something shift.

Suddenly, she could see in a way she never had before. She could see Madrigal's thoughts, like a cloud of locusts, buzzing around his head. Each thought shouted at her, one after another.

I know you are in here, fool-girl, the familiar was thinking. *I know you are in here and you are not welcome.*

She withdrew from Madrigal's head and immediately delved into the mind of Widdershins. His thoughts were heavy and clunky, like great stones or hunks of metal. *I must help. I must help. How can I help? I cannot help. I am useless. I am a lump of clockwork. Useless, useless, useless.*

She could not bear another second of it, so she retreated and forced her attention elsewhere.

Her vision expanded, shooting through the different carriages of the Goblin Market. *How many teardrops did I acquire today?* thought one shopkeeper. *If I can sell twenty more nightmares, I can buy that staff I've always wanted,* thought another.

Entirely by accident, she found the thoughts of a pigeon swooping overhead. *Worm!* its mind screamed as it dived down for a catch.

Yesterday felt such power that she was sure she could have taken control of the pigeon's mind, manipulating its wings and beak and claws, if she fancied. But she stopped herself from indulging that interest.

Instead, she kept on searching the length of the train until at last she found what she was looking for: the mind of an imp, sitting on top of the train, a few carriages down.

The imp was talking with two other demons just like herself, and they were passing around a goblet of something.

'I propose a toast, lads!' Pyewacket announced. 'To us – for stopping the girl from finding the last mournful rose! Except for the ones growing at Thistle Hall, o' course.'

'To us!' the other two cheered. 'Pass us that ghastly goblin rum, then, Pye . . .'

Yesterday gasped as she pulled out of the imp's mind. 'There's three of them, up on the train roof,' she said. 'They've got the rose.'

Yesterday noticed a ladder on the wall leading up to a little trapdoor. She scrambled up it and, pushing the trapdoor open, emerged on the roof of the train. Jack, Madrigal, and Widdershins followed promptly after her.

'Fool-girl, you can't just go clambering around on the roof of a train!' Madrigal was saying, but Yesterday was off, tearing along the top of the carriage, until she spotted three rat-like figures up ahead. Her fox ears stood up as she heard a snickering, sneering voice.

'Well, well, well. Look who it is,' said Pyewacket, standing and brushing herself down. The other two imps stood either side of her and eyed Yesterday menacingly. 'I had a *feeling* you were still around here somewhere. The name's Pyewacket. This is Lachrimus and Bread-and-Slug. It's a pleasure to meet you, Yesterday Crumb.'

Lachrimus chuckled. 'It'll be a pleasure plucking out your eyeballs and swallowing them whole, too,' he said.

Yesterday rolled her eyes at them. 'Talk all you want,' she said, 'but all you will ever be is a monster's servants, and I can't think of anything more pathetic than that.'

'We're his secretaries, *actually*,' said Bread-and-Slug, sticking out his blue tongue.

Pyewacket gave him a shove. 'Shut it,' she told him, and cocked her head at Yesterday. From behind her back, she produced the thing Yesterday had most wanted to see – the mournful rose, sparkling silver in the moonlight. 'You want the rose? You want to break Mr Weep's pesky little curse? Well, why don't you come and get it?'

'How about this instead?' said Yesterday, smiling the sweetest smile she could manage. 'Why don't you –' she reached out with the Clairvoyant Coffee's magic, trying to find her way into Pyewacket's thoughts – 'just give it to me?'

She saw the imp's thoughts in the air, and tried to seize them, to pluck them like the strings of a marionette. 'Watch out, Pye,' warned Lachrimus, tapping his sister's shoulder. 'Her forehead.'

'She's a tea witch, ain't she!' said Bread-and-Slug, backing away. 'Let's get out of here!'

Pyewacket kept smiling. 'Bread-and-Slug, why don't you show our friends here what you procured from the Goblin Market this evening before we go?'

Bread-and-Slug grinned. 'Happy to, big sis,' he said, and produced a pale blue fan. 'Made from thunderbird feathers, this is. Know what that means?'

'Get down!' Madrigal squawked, but it was too late.

The imp waved the fan and unleashed a great blast of wind. The force of the gust swept Yesterday clean off her feet. It sent Madrigal, Jack, and Widdershins flying across the roof of the carriage. Stomach lurching, Yesterday tried to stop herself from skidding over the edge of the train.

'Grab on to something, quick!' shouted Jack, but before she could, Yesterday went tumbling over the edge with a scream.

As she went, she reached out and caught hold of a pipe. Swinging wildly, legs kicking through empty air, she clutched on to it desperately. Her arms burned as she tried to hold up her weight. Her fingers started to slip. If she fell, it would shatter every bone in her body. Some of the Goblin Market's shoppers gasped and pointed from below.

'Miss Yesterday!' said Widdershins, his head appearing over the edge of the train. 'Thank goodness I wasn't too late!'

Grasping on to her arm, the automaton pulled her back on to the safety of the train's roof. 'Thanks,' gasped Yesterday, scrambling to her feet. The imps were dashing down the train, snickering as they went.

Madrigal swooped after them, shrieking, 'Stop, you bandits!'

'Daft bird,' snarled Lachrimus, drawing a bone-handled knife.

The blade sparkled in the light of the streetlamps. The imp slashed madly at the familiar, but Madrigal pirouetted in the air, flourishing his wings. Yesterday didn't know how, but when the blade touched the familiar, it did not cut. The blade simply crumbled into a cascade of brown sugar.

Madrigal retreated to Yesterday's side. At that moment, the train beneath her juddered. 'What was that?' she said, staggering.

She looked all around. The city of York was churning slowly past.

The Goblin Market was moving.

'The Market has a schedule to keep, fool-girl,' said Madrigal, flapping in mid-air. 'We must leave now, before it is too late.'

'But we have to get the rose!' Yesterday shouted, starting after the imps, who were still sprinting down the train.

The Goblin Market rattled along, picking up pace

as it laid its own tracks in front of itself and puttered out of the town square. At the end of the square, it turned swiftly to one side and began racing towards a coffee-house. Yesterday was certain they were going to crash right into it. But then at the last second, the train tilted upwards, and it started climbing the side of the building.

Up the train went, up and up the walls. Jack and Yesterday screamed as they slid and fell backwards, the smooth surface of the metal offering little purchase as they clung on to whatever they could. But then, just when they could hold on no longer, the train righted itself, and the Goblin Market carried on its journey, chugging away over the rooftops of York's shops and houses.

The wind was bellowing all around them now, like the roar of a lion, lashing Yesterday's hair wildly about. The world raced past at a dizzying speed.

Yesterday gritted her teeth and got to her feet yet again. 'Those imps aren't getting away *this* easily,' she muttered, and began to run.

She reached the gap between two carriages. Sprinting at full pelt, she leapt right over it, landing firmly on the other side. Laughter escaped her throat. *I just jumped between moving train carriages,* she thought, and on she went, not a moment to waste.

As she ran, she kept reaching out with her mind, trying to get to Pyewacket. Instead, she found wasps' nests in the carriage beneath her, with a thousand buzzing creatures, their gossamer wings fluttering, their antennae twitching. Acting on instinct, she flooded their weak minds with her own will.

Stop the imps, she ordered. The swarm complied, buzzing out of its nest, streaming out of the window in a blitz of black and yellow until they reached the imps further up the train.

And then, the imps screamed.

The wasps had descended upon them and sank their stingers into exposed flesh. Bread-and-Slug flapped his fan at them, blasting the wasps away. The chaos gave Yesterday enough time to catch up. But then, the imp aimed his fan at Yesterday and the others for another strike.

'Oh, no, you don't!' said Jack, producing a rope of stretchy pink candy from his pocket – like the one Yesterday had seen in his confectionary laboratory holding up his bed. Whipping it through the air, he launched the candy like it was a lasso. It wrapped itself around the fan and Jack yanked hard, flinging the device off the train and into oblivion.

Pyewacket grunted in frustration. Angry red spots

covered the rat-creature's skin where the wasps had struck. The imps turned and bolted, racing further down the train. Yesterday pursued, jumping between train carriages, adrenaline thrumming through her, the world blurring past.

Soon, they neared the front of the train. The imps had nowhere else to run.

'Boys, time for Plan B I'd say?' said Pyewacket, glancing over her shoulder at Yesterday.

'Plan B it is, Pye,' said Lachrimus, with a wink.

The ratty imps darted onward, bounding over the gap between the last two train carriages. They reached the locomotive at the front, at which point they disappeared through an open trapdoor, down into the engine room.

Yesterday tore after them. She vaulted on to the roof of the locomotive. Then, she slipped down the ladder into the smoke-filled chamber below.

At the bottom of the ladder, she whirled to face the imps, gathered around the door to the engine's firebox. 'For the last time,' said Yesterday, reaching out with the power of the Clairvoyant Coffee, 'hand over the mournful rose.'

But to her distress, she realised that the magic had faded.

The imps could see it too. The eye on her forehead must have disappeared. 'Oh, we do love a fighter,' said Pyewacket.

Yesterday's stomach knotted. 'Give me that rose, or . . . Or I will make sure you regret it.'

Bread-and-Slug grinned as he opened the firebox door. Heat surged up from its fiery, glowing belly.

'I cannot fathom you, girl,' said Pyewacket. 'Why would anyone turn down the gifts of Mr Weep for a job in a teashop? You could've owned crowns and kingdoms!'

'Jewels and riches!' added Lachrimus.

'Feasts and fine things!' said Bread-and-Slug.

'But *why*?' asked Yesterday. 'Why offer me these gifts, then put a splinter of ice in my heart? What game is he trying to play?'

Pyewacket shrugged. 'I wouldn't ask too many questions, if I were you. In any case, we've got places to go, people to exsanguinate. You know how it is. So, let's get on with it, shall we?'

'Can't we just discuss this?' Yesterday pleaded.

Pyewacket simply smiled and tossed the rose over her shoulder. 'Oops.'

'No!' cried Yesterday, lunging for the rose. But it was too late. The mournful rose fell through the air and an updraft sucked it down into the firebox.

The flames immediately turned a bright and crackling silver.

There was a deep rumbling sound.

'Miss Crumb, I really must insist now ...' squawked Madrigal, his head appearing from the open trapdoor on the roof.

An enormous boom erupted from the furnace. Its casing ruptured open, fragments of metal firing outwards. Yesterday managed to leap on to the ladder just in time to dodge a splinter of steel that shot past her and buried itself into the wall.

The train shook as it swerved to one side and began skidding wildly over the rooftops, crashing through chimneys in explosions of smoke and bricks.

'Time to go,' said Pyewacket with a grin.

The three imps darted over to the carriage door. Pyewacket kicked it open. The world whizzed past as the Goblin Market veered wildly and unpredictably over the rooftops, the road below a blur of paving stones. The train teetered to and fro, dangerously close to tipping into the silvery-black river running alongside.

'Mr Weep sends his regards!' snickered Lachrimus.

And with that, they leapt through the open door and out into the night, abandoning Yesterday and the others to their runaway train.

Yesterday immediately dropped back down from the ladder and set about pulling levers and pressing buttons at random.

'There must be a brake here somewhere,' she said as the others clambered down into the locomotive to help. If anything, she seemed to be making things worse, as the train thundered onwards faster and faster.

Then, just when she was beginning to despair, a splendid voice sang to them from the other side of the open door. 'I say, my darlings! It appears you are in need of some assistance!'

Yesterday peered out. Dwimmerly End itself was dashing alongside them across the tops of the houses on its long flamingo legs, doing its best to keep up with the Goblin Market. Miss Dumpling was standing in the front doorway.

'There's only one thing for it,' said Jack. 'We need to jump.'

'*Jump?*' replied Madrigal. 'Have you gone *quite* round the bend?'

Widdershins piped up. 'Miss Yesterday, if you climb on to my back, I can carry Mr Jack in my arms,' he suggested earnestly. 'Then Mr Madrigal can fly, and we'll all jump together.'

'It will take but a leap of faith!' the tea witch called out to them.

'That woman has a hideous approach to workplace safety,' huffed Madrigal.

It was hardly ideal, but Yesterday could see no alternative. She nodded to Widdershins and the automaton hoisted her on to his back. Scooping up Jack in his arms and carrying him like a child, he bolted for the train door.

And then, he jumped.

Yesterday held her breath.

She closed her eyes.

And *whoosh*.

Then, a great thump.

Her ears rang. Her head pounded. But when Yesterday opened her eyes, she found that she was on the floor of Dwimmerly End's tearoom, a bit bumped and bruised, but otherwise safe and sound. She had somehow survived.

Looking around, she could see the others were OK too, all save for Widdershins, whose arm had snapped off upon impact.

'Never mind!' he said merrily, picking up his dismembered arm and fastening it back in place. 'I'm much easier to repair than most folk.'

'Miss Dumpling, meet Widdershins,' said Yesterday, getting to her feet. 'Widdershins, Miss Dumpling.'

Miss Dumpling gave him a curtsey. 'How do you do, darling?' she said, and the automaton, not knowing what else to do, gave a quick bow.

There was a screeching sound from behind. Yesterday turned and looked out of the teashop door to see the Goblin Market topple over the edge of the rooftops. With an almighty splash, it crashed down into the deep, dark river below, the goblins scrambling out of the windows to safety.

'Goodness me,' said Miss Dumpling, glancing at the sinking train. She turned to Yesterday. 'Well, don't keep me in suspense! Was your daring mission a success?'

Yesterday shook her head heavily. She wanted to cry out her apologies that the goblins' wonderful market had ended in the river.

'Ah, my dears,' said Miss Dumpling in a warm, gentle voice. In an effort to lift spirits, she spun around and clapped her hands. The teapots lifted off their shelf at the back, whizzing into action. 'Pop the kettle on and get out the cake – whatever else happened, I bet you've got a wonderful story to tell.'

Chapter Fourteen

Neither-Nor

Once everyone was gathered around the kitchen table with their mugs and teacups, they set about telling Miss Dumpling and Mr Wormwood the full story. Yesterday began the tale, then Jack picked it up with their chase across the train carriages, Madrigal tutting disapprovingly now and then.

'And that's the whole story,' Jack concluded, taking a sip of hot chocolate. 'Easily in my top-ten favourite adventures.' He glanced at Yesterday, and his glee faded a smidge. 'Other than the fact we lost the rose, of course.'

Miss Dumpling set her cup on its saucer and gave Yesterday a knowing smile. 'So, the Clairvoyant Coffee was a success, darling?'

Yesterday smiled back at her teacher. 'You should've

seen the looks on these two when they saw my third eye,' she said. Then, under her breath, 'Eat your heart out, Lady Saturnine.'

It was Jack who asked what everyone was thinking. 'Mr Wormwood,' he said in a quiet voice, 'are you any closer to finding out where mournful roses grow?'

The dryad shook his head gravely. 'I'm afraid not, boy. That knowledge appears to be lost.'

Jack put his head into his palms.

'Do not wilt, Mr Cadogan!' said Mr Wormwood, in a philosophical tone. 'Our universe is poetry, written in stars and mountains and forests. Some poems are tragic. That is what makes them beautiful.'

Miss Dumpling nodded along. 'Terribly sage, Mr Wormwood, I'm sure. Though I should quite like to prevent Yesterday's particular tragedy from coming to pass, if I can help it. There's got to be *something* out there that'll help us find those elusive roses.'

'The imps knew,' said Yesterday, scratching her chin. 'They were being all smug about it.' She wracked her brains for a clue, raking over everything that had happened. 'What did they say? Something about that being the last rose, except for the ones that grow at a place called . . . Thistle House? Thistle Hall? That's it! That's where they grow. Thistle Hall, wherever that is.'

Miss Dumpling stared at her, wide-eyed. 'Are – are you quite sure about that?'

'Yes, Thistle Hall, that's definitely what they said.' Yesterday's smile began to fade as she realised Miss Dumpling and Mr Wormwood were looking at each other with expressions of dread.

'What's wrong?' she said. 'Where's Thistle Hall?'

Miss Dumpling hesitated for just a heartbeat. 'It's in the Land of the Dead, Essie. Thistle Hall is the name of Mr Weep's ancestral home.'

Yesterday's stomach went all wobbly, like a cheesecake.

'Of course! How did I not see it for myself?' said Mr Wormwood, smacking his palm on the table. 'Few plants with such power over life and death would deign to grow anywhere else.'

Yesterday did not know what to say. 'Then it's over,' she said. 'We're not going to find a mournful rose by the winter solstice, because it's completely and utterly impossible.'

'Darling, I thought you knew better than to use words like *impossible* in a place like this,' said Miss Dumpling primly. 'We said we'd find a mournful rose, and that's exactly what we're going to do.'

Yesterday blinked very rapidly. 'You're suggesting we go there? To the Land of the Dead?'

Miss Dumpling simply nodded.

'But wouldn't that be outrageously dangerous and stupid?' Yesterday asked.

'Dangerous?' said Miss Dumpling. She looked genuinely puzzled. 'When has that ever stopped us? If travelling to Mr Weep's garden is the only sure-fire way to find a mournful rose before the solstice, then that is exactly what we are going to do.'

'But Miss Dumpling,' said Madrigal, hopping from the windowsill on to the table, 'we don't even know where an entrance to the Land of the Dead is! The Infernal Embassy in London was shut down long ago. All the other gateways have been hidden. And we have less than two weeks before the winter solstice arrives.'

'If memory serves,' said Miss Dumpling, thinking carefully, 'the Museum of Entirely Unnatural History has a map depicting Britain's magical portals in its archives.'

'Yes, but the archives are strictly closed to the public,' Madrigal pointed out.

'I am well aware of that,' said Miss Dumpling. Pascal floated on to her lap and she stroked his shell.

'So, what are we supposed to do?' said Madrigal, his head cocked to one side. 'You think they'll just hand this map over to us?'

'Oh, now, don't be preposterous,' chuckled Miss Dumpling. 'We're not going to *ask* them for it. We're going to steal it.'

Yesterday stared at her teacher. 'We are?'

'We're already planning to steal a rose from Mr Weep,' Miss Dumpling pointed out. 'I say, in for a teacup, in for the whole pot. We'll be veritable career burglars by the time this is all over!'

Madrigal gave his longest, deepest sigh yet. Yesterday could not help grinning. 'What *is* the Museum of Entirely Unnatural History, anyway?' she asked. 'It's not in any of the books in your library.'

'It was built years ago by an old flame of mine, Maggie Hollybones,' said Miss Dumpling. 'She lamented the fact that faeries didn't have any museums, so she built one of her own, dedicated to unnatural history. Magical science, that is, not history in the *kings and queens* sense. An answer to the humans' Natural History Museum in London, if you like. Maggie had one of Queen Titania's dreams on display last time I visited.'

Jack stood and stretched his arms in a yawn. 'Well, I for one am all for it,' he said. 'I'll be in my lab if you need me. The Goblin Market gave me more than a couple ideas I want to try out before bedtime.' He shot Yesterday a grin.

Yesterday grinned back at him; she could only imagine what kind of ideas he was talking about. 'I'm on board too,' she said. 'Not that I have much choice. Let's steal that map and find a way to the Land of the Dead.'

She realised how ridiculous it sounded when she said it out loud.

To calm her nerves, she shared some carrot cake and a pot of Wayfarer's Blessing (*a whole night's sleep in a single cup!*) with Miss Dumpling before heading up to her bedroom to get some reading done. As she climbed the stairs, she heard noises coming from the confectionary laboratory. Curious, she knocked on the door.

'Come in!' came a muffled voice.

Buried among his machines and peculiar experiments, she found Jack tinkering at what looked to be a small oven, a haphazard array of pipes and valves coming off it.

'Close the door! Close the door! Watch this,' said Jack, pushing up a pair of goggles on to his head. 'I've just put the ingredients in . . .'

Yesterday shut the door behind her. 'What *is* it?' she asked.

'It's a Cake-O-Matic,' said Jack proudly, hands on

his hips. 'Or maybe a cake-crafter. Or a caker-maker. I haven't settled on a name yet. All you have to do is put in the ingredients and the machine will do the rest.'

'And this is safe, is it?' asked Yesterday, raising an eyebrow.

Jack replied, 'It's my Christmas present for Miss Dumpling.' Yesterday couldn't help but note he hadn't *really* answered the question, but Jack was already pulling levers and tugging valves. The machine rattled and whirred, before erupting with a loud bang and splattering warm chocolate all over Yesterday's hair.

'Oh, sweetmeats, not again,' Jack muttered, frantically scrambling to turn off the device, but not before he received a face full of flour. Yesterday burst out laughing.

Jack opened the window to let out some of the smoke, then clambered out on to the windowsill for some air. Yesterday joined him, the pair of them sitting on the sill, their legs dangling over the edge. Dwimmerly End had settled itself down for the night under a huge oak tree in the middle of a heather-laden moor, beneath a sky full of stars.

'What's Christmas like here?' asked Yesterday. She tried to picture Christmas Day in the teashop, all cinnamon scented and decorated with snow. Would there be a tree? Would there be gingerbread men and Christmas pudding and mince pies? Would there be *presents*? 'We never really celebrated it at the circus.'

'Never?' Jack said, his eyes widening. 'Well, luckily for you, nowhere does Christmas like Dwimmerly End! Mr Wormwood grows us a Christmas tree, Madrigal eats too much fudge, and Miss Dumpling takes care of most of the cooking, of course. Last year, she made a Christmas pudding that never ran out, no matter how many bites you had of it – I was so stuffed I thought I was going to explode. And don't get me started on the presents. Miss Dumpling absolutely spoils us. My first Christmas at Dwimmerly End, she got me a storm-catcher. It was my *dream*.' Yesterday was silent. 'Are you OK, Essie?'

She nodded. 'I suppose,' she said. 'I just . . . I just hope I actually *make* it to Christmas.'

Jack took her hand and gave it a squeeze. 'You're not in this alone, you know. We're not going to let anything awful happen, Essie. No way.'

Yesterday smiled at that. 'Seems like not many care about people like us, outside Dwimmerly End,' she said. 'Like that horrible goblin. What was that word he called us? Neither-nors?'

'It's another word for *strangeling*,' Jack explained.

'And not a very nice one. In a way, it's not wrong. We *are* neither one thing nor the other – not quite faeries, not quite humans – since we grew up outside the faerie world. But at the end of the day, it's a horrible, stupid word, used by people who think we're different and therefore must be *dangerous*. The truth is, once we've gotten the hang of our magic, we aren't really any more or less dangerous than anyone else . . . *unfortunately*,' he added with a grin.

Yesterday felt tears pricking her eyes. She turned away from Jack so he wouldn't see. 'No matter where I go, it feels like there's always someone who thinks I'm a monster.'

'Is that such a bad thing?' Jack said gently. 'Some of my best friends are monsters.'

'Well, yes, it is a bad thing,' said Yesterday, looking out on to the field of heather. There were will-o'-the-wisps gliding over bogs, illuminating the darkness with green and purple light. 'I was ditched by my mum and dad at the circus, and now I might get ditched by this world too. Or else end up in the Land of the Dead.' She let out a big sigh. 'If I didn't have these silly fox ears, maybe my whole life would've been different.'

'Maybe,' Jack admitted. 'But would you be Yesterday without them? It's like my wolf snout. Maybe it looks a bit weird, but I can smell things no one else can: I know exactly when a batch of caramel is about to burn, or when the sherbets need an extra teaspoon of lemon. Sure, there are people who have normal-looking noses and normal-looking lives. But normal's just another word for boring, if you ask me.'

Yesterday smiled. 'I never thought about it that way before,' she said. She went quiet for a minute as she gazed out at the moors. It was true, in a way, what Jack was saying. If she had been born an ordinary human, she wouldn't have been able to do the magic she'd done today. And she would never have found her way to Dwimmerly End, to Miss Dumpling, to Jack.

Yesterday felt a warmth spreading inside her. On impulse, she leant over and gave Jack a quick hug. Then, she pulled away from him.

'Sorry,' she said, looking anywhere but Jack's direction. 'I'm not really a hugger. It just felt like the right thing to do. That was my first hug, actually. I hope I did it properly.'

'That's OK,' said Jack, his cheeks going a bit pink. 'I think it was a very commendable hug.'

'Good,' said Yesterday, her cheeks turning a little pink, too. 'Goodnight, Jack.'

And then she scurried off the windowsill and up to her bedroom.

*

Yesterday stood in the teashop's doorway, watching as it trundled into the village of Spoonsbury. Over the last few days, Miss Dumpling had been burrowed away in the tealeaf reading room, trying to find out the museum's current address. Between the time it took her to do so, and Dwimmerly End having to walk all the way there by foot, they had only a week left until the winter solstice – until Mr Weep's curse took its wicked effect.

With sleep-heavy eyes and aching muscles, Yesterday had been up early on bread duty in the kitchen, kneading dough and letting it rise. Then, Madrigal had appeared by her side, and told her to come and see.

It was a charming place, especially when cast in the pale blue light of dawn. There was a bridge over a trickling river, a quaint hall overlooking the village green, and handsome little avenues festooned with cottages.

On top of a hill peppered with trees and bushes was the Museum of Entirely Unnatural History. Like Dwimmerly End, it was cloaked under magical veils that kept humans from perceiving it. At the base of the hill, twinkling early morning sunlight danced across the surface of a lake.

The museum building itself was a tangled mess of different architectural styles. The centre resembled a Greek temple, with thick columns holding up a mighty pediment, all rendered in gleaming white stone. At the front were two vast mahogany doors, and carved into a stone archway around them were statues of magical beasts: gryphons, pixies, werewolves, sphinxes.

On one side of the main temple was a vast metal dome, etched with images of planets, stars, and moons. From another protruded a great marble pyramid, and a stone tower rose up at the back, with a great clock chiming at the top.

Then Yesterday noticed something even more peculiar – the museum wasn't actually touching the ground. A pair of enormous hot air balloons seemed to be holding it fifteen feet in the air. It was anchored to the earth by a long, rusting chain that went all the way down into the bottom of the lake, though it looked quite as if it might go sailing off if a strong gust blustered its way towards.

Miss Dumpling and Widdershins entered the tearoom. The automaton set about tidying up the ashes in the fireplace, humming merrily to himself; he had been eager to make himself useful from the very moment he'd arrived at Dwimmerly End, and Miss Dumpling had given up trying to stop him.

'The museum looks extraordinary!' said Yesterday. 'Even if it does seem like someone cobbled it together without a second thought.'

'Well, dear Maggie Hollybones was rather unique amongst museum curators,' explained the tea witch. 'She argued with the Faerie Queen's botanist after he slighted her at a ball. Maggie's response was to pinch part of the Royal Botanical Gardens and add it to her budding collection.'

'She stole a *museum*?' Yesterday said.

'Indeed, and that was only the beginning!' said Miss Dumpling, leading Yesterday through to the kitchen. 'After that, she started pilfering galleries and exhibition halls from all her enemies, and adding them on to her beloved Museum of Entirely Unnatural History.'

Yesterday arched an eyebrow. 'What about the balloons?'

'Ah, those,' said Miss Dumpling, reaching for a teapot from the shelf as they went past. 'One day, Maggie decided to strap some balloons to the roof, planning to take her museum on a world tour. Trouble was, she got bored of that idea after a couple of stops, and went off on an adventure, entrusting the museum's care to a new curator. The place has been moored here ever since, and Maggie's been missing in action.'

'And are you quite sure this map to the Land of the Dead is still in there, in the archives?' asked Madrigal.

'Quite sure,' said Miss Dumpling, as they went into the kitchen. 'Maggie showed me it herself, once upon a time. Now, to break into the Museum of Entirely Unnatural History and find the map to the Land of the Dead, you will, of course, need magical assistance. A Jumbling Jasmine should be just the ticket. And I want you to concoct it.'

Yesterday was not sure she had heard her correctly. 'Miss Dumpling, have you forgotten that the last time I tried a Jumbling Jasmine, it nearly destroyed the teashop?'

'Don't worry about that,' said Miss Dumpling brightly. 'The truth is, I'm sorry to have missed seeing your Clairvoyant Coffee work so splendidly and I want to see your tea witchery in action for myself.'

Yesterday drew in a deep breath. 'OK, but . . . don't say I didn't warn you.'

Miss Dumpling grinned and presented Yesterday with her favourite pink teapot. Pascal filled it with warmed unicorn milk, then Yesterday added the toothweed, the jasmine petals, and a pinch of powdered cinderspice from the pantry. Finally, she cupped her hands around the teapot and prepared to say the incantation.

'Think of the sparrow in the air,' Miss Dumpling murmured in Yesterday's ear. 'Think of the wolves on the steppes, of the dolphin in the waves. Know that you have a part in the splendid dance of the world.'

Yesterday smiled, and closed her eyes as she spoke the words of the spell. *'Tea before me, change my shape, from bird to beast, from fish to ape.'*

She opened her eyes and saw Miss Dumpling watching proudly. Even Madrigal, perched on the windowsill, looked hopeful.

A surge of magic burst through her belly. Her fox ears twitched and she heard the great rhythms of the world: the wingbeats of soaring geese, the song of whales in the sea, the chirping of the crickets in the meadow. She didn't know where the sounds were coming from, but she was listening, and she felt them all in her heart.

She could hear the tea in the pot too, bubbling away. She took the lid off and beamed at the sight of the thick, brown brew.

'Something smells good!' said Jack, appearing in the doorway. 'Let me guess: Jumbling Jasmine?'

'In theory,' said Yesterday. She breathed in deeply. Spice and sweetness, warmth and sugar – it smelled just right. But still, she would only be sure if she tried it.

Yesterday poured a cup and took a few careful sips. One moment she tasted custard; the next, the sweetness of apples. Then there was spinach. Then cheddar cheese. Then toffee. She handed the cup to Jack, who also took a sip.

'Now what happens?' she said. 'How does one actually go about turning into a beast?'

'It's quite simple, really,' said Miss Dumpling. 'To become a bird, for instance, one must think like a bird. Become untethered from the earth. Let nothing hold you down, and you shall fly.'

'And what happens to your clothes when you change shape?' Yesterday asked. 'Do they just vanish? Do they turn into fur and feathers?'

Jack leaned in and whispered, 'It's best not to overthink it.'

'Suppose not,' said Yesterday. 'All right, then. Let's do this. Let's steal ourselves a map.'

Yesterday closed her eyes and pictured the first creature that popped into her head: a sparrow. She imagined it in every detail – its beak, its delicate feathers, its fast, fluttering wings. She pictured how it would feel to lose touch with the earth, to swoop beneath a canopy of stars with no weight upon her shoulders. To feel free.

Her body felt electrified. She opened her eyes and lifted her arm, examining it carefully. She gasped as feathers sprouted from her skin. A sharp pain lanced from her shoulder blades. She glanced over her shoulder to see actual wings unfurling and splaying out. A beak shot from her mouth and took its place. Her ears shrunk, and her whole body followed, the cupboards and the chairs and the whole kitchen soon towering over her.

In a matter of heartbeats, where Yesterday Crumb had once stood, was a little sparrow with ginger feathers.

Chapter Fifteen

The Museum of Entirely Unnatural History

Yesterday's whole body felt weightless. Her new wings itched to spread out and fly. Her legs, on the other hand, were like fragile matchsticks, brittle and shaking. She had an almost irrepressible need to hop on the spot.

She tried to ask Miss Dumpling how to use her wings, but it came out as a string of merry cheeps. 'Fly, my darling,' said the tea witch, giddy with delight. 'Fly!'

Yesterday flapped her wings experimentally, and at once she was in the air. Flight was as effortless to her now as walking or breathing, and it was wonderful. It was as if an immense burden she had not known was there had been lifted from her shoulders. Now she had broken the shackles of gravity, she couldn't contain the joy of swooping up to the ceiling, fluttering over the kitchen counters, diving and rising and plummeting. She was *free*.

What other beasts could she become? How would it feel, she wondered, to become a fish, to breathe through gills instead of lungs, to swim through water and live in a world of coral and sand? How would it feel to become a leopard, bounding across the savanna faster than a thunderclap? A carnival of possibilities danced in her mind. The joy of magic inflated her; she felt untouchable, undeniable, unstoppable.

Jack was enjoying himself too, rapidly shifting between forms, morphing from a basset hound to a crawling iguana to an Arctic hare to himself again. 'This is *much* better than a boring old cup of Earl Grey,' he chuckled, as he turned into a cormorant.

Yesterday swelled with pride. Her tea had worked. For the first time, she felt like she truly was a tea witch's apprentice.

'Now remember,' said Miss Dumpling, flinging open the kitchen window, 'first, you must find the archives. Then, track down Wirry-Boggle's *Guide to the Portals and Passages of Britain*. It should lead us straight to the entrance to the Underneath. Break a leg out there, my darling dears!'

Jack became a sparrow too and the pair flew out of the kitchen window and off into the misty blue haze of dawn. Yesterday revelled in the wind against her claws. She eddied and glided with the breeze, twirling mist between her claws.

Onwards they flew, soaring up the hill, flying over the enormous chain that tethered the hovering museum to the earth, and on towards its grand front doors. The hodgepodge building was even more bewildering up close: a glasshouse here, a bronze dome there, a Greek temple in the centre, all stuck together without any sense of unity.

They landed on the porch in front of the entrance and turned back into themselves. Jack tried the door handles. 'It's locked,' he said.

'Hm,' muttered Yesterday. Her eyes were drawn to a small crack at the bottom of the doors. 'How about . . .'

She imagined herself terribly small and unseen (which was not very difficult, given her years of practice in Skelm's circus). She let herself feel humbled by the majesty of the museum, dwarfed by its enormity. Then, she pictured herself covered in fur, with twitching whiskers and soft, velvety ears.

And a moment later, she became a dormouse,

shrinking down and down and down, until Jack's boots loomed over her like those of a giant. Jack giggled and became a dormouse as well. The two tiny rodents trundled towards the door, scurrying under it with ease and emerging into a vast exhibition hall. They returned to their ordinary forms and peered around.

In the centre of the hall was a statue of a lady wearing smart riding gear. A plaque read *Miss Maggie Hollybones, Creator of the Periodic Table of Magic and Founder of the Museum of Entirely Unnatural History.*

Hanging from the ceiling was a great skeleton of a sea serpent, while all around the sides of the hall, curious objects were on display. A sword was mounted upon the wall, little rainbow swirls dancing along the blade. *Caladbolg,* the plaque read. Jack yelped in excitement.

'That's the sword first wielded by King Fergus mac Rossa, and later the faerie knight Althias at the Battle of Dragon's Roost,' he said, his eyes as wide as saucers. 'And look over *there*. The magician Pottinger bound the demon Varax in that very deck of cards.'

They walked past what looked like a furry, golden rug in a cabinet (*The Golden Fleece: exhibit made possible by the generous donation of Medea, sorceress*) towards a map of the exhibition halls. Jack tore off some cobwebs so they could read what it said. There was the Hall of Artistic Musings, the Hall of Historical Curiosities (in which they were currently standing), the Hall of Botanicals, the Hall of Beasts, the Hall of Stars, and the archives.

Above the map was a rather perturbing note, which read: *The Museum of Entirely Unnatural History takes no responsibility for any personal items that are lost or damaged while on the premises, nor for any hauntings, bouts of madness, disappearances, or coronations that may occur during your visit.*

The place was so covered with dust that Jack sneezed furiously. 'I'm fine, no worries,' he said, rubbing his snout. 'Looks like the archives are just past the Hall of Stars.'

They crept on through the Hall of Historical Curiosities. They passed the Theatre of Time, where ancient battles and other important moments were frozen in mirrors for visitors to observe, and the Dreamer's Walk, where one could step into the dreams of important figures like Merlin or the faerie playwright Mustardsocks.

As they headed into the Hall of Artistic Musings, they walked by a number of sculptures. A pair of bronze soldiers barked insults at each other and clashed with swords, locked in an eternal duel. The marble statue of a faerie princess sobbed into her hands, and asked Jack and Yesterday if they'd seen her missing lover.

'Most of the paintings in the museum are enchanted, you know,' said Jack, as they hurried past the sculptures and into a portrait gallery. Framed paintings lined the walls. 'You can step right into them and wander around the world the artist created.'

He approached a lightly shimmering painting of a meadow of wildflowers and scaled a small ladder leading up to its frame. Plunging his hand through the canvas, he reached into the painted world on the other side and pulled out a slightly blurred flower.

'Very nice,' said Yesterday. 'Now stop messing around. We've got a map to steal. Now if I remember rightly, this way should be the Hall of Stars . . .' Just then, though, another painting caught her eye. Unlike the other paintings, its surface didn't shimmer. It was an ordinary painting, not one you could enter and explore.

The painting depicted a pair of luminously beautiful women with pointed ears and gnarled antlers. They looked almost identical, though one had a golden crown over her head, while the other was shrouded in shadow. They were duelling with swords, astride winged horses.

'That's a scene from the Unseelie War,' said Jack, and Yesterday caught the note of pain in his voice. *The war that killed his parents.* 'You know, that big civil war between Queen Titania and her sister, Mab? They were best friends when they were kids.'

'So why did they go to war with each other?' Yesterday asked.

'Officially, it was because Mab thought Titania was picking on strangelings and faeries who she didn't consider pretty enough to be part of her court – the Seelie Court,' said Jack. 'But some people say there was a witch who turned them against each other for reasons of her own.'

'And what do *you* think?' said Yesterday.

'Me?' said Jack, letting out a breath. 'I think as soon as someone starts fighting for justice and equality, other people will always search for ways to make them look bad.'

They continued on, out of the gallery, passing through an archway littered with cobwebs into the Hall of Stars. 'They really have let this place go,' said Jack, sneezing again at the thick dust. They walked beneath a dark ceiling dotted with pinpricks of starlight, colourful little planets wheeling through the air above them. 'It looks like it's been abandoned.'

Yesterday frowned, watching as constellations lit up in the stars overhead. 'Miss Dumpling said there was a new curator. Whoever it is, they aren't doing a very good job.'

Yesterday froze, a sudden pain lancing through her. She clutched her chest and groaned. 'Essie!' cried Jack. 'Essie, what's wrong?'

'It's my . . . heart . . .' she said. As quickly as it came, the pain subsided. 'I think the splinter of ice Mr Weep put in there is growing. The solstice is just over a week away. We should hurry.'

Beyond the Hall of Stars was a plain-looking corridor that ended in an unassuming locked door.

The archives, said a sign beside it.

Yesterday's pulse quickened. They ran over to the door and Jack tried the knob. 'Locked, again,' he grumbled.

'But there's no lock or keyhole,' Yesterday pointed out.

She glanced up at the door frame. Spreading its wings over the door was a statue of an owl. A message was carved into its pedestal. Yesterday read it out loud.

'I awaken sleepers, I turn peasants into kings.
I name the stars, I give the flightless wings.
My heart is truth, my blood is ink.
What am I? Have a think.'

'It's a riddle!' Jack said excitedly. 'What do you reckon the answer is?'

Yesterday thought about it for some time. 'Well, museums have planetariums – maybe that counts as naming the stars? No, it can't be. Far too easy. Magic can give you wings. Maybe that's it?'

'Nothing's happening,' said Jack.

'Yes, I can see that,' Yesterday muttered. 'Come on. Think . . .'

Then, it came to her in a flash. 'Oh, of course,' she said. 'Reading books teaches you things you didn't know before. It's like waking up from being asleep. Learning gives you power, regardless of who you are – a peasant can turn into a king, and someone who can't fly can suddenly gain wings. Don't you see?'

Jack exhaled slowly. 'Um . . . no?'

Yesterday let out a sigh. 'It's *knowledge*!'

As she said the word, the door swung open.

Immediately, they were enveloped in the glorious smell of old parchment. Beyond the room was dark, but as they stepped inside, torches suddenly came alight, flickering with pale pink flames, illuminating stack upon stack of books. Between them and the books, though, was a deep, dark pit.

'How do we get across to the books?' asked Yesterday, but even before she'd finished the sentence, something strange started happening. Books began to jump off the shelves and march along the floor in a peculiar literary parade. One by one, they placed themselves at the edge of the pit, layering on top of each other.

'What do you think they're doing?' Jack said.

Yesterday stared, amazed, as the books slotted together in an elaborate mosaic. 'They're building a bridge,' she realised aloud, as the assembled books began to arch over the great pit towards the strangelings.

Once the books had reached them and settled into their positions, Jack took a tentative step on to the makeshift bridge. 'Seems stable enough,' he said, so Yesterday followed. They crossed the bridge one book at a time, peering nervously over the edge and into the darkness below.

At last, they were over the bridge and standing in the archives. It made Dwimmerly End's library look downright pitiful.

Bookshelves were stacked so precariously high that they seemed to disappear out of sight. There was an immense pile of books under a sign marked *Returns*. It became quickly apparent that the shelves were not arranged in well-planned rows, but instead meandered and twisted, a maddening maze rather than an organised collection. There were display cases here and there, with old and precious tomes resting inside.

Yesterday gazed around in wonder. To see so many books in one place, so many worlds and stories waiting to be explored, was enchanting. She read the spines hastily as they hurried through the collection: *A Thousand and One Enchantments You Need to Know*; *Precautions for Summoning a Fire Spirit*; *The Art and Practice of Automaton Sculpting*.

Other peculiar documents were strewn about, including a pamphlet that read, *Are you a, spirit, familiar, or demon in service to a witch? Join the Union of Magical Minions today – we have nothing to lose but our pentacles!*

Before long, they were lost in the literary labyrinth. Yesterday ran her finger along the shelves, scanning the titles. Jack, meanwhile, was darting from row to row, saying things like, 'Here's one about how to grow stormblooms – Mr Wormwood would love that! And here's a book about the cucumber tea recipes used by the kappa of the Kamo River. Miss Dumpling could use those, don't you think?'

'Jack,' said Yesterday, trying to focus, 'we can't just go around taking whatever books we want – as fun as that would be. Now, let's see here. *How to Raise a Zombie in Ten Days*, *The Nautical Markets of the Merfolk* – Jack, we're going to be searching here for days at this rate!'

They had circled around and found themselves back at the entrance. Yesterday groaned. 'Which shelf should we try next?' she asked.

'Hang on,' said Jack. He was standing beside the display case next to the enormous pile of Returns. He tapped on the glass and gestured to Yesterday. 'Look at this!'

Yesterday hurried over. Inside the display case was a leather tube, with straps for carrying it upon one's shoulder. The plaque read, *Wirry-Boggle's Guide to the Portals and Passages of Britain – First and Last Edition.*

'That's it!' Yesterday said, almost in disbelief. 'The map's in that tube! But how are we meant to get at it? This glass must be protected by powerful magical wards, shielding spells, defensive enchantments . . .'

'I have an idea,' Jack said. He lifted up a heavy book and brought it down on the glass. It shattered immediately. He put his hand in and took out the leather tube.

'*Jack!*' said Yesterday. 'You could've really hurt yourself if it was bewitched! Besides, we're trying to be subtle—'

She broke off. Her attention was drawn to the large pile of Returns books that appeared to be . . . *breathing*. 'What on earth . . .' she murmured.

The pile of books began to rumble and shake as the ones at the top came crashing to the ground. Then the whole edifice came apart in the middle – revealing *something* underneath.

Its head rose first – blue-black eyes, like the ink of a pen; then a pair of wings, as brown as the pages of an ancient text; then a body, huge and covered in shining bronze scales, like the gilded lettering along the spine of a leather-bound book.

It was a dragon, and it was waking up.

Chapter Sixteen

Exit, Pursued by a Dragon

As the dragon reared up, books tumbled from her scales, revealing that she was even larger than Yesterday had first thought. The mighty reptile used her claws to place a pair of spectacles hanging from a chain around her neck on to her snout. She gazed down through them at the intruders.

'*Hush*, children,' she rumbled. 'The archives are a place for quiet study and reflection. Not clamouring around like barbarians.'

Yesterday gawped at the beast in stunned silence. She had read about dragons – but she hadn't imagined meeting one, let alone being told off by one.

'Amazing,' breathed Jack, stepping back to get a full view. 'Never thought I'd get to see a dragon up close.' Then, addressing the creature herself, he added, 'Sorry for waking you up. We'll be going immediately.'

'Young man,' said the dragon, in the sort of tone that would usually be accompanied by a raised eyebrow (if dragons had eyebrows), 'I can plainly see you are trying to steal from the Museum of Entirely Unnatural History. As its curator, I must insist that you do not. Otherwise, things might get unpleasant.'

Plumes of smoke trailed from the dragon's jaws. Orange light glowed in her throat.

I was worried about my heart turning to ice, Yesterday thought. *Turns out I'm going to be burned alive by a dragon instead.*

'Oh, you mean this?' said Jack, indicating the map under his arm. 'I can understand why it may *look* like we're stealing from you. But I promise – and you can trust me – you're quite mistaken.'

The dragon looked sidelong at Jack. 'Oh, why do I even bother? Let me save us both some time. You are going to spin a wild and riotous lie. I will pretend to believe it, so I don't have to do any *incineration* nonsense. Take the map, if you must. All I ask is that it ends up in a good home.'

Jack blinked at the dragon, puzzled. 'That was . . . surprisingly easy.' He slung the map case over his shoulder and turned to Yesterday. 'So, do we just leave?'

Yesterday frowned. Something didn't feel right to her. 'Why aren't you going to burn us alive?' she asked. 'Not that I *want* you to. But we did break into your museum, after all.'

The dragon's eyes lingered on her for a moment. Then, she gave a weary sigh. 'A year ago, when I became curator,' the dragon said, 'I would have never let a pair of thieves waltz in here and pilfer Miss Hollybones' archives. She left me to run this place precisely because I was such a good librarian, after all.'

'I didn't know there were dragon librarians,' said Yesterday.

'My kind are renowned for hoarding treasures – and that includes books, not just gold and gemstones,' said the dragon. 'I began my own collection of written wonders when I was only a dragonling, beginning with discarded letters and business notes – all sorts of things that I thought might be interesting. But the village-folk thought I was trying to eat their sheep, so they came after me and torched my hoard. I vowed to guard my future books with a ferocity unprecedented even amongst librarians, who are known for being a ferocious bunch. That's why Miss Hollybones hired me to be her librarian in the first place.'

'So when you were made curator, I suppose that was a dream come true?' asked Yesterday.

'Oh, yes! She was trusting me to protect the whole museum! But when word got out that a dragon was running the place, no one wanted to visit any more. Haven't had a visitor in months, in fact. These may be the museum's final days.'

'But why?' said Yesterday, a mix of sympathy for the dragon and fury at the injustice of it all rising up in her. 'Why does no one want to come here? This place is wonderful.'

The dragon, for a moment, looked radiant with pride. Then, sorrow crept back into her blue-black eyes.

'No parents want their children anywhere near a dragon,' she said. 'Perhaps I may accidentally scorch them. Or eat them. Or crush them under my tail. All highly unlikely, but some faeries have backwards views about monsters like me.'

'That's just ridiculous!' Yesterday said. 'I know how it feels, everyone thinking you're dangerous. The Royal College of Witches are trying to take my magic away because they think I might blow someone up by mistake.'

The dragon looked at her over her spectacles. '*Have* you ever blown anyone up?'

'Well ... almost,' Yesterday said. 'But never intentionally! Though I might someday, if the mood takes me.'

The dragon chortled at her and Yesterday smiled back. Yesterday was no expert in comforting others, but she reached over and touched the dragon's scales, like patting a friend on the shoulder. They were rough and hot beneath her touch, but she kept her hand there anyway, and the dragon allowed her to.

The dragon considered Yesterday with her blue-black eyes. 'What is your name, fiery one?'

'Yesterday Crumb,' she said. 'You can call me Essie, though. This is my friend Jack. How about you?'

'Pepperprew,' said the dragon.

'Maybe you can change people's minds, Pepperprew?' said Yesterday. 'Lots of people don't like strangelings, but not everyone. Plenty of faeries visit our teashop, even though it's full of strangelings. If some minds can change about us, maybe they could change about you too?'

Pepperprew looked away. 'Perhaps the fear of my kind is not so unwarranted,' she muttered. 'We burn. We destroy. For centuries, dragon-slaying has been a noble profession amongst faerie folk for this very reason. How could we ever undo such hate?'

'Maybe,' said Yesterday slowly, 'if you invited some people round for tea at the museum, they would get to know you and see that you might be a monster, but you're not *monstrous*.'

The dragon tilted her head at Yesterday. 'Did you say *tea*?'

Yesterday nodded with a smile. 'A friend once told me that nothing can't be solved with a cup of tea, a slice of cake, and a very dear friend.'

Pepperprew chuckled. Then, she gestured with her snout. 'Why do you need that old map, anyway?'

Yesterday told her all about Mr Weep and the splinter of ice he had lodged in her heart, how it would claim her life in one week's time. The dragon bowed to her when the story was finished.

'It takes some courage to hold a conversation with a dragon,' said Pepperprew. 'And twice as much to stand up to Mr Weep, not to mention the goblins of the Goblin Market. Perhaps you have the heart of a dragon in your chest. Essie the Dragonheart sounds very well, do you not think?'

Yesterday felt a ripple of pride. 'Essie the Dragonheart,' she repeated, revelling in her new title.

'It would be a tragedy for a dragon's heart to freeze,' Pepperprew mused. 'You are welcome to the map, if it will help you thwart such wickedness.'

'Thank you,' chorused Jack and Yesterday.

Jack stepped forward and added, 'Pepperprew, I'd say you're the most honourable dragon anyone could hope to meet.'

'If only I could join you on your quest.' The dragon sighed. 'I should like to sink my jaws into Mr Weep for inflicting such darkness upon you. Indeed, I fear a map alone will not be enough. Mr Weep is not a foe you can face unarmed. But perhaps I can help in that department.'

The dragon lifted up off her haunches and strode away, the floor shaking with every step she took. Jack gave Yesterday a shrug, and they followed Pepperprew through the archives.

'There are texts in this place that creatures like Mr Weep would very much like to see forgotten or destroyed,' said Pepperprew. 'What a blessing that he tends to overlook that which he sees as beneath him.'

'What sort of texts?' said Yesterday curiously.

'Histories. Journals. Essays,' said Pepperprew. 'Including works by those brave souls willing to travel to the Land of the Dead and document the secrets they uncovered there.'

'I heard that ghosts used to travel freely between our world and the Land of the Dead,' said Yesterday. 'Jack tells me they would come and do their Christmas shopping at Dwimmerly End. Why did Mr Weep close the borders?'

'Perhaps you can learn that answer for yourself,' said Pepperprew. 'Ah, here we go.' She stopped in front of a stack of particularly dusty books right in the corner of the archives chamber. Pepperprew traced along the spines with her claw until she found what she was looking for. She took the book down and handed it to Yesterday.

'*The Tragic Tale of Mr Weep*?' Yesterday read, taking the book from the dragon's claws. 'Sounds cheerful.'

She flipped open the plain, black book to its first page, Jack peering over her shoulder so he could read along with her.

The creature that calls itself Mr Weep was not always the wicked demon he is now, she read. *The Land of the Dead was not a realm of ice and shadow, but one of golden grasses and pomegranate groves, of trickling streams and endless peace. There were no demons, and ghosts did not renounce their faces and their magic when they entered.*

Then one day, Mr Weep sealed the borders. He would stalk the Land of the Living, freezing the hearts of faeries and taking them into his service – as demons.

At this time, I – Threnody Gravesbait – was in the employ of Mr Weep, as his music teacher. This was also the time when he sought a way to impress the one now known as the Nameless Queen. I believe it is essential that I tell this story and that I am uniquely placed to do so . . .

'The Nameless Queen?' Yesterday read aloud. 'Who's the Nameless Queen?'

'You have never heard *The Ballad of the Nameless Queen?*' said Pepperprew, quite astonished. 'I thought it was sung to all faerie children.'

Yesterday winced. 'I'm a strangeling, remember?' she said. 'I grew up around humans. What *is* the Ballad?'

'Something that I ought to have stamped out years ago,' said a voice of pure ice.

Yesterday's heart squeezed around its frozen splinter. She would have known that voice anywhere.

She turned slowly. There, hovering in the middle of the archives, was a door made of silver wood, and in the doorway stood Mr Weep. In his hand was the iron key Yesterday remembered seeing around his neck.

'A witching door,' Jack murmured.

'I thought I was being overly cautious when I had my imps keep an eye on you after that trouble in the Goblin Market,' he said, his lips gnarling into something that called itself a smile. 'But clearly I underestimated you. Look at you, Yesterday! Finding the map to my kingdom, discovering rare texts that might expose my weaknesses. I thought I'd destroyed every measly copy of that ghastly book before it was even published. We'll just have to tidy up the loose ends, now, won't we?'

The book in Yesterday's hand went cold. She looked down at it. Spidery blooms of frost spread over the cover as the book turned to ice. Then, with a sharp crack, it shattered, countless fragments cascading to the floor.

Fury raged inside her – yet another chance at saving her life, completely lost. 'What do you *want* from me?' she bellowed. 'Why can't you just leave me alone?'

'Stand aside, Demon King,' said Pepperprew, towering over the silver-haired figure. 'You will not harm the books – or this child!'

Mr Weep ignored the dragon. 'Tell me, Yesterday, why would you want to live a quiet life in a teashop? Such a small, meaningless existence? You could rule.

You could be magnificent. Poets would write epics about you. Festivals would be celebrated in your name!'

'Maybe I'm just not really a festival person,' snapped Yesterday. 'And you haven't answered my question. Why are you so interested in me? What game are you trying to play?'

'I do not show my hand so easily, little cub,' Mr Weep taunted, but, in his eyes, she saw something flicker. 'You're frightened of me, yes? I don't blame you. I am the King of the Dead, after all. Call a man *monster* enough times, and that's exactly what he becomes.'

He took another step towards her.

'You're playing my game quite impressively,' said Mr Weep. 'It's that teashop, isn't it? And that ridiculous tea witch. Making my challenge a little too easy for you. Well, that's no fun. I want to see what *you* can do, Yesterday. What *you*'re made of. Nobody else.'

Pepperprew let out a bellow. 'Her life is not your plaything, Demon King. Step back, Dragonheart,' she roared. 'Let me defend my archives from this trespasser!'

With that, the dragon opened her huge jaws and unleashed a breath of pure flame. The light shimmered across her bronze scales as the fire tore towards Mr Weep.

But before the flames could reach him, Mr Weep opened a silver umbrella to shield himself. The blaze bounded against the umbrella, turning to cinders and smoke.

The burning embers fell to the floor, where a pile of dry papers lay. They caught, the flame leaping to other scattered books and parchment that lay around the archives. In seconds, everything went up in twisting flames.

'*No!*' said Pepperprew, desperately swiping at the fire with her tail. 'What have I done!'

Smoke filled the room, choking and dark.

'This has given me a marvellous idea,' said Mr Weep, who had not taken his eyes from Yesterday. 'How about I burn your teashop to the ground too? That way, you won't be able to *cheat* any more.'

Yesterday's heart began to thunder in her chest. *No, she thought. No, please.* But she would not give him the satisfaction of begging.

'Don't worry, Essie, he can't do that,' whispered Jack. 'Ice is his thing, not fire.'

'Hmm, true, I'm not much of a fire person,' said Mr Weep. His eyes went to Pepperprew. 'But *she* is.'

Mr Weep's umbrella disappeared, and he pulled out his white violin with purple-black strings.

'The Demonheart Violin,' Jack gasped. 'They say it's strung with the heartstrings of a powerful demon. No being of flesh and blood can resist it! We need to get out of here.'

'But we can't leave her!' said Yesterday, looking at the wailing Pepperprew.

'We have to, Essie,' said Jack, taking her hand. 'We don't have a choice!'

'I'm sorry, Pepperprew,' Yesterday whispered. She could feel some Jumbling Jasmine still burning inside her belly. She created a picture in her mind, calling upon the last of her tea's magic. As adrenaline churned through her, she imagined how it would be to charge, to sprint, to bound endlessly to freedom.

Her body began to sprout gingerbread-coloured fur. She grew larger, then tumbled on to all fours as her hands and feet became paws. She stretched her neck and held her head upright, her ears flexing as she became an enormous, pony-sized fox, tall and maybe even a little proud for the first time in her entire life.

And then the notes began to play. Jack stood, mesmerised, unable to change as the music of the violin took hold of his senses. But Yesterday was already in flight – the blood pounding through her ears loudly enough to block out the music. Or perhaps Mr Weep was simply *letting* her go? Either way, nothing would stop her now.

She flung Jack on to her back. Then, she galloped off, her feet padding soft and silent across the floor, her great tail swishing behind her, as she dashed past the bookshelves, past Mr Weep.

She peered over her shoulder. Pepperprew was straining against Mr Weep's violin.

'Run, Dragonheart! *Run!*' roared the dragon, doing her best to resist with her mind, even as her body fell under Mr Weep's command.

'Follow them. Destroy their teashop,' Mr Weep commanded the dragon. 'Reduce it to ash and nothingness! Spare the girl and no one else!'

Yesterday flew back through the archives, over the bridge of books. She glanced backwards to see Pepperprew slithering after her. Her eyes were bulging with panic, with fury, but the rest of her was clearly under Mr Weep's control. She spotted Yesterday and began thundering after them.

Yesterday bounded onwards, out of the archives, through the Hall of Stars and the Hall of Artistic Musings, smashing into a vase and unleashing long-trapped spirits that moaned gratefully; knocking over a statue of the late Faerie Queen Titania – a crime punishable by death, if the Seelie Court found out.

On and on and on she went. Soon, they were back in the museum's entrance hall. The great double doors stood ahead, and she careered towards them. 'What are you going to do?' said Jack, coming to his senses now the violin was out of earshot. 'Essie, I'm pretty sure those doors were locked!'

Yesterday clenched her jaw. *Hold on tight,* she thought.

She bolted headlong towards the locked doors, her claws outstretched. She crashed straight through them in a shower of splinters, quickly morphing into a giant eagle as they went hurtling off the edge of the museum's front steps.

But she couldn't get any height. Struggling under Jack's weight, Yesterday began spiralling down to earth. She crashed into the grassy hill, the wind knocked from her belly, the shock of it burning away the last of the Jumbling Jasmine. She turned back into a girl, and when she tried to transform again, the witchery would not work.

'I'm all out of magic,' she told Jack as they scrambled to their feet. 'We have to get back to Dwimmerly End!'

'Look!' Jack called. 'It's come to meet us!'

Yesterday turned and saw the great flamingo legs of Dwimmerly End racing towards the museum. Jack and Yesterday sprinted for the front door. Widdershins reached down and hauled them into the safety of the teashop, where they tumbled to the floor in a heap.

'Miss Dumpling,' gasped Yesterday. 'Mr Weep has enchanted a dragon, and she's coming to burn Dwimmerly End down!'

Miss Dumpling blinked. 'You're telling me a possessed dragon is on its way to set fire to the teashop?' she said. Jack and Yesterday nodded. 'Goodness! How incredibly unexpected.'

A moment later, Pepperprew tore out of the Museum of Entirely Unnatural History. She swooped down towards them, beating her tremendous wings. Then, she opened her jaws, and out came a flood of fire.

Dwimmerly End leapt out of the way, throwing everyone off their feet. The teashop raced back down the hill, narrowly avoiding the inferno as, all around them, bushes and trees caught fire, tangerine flames lighting up the mid-morning sky.

'Can't this teashop go any faster?' Madrigal squawked.

Jack snorted with displeasure. 'Um . . . what's that smell?' he said.

Yesterday sniffed the air; it was full of the undeniable scent of smoke. 'I am sorry to report that the teashop appears to be on fire, Miss Dumpling!' said Widdershins, peering out of the window.

Yesterday ran to join him. Flowers all along the teashop's east wall were scorched, feathers of smoke trailing off them.

In the distance, at the bottom of the hill, she saw the lake's shining surface. 'Miss Dumpling, the lake!' she said, pointing. 'I don't suppose Dwimmerly End . . .'

Miss Dumpling grinned. 'Darling, I like the way your mind works.'

The tea witch murmured something under her breath.

The dragon was gaining on them now, bashing trees aside as it tore after them down the hill. Pepperprew roared. She opened her mouth and released the greatest outpouring of fire Yesterday had seen yet.

At that moment, Dwimmerly End took a running jump off the base of the hill and propelled itself towards the water.

For a moment, the teashop flew. Then, it plummeted. Water splashed around them as they struck the lake's surface. The teashop plunged into the black, murky depths and columns of bubbles rose up around the windows.

The bewitched dragon let out a muffled bellow of frustration as Dwimmerly End sank to the bottom of the lake.

Chapter Seventeen

Steeped Storms

'That's all the leaks plugged up,' said Jack, drying off his hands.

It was early the next morning and Dwimmerly End was marching along the bottom of the lake. They had spent the whole night underwater just to be safe, hiding from Mr Weep and the bewitched Pepperprew.

Now, they gathered around the kitchen table. Little fishes peered in at the window, perplexed by the sight of a teashop where no teashop ought to be. A half-man, half-frog faerie with bulbous eyes and slimy skin was shaking his webbed fists at them, ranting in a language full of croaks and gurgles.

'Why is there an angry vodyanoy outside?' Yesterday asked, pulling out her chair.

'Seems we broke the gate to his eel farm when we landed,' Jack explained as he joined her.

'Oh, let him tire himself out,' said Miss Dumpling, waving a hand. 'I've already promised to fix it for him *and* give him a lifetime supply of Bubblious Tea. Some faeries can be terribly unreasonable!'

They sat and ate their breakfast, doing their best to ignore the faces looking in on them. Widdershins had made everyone pancakes, and the enchanting aroma of fried unicorn butter wafted through the air.

As they ate, Miss Dumpling pored over the map. 'Well, this *is* splendid news, darlings!' said the tea witch, skimming a finger across the yellowy scroll. 'It seems there are a few portals to the Land of the Dead nearby. Trouble is, most of them have simply stopped working. Magic is a muscle. It must be exercised, or it fades, as it does with faeries lost in the human world.'

Pain spiked briefly through Yesterday's chest again – the splinter of ice, reminding her that it was there, getting larger all the time. Yesterday winced. 'So . . .' she managed to say, 'we have no way of knowing which portals work?'

Miss Dumpling gave a hint of a grimace. 'We still have six days until the winter solstice. More than enough time to find a functioning portal!'

That didn't seem like a lot of time to Yesterday, but at least they had a chance.

The teashop set off to the nearby county of Lancashire, walking across the lake's dark bed for some time and eventually emerging on a thin beach. Water streamed off the walls and the flowers, and the teashop shook itself dry. To everyone's relief, the dragon and Mr Weep were nowhere to be seen.

Yesterday wished she had got to read a bit more of the book in the archives – *The Tragic Tale of Mr Weep*. Maybe she could have learned Mr Weep's secrets: where he came from, what kind of a game he was playing, and why he cared so much about Yesterday in the first place.

But now the book was gone, and she felt as though her one advantage had been snatched away.

Still, they had a plan, and Dwimmerly End was heading off to meet it.

But the weather had other ideas. Around mid-afternoon, the clouds opened up and began lashing the hills and the teashop with sheets of rain. Soon Dwimmerly End was wading slowly through deep, thick mud.

'I do adore the rain,' said Miss Dumpling, blowing on her tea as the gentle pitter-patter against the windows steadily increased. 'Can you name two things better made for one another than tea and rain? But it must be said, Dwimmerly End is going slower than a slug through syrup with all this wind and mud about!'

'Is there any way we can make the teashop go faster?' Yesterday asked.

Miss Dumpling had a wicked look in her eye. 'There certainly is,' she said. She set down her teacup. 'Fancy learning a new tea, my apprentice?'

Yesterday's ears pricked up. 'What sort of tea were you thinking of?'

An excited smile crept across the tea witch's face. 'As you may have learned from your studies, the Steeped Storm, sometimes called the Storm in a Teacup, is a tea that gives the drinker some control over the weather – you'll never have a picnic spoiled by rain once you've mastered this one! If we can harness this storm to *propel* us, rather than get in our way, Dwimmerly End will reach Lancashire in no time. Now, the first ingredient we need is a freshly bottled rainstorm.'

'Enter Jack Cadogan,' said Jack to Yesterday. 'I catch rainstorms for Mr Wormwood to water his plants with all the time.'

Yesterday followed Jack to the storm-catching chamber. At one end there was a large window with an enormous mechanical crossbow in front of it. Jack opened the window, sat behind the crossbow, and took aim at the clouds, before firing a net on an extremely long cord towards the sky. The net caught a little grey thundercloud. Jack reeled it in, then stowed the cloud in a stoppered bottle and gave it to Yesterday with a little bow.

Yesterday returned to Miss Dumpling in the kitchen. The tea witch rustled up a pot of ordinary jasmine tea, along with a slice of carrot cake each so they could have a nibble and a drink while they went over the basics.

Miss Dumpling clapped her hands and her copy of *The Tome of Terrific Tea Witchery* shot out from its cupboard, opening to a certain page as it floated over the table.

Steeped Storm, or
the Storm in a Teacup
Difficulty Level: Considerably Tricky

Ingredients

One freshly bottled rainstorm
A pinch of will-o'-the-wisp sugar
A teapot's worth of water (boiled, preferably by tea spirit, salamander, or dragon)

'Now, a word of warning,' said Miss Dumpling. 'The magic of the Storm in a Teacup can be rather . . . *chaotic*, shall we say.'

'Chaotic?' said Yesterday, through a mouthful of carrot cake. She did not exactly like the sound of that, since her magic was prone to chaos at the best of times.

'In the hands of an inexperienced witch, this tea would be perilous both to the caster and to anybody who gets too close,' Miss Dumpling went on. 'But you are not inexperienced, are you, darling? Your magic has come along much faster than any apprentice I have ever encountered. It must be because of your delightful fox ears – you're more attuned to the melody of magic than most.'

Yesterday blushed. 'Why is the Storm in a Teacup so risky?' she said.

'As I taught you in one of our first lessons, all tea witchery depends on the witch calling upon a memory or a feeling and channelling it into her brews. That's why the magic works best when you think cheerful thoughts, darling, and goes wrong if you let the darkness in. Things get even more complicated with the Storm in a Teacup.'

Even more complicated? Yesterday thought uneasily.

'The emotion a Steeped Storm demands is passion,'

Miss Dumpling continued. 'Unfortunately, many people get passion confused with anger, clinging on to rage and letting it consume them. Anger is unproductive, but it can be transformed into something useful – that is, *righteous* passion.'

Yesterday frowned. If anything, she was now more confused.

'What makes you angry, Yesterday?' asked Miss Dumpling.

Yesterday glanced out of the window, watching raindrops race down the glass. 'Everything makes me angry,' she muttered. 'I'm angry at how some faeries would rather kick strangelings out of their world than help us, and how humans take advantage of us because we look peculiar. I'm angry at being kept in a cage at a circus. I'm angry at myself too. How easily I let Mr Weep trick me into signing his contract.'

'You mustn't beat yourself up for doing something perfectly and incredibly normal,' Miss Dumpling said gently. 'I do not mean this unkindly, but it simply has to be said: Mr Weep could only put ice in your heart because it was on the chilly side to begin with.'

Yesterday felt a shiver run through her.

'So often, anger is just fear flying its colours and making a fuss,' said Miss Dumpling. 'You mustn't be like

Mr Weep. Don't let heartbreak turn you into something cruel. Let it simmer into a taste for wonder and justice.'

'Did you say Mr Weep is . . . heartbroken?'

'Well, of course, darling,' said Miss Dumpling. 'It is a tale many faeries tell in the dead of night.'

Yesterday remembered what Pepperprew had said. *'The Ballad of the Nameless Queen . . .'*

Miss Dumpling nodded. 'Indeed,' she said. 'It tells the story of Mr Weep . . .'

As she said his name, Miss Dumpling passed her hand over the steam coming from the teapot. Yesterday gasped as the steam gathered itself into the shape of a figure in a suit, clutching a violin.

'. . . And his runaway bride: the Nameless Queen.'

Again, the steam coalesced into a second figure, one in a long and streaming wedding dress. The figure of Mr Weep took her hand and the two danced and twirled and pirouetted together.

'Mr Weep got married?' said Yesterday. 'Who'd ever marry someone like *him*?'

'Who knows?' said Miss Dumpling. 'She wore a mask to their wedding, and spent all her days in her chambers, then ran away before they'd even taken their honeymoon.'

'Why did she wear a mask?'

'Nobody knows for certain,' Miss Dumpling admitted. 'If you ask me, I think she was fleeing from something, and didn't want to be caught. Maybe she was already married to someone else. Or maybe she was ashamed, for one reason or another. Who can say?'

'Does anyone know why she ran away, at least?' asked Yesterday.

Miss Dumpling paused, thoughtful. 'Everyone tells a different story, though all agree that she vanished on their wedding night. The Ballad itself is rather ambiguous:

> *'The King found the secret she tried to have banished.*
> *They duelled, they fought; he wept, she vanished.'*

Yesterday gave a small wince. She was desperate for answers but found herself with only more questions. 'So what else does the Ballad say?'

'Let me see if I can recall,' said Miss Dumpling.

> *'Old Mr Weep, he was torn apart,*
> *From the pain that had stained his ancient heart.'*

The tea witch waved her hand over the steam. The bride vanished, and Mr Weep fell to his knees, sobbing.

'In sorrow, he took his heart full of pain
And froze it, so it could never break again.'

Yesterday stared at the sobbing man made of steam. 'He froze his own heart? Literally?'

Miss Dumpling nodded gravely. 'Ice preserves, or so they say. I'd personally recommend a nice pot of tea and a slice of chocolate cake, but to each's own, I suppose. To my mind, the trick to letting go of anger is to stop feeding it . . .'

She passed her hand through the steam a third and final time. It transformed into the figures of a raven, a man with hair made of leaves, a second man made of cogs, a boy with the snout of a wolf, and a girl with pointed fox ears.

'. . . And to gorge yourself on love, instead.'

Yesterday smiled, and hope blossomed in her chest.

'Let's build up to the Storm in a Teacup,' said Miss Dumpling. 'Why don't you try having a conversation with Madrigal without wanting to pluck out his feathers one by one?'

Yesterday looked up at Miss Dumpling, then looked away again. 'What good would that do me? Besides, it's Madrigal who hates *me*. Not the other way around.'

'I don't think Madrigal hates you in the slightest,

not really,' said Miss Dumpling. She finished her tea. 'He just has his ways. If you can make peace with him, mastering the Storm in a Teacup will be a breeze. If you can tame your anger, you can tame a storm. Do what you do best. Listen past his words and hear the beat of his heart.'

Yesterday sighed. 'All right,' she said reluctantly, and went to look for the familiar.

She found him in one of his usual spots, perched on his podium by the tearoom's front door, reading a newspaper. Jack was lying on the floor next to him, chatting away while Madrigal made the occasional weary comment.

'Hello, Jack . . . and Madrigal,' said Yesterday. She folded her arms, taking a deep breath.

'Hello,' said Jack, propping himself up on an elbow.

Madrigal looked at her for a second, then went back to his paper. 'What do you want now, fool-girl?'

She stifled the urge to snark back. 'Madrigal,' she said, 'you have nothing but nasty things to say to me, and you know very well that I'm not exactly your biggest fan either.'

'Hmph,' said the not-raven, still not looking up at her.

She bit back a surge of irritation rising up from her

belly. *If you can tame your anger, you can tame a storm,* she thought. 'I suppose I never made things easier for you,' she continued, undeterred. 'It's been said from time to time that I can have a bit of an attitude.'

'A *bit* of an attitude?' Madrigal protested.

'Shush. I'm trying to build a bridge here,' said Yesterday. She paused to breathe and let her nerves settle before going on. Her ears twitched, picking up on unsaid words hanging in the air. She recalled her argument with the familiar and what he had said that day. 'I . . . I know why you don't like me. It's because you don't want Miss Dumpling to get hurt.'

The familiar looked away, out of the window.

'I think that's pretty noble of you, to be honest,' she said, letting the bitterness underneath her words dissolve, 'to care about your friend that much. But it doesn't make it right for you to keep calling me a fool all the time and to act as if I'm a terrible person.'

There was a long pause. Then Madrigal, to Yesterday's surprise, nodded and let out a sigh. 'Maybe you are right, fool— . . . Miss Crumb, I mean. After what I've seen, it's *possible* that you are more capable, and more considerate, than I gave you credit for. Perhaps I was defending Miss Dumpling against a threat that never existed. I may have misjudged you.'

Yesterday, without meaning to in the slightest, gave Madrigal a small smile. 'Did I just hear an apology?'

The not-raven gave a small chortle. 'Perhaps.'

'Oh, Madrigal,' said Miss Dumpling, who, it turned out, had been watching from the door to the kitchen. 'A witch couldn't ask for a more obliging familiar.'

She gave Yesterday a wink.

'Now, darling,' the tea witch continued. 'What do you say? Shall we cook up a Storm?'

*

Pascal boiled some water for Yesterday while she studied the recipe from *The Tome of Terrific Tea Witchery*. The tea spirit poured the water into a green teapot that looked like it had once been smashed on the floor then pieced back together. Along the fractured lines where it had been broken were veins of pink glue.

As Yesterday unstoppered the bottled rainstorm Jack had caught for her, a little jolt of lightning burst out and almost scorched her skin. She carefully tipped the foggy contents into the teapot, along with a sifting of will-o'-the-wisp sugar.

Lastly, she clasped her hands around the teapot.

'Remember, Yesterday,' said Miss Dumpling, holding

Pascal in her arms. 'Draw upon your passion, not anger for anger's sake, or else the storm will tear you apart.'

Yesterday let her mind fill with thoughts of Mr Weep, the Royal College of Witches, and Skelm's circus. A tempest of hate roared inside her, with the splinter of ice at its core. *I know you're there, anger,* she thought. *I know you're there, and I'm not going to feed you.*

Her mind turned from her life in the cage, the whispering crowd and the scowling Mr Skelm to the moment she had first met Madrigal. To when he had waved his wing over her padlock and she had stepped out, tasting freedom for the first time and feeling as though magic lay just within her reach.

A smile came to her lips. Defiance and hope and passion rolled through her body.

And she said the words of the spell.

'Tea, tea, sizzle and steep, may thunder crash and skies weep!'

There was a lightning flash and a thunderclap. Clouds of fog rose from the spout of the teapot.

She poured the teapot's contents into two rose-gold teacups on the kitchen table. The tea was misty grey, with a swirling vortex of blue in the centre. Miss Dumpling nodded at Yesterday, and they each took a sip.

It was a little flavourless, with traces of something like burnt wood. Once Yesterday had drained her cup, the sound of something crackling came from her belly. Her hair immediately stood on end with static.

'*Something* is happening, at least,' she said, patting her hair flat. Widdershins scuttled over with a hairbrush, and gave her ginger tangle of curls a quick, helpful comb.

'Why don't we try it out and see?' said Miss Dumpling. She led Yesterday through the tearoom and opened the front door. 'Now, remember,' she said, 'to bend the wind to your will you must seize on to your passion, your sense of power, without letting it turn into destructive anger. Allow the tea's power to churn through you, and then release it into the air, bit by bit. It will draw the wind like a hobgoblin to coffee cake.'

Yesterday did as her teacher instructed. Her fox ears stood upright as she listened to the rumble of the thunderclouds above and the spark of power sizzling inside her. The rain sprayed against her face, but still she listened to the spark. She fed that spark her energy, let it draw upon her strength, and it started to grow. Her veins began to glow a brilliant lightning-blue.

And then, everything went still.

'The wind awaits your command, darling,' Miss Dumpling said, gesturing to the sky with her open palm.

Yesterday felt like she was bursting with power. She flicked her wrists and the wind followed the curve of her hand, like a puppy being led by an invisible lead. She guided it round behind them, motioning for it to push them on, to give Dwimmerly End great speed, to carry them to the portal.

The wind behind the teashop grew and grew in fury as Yesterday fed it the energy coiling inside her. Soon the wind became a gust, a gale, a *hurricane* – the strongest wind that Yesterday had ever known. The teashop seemed not so much to run as to glide across the ground.

'Do you think the Storm in a Teacup could make the teashop fly?' Yesterday suggested, shouting over the thunderous wind. 'Then we'd make it to the portal even faster?'

Miss Dumpling grinned. 'I think attempting to make a teashop fly with your first Storm in a Teacup may not be the most sensible thing in the world. But I like the way your kettle boils, darling!'

Yesterday smiled up at her teacher. Her mind was swirling with ideas of all the different things the various brews in *The Tome of Terrific Tea Witchery* could do if they were really pushed to their full potential. What about combining different teas? What about mixing a

Storm in a Teacup with a Jumbling Jasmine? Could that let you turn into a cloud yourself? Into a wolf made of mist? Into an eagle with wings of lightning?

There were so very many options out there and Yesterday's soul filled with a whole universe of dreams, a pantry of possibilities.

She was going to try it all, eventually. She would not just be a great tea witch; she would change tea witchery for everyone, inventing her own brews and discovering new uses for old ones.

But first, she had to survive past the winter solstice.

Chapter Eighteen

The Afterlife's Immigration Bureau

With the wind of the Storm in a Teacup behind it, Dwimmerly End sped across the North of England, following the directions from Wirry-Boggle's map. First they visited Lancashire, then a small town called Beverley, then the tumultuous city of Newcastle.

At each place, Yesterday watched, puzzled, as the teashop trotted into one graveyard after another. Each time, Madrigal would swoop out of the window and return moments later, shaking his head somberly and saying, 'Out of order' or 'Not a hint of magic left in it.'

'What's out of order?' Yesterday asked in Newcastle. She peered out of the window at the graveyard beyond, in the shadow of a towering cathedral. 'From what we've seen so far, I'm guessing all the portals to the Land of the Dead are in graveyards, but what's the portal meant to look like? A tombstone, or something? And how do you know if it isn't working?'

But Miss Dumpling seemed far too distracted to give her a straight answer.

'Oh, bless my crumpets,' the tea witch murmured distantly to herself as she studied Wirry-Boggle's map for the five hundredth time. 'Maybe the graveyard in Edinburgh will have an operational portal? I suppose it's worth a try . . .'

Soon, the day of the winter solstice came, and they still hadn't found a working portal. Yesterday could barely say a word over breakfast, she was so choked up with fear.

Dwimmerly End arrived in Edinburgh in the early afternoon. Jack's bossy-watch had started barking about how little time they had left till sunset. *Hours! Only a few hours!* it howled at them, the sun already beginning its descent towards the horizon.

Edinburgh seemed like a city born out of a fairy tale, all winding cobblestone streets and dark, hidden corners. Its castle presided over the edge of a cliff, like an ageless king gazing jealously down on his subjects from a mountainous lair.

The place was hauntingly beautiful in the soft light of afternoon, yet Yesterday couldn't enjoy it. The splinter was growing larger and sharper in her chest, and with every step she felt a sting of pain as it bored deeper into her heart.

Yesterday and Miss Dumpling spread the map over the table in the kitchen. 'Looks like it's in a place called Calton Hill,' said Yesterday. 'Another graveyard?'

'Quite,' said Miss Dumpling. 'Onward, Dwimmerly End, to Calton Hill!'

The teashop climbed a steep road and hopped over a wall. On the other side, Yesterday peered out of the kitchen window at tombstones jutting from the earth like broken teeth, ensnared by moss and ivy. Madrigal circled around the cemetery. When he returned moments later, he said breathlessly, 'It's *alive*. The portal is alive.'

Miss Dumpling lit up and gave Yesterday's shoulder a little shake. 'Did you hear that, darling? The portal works!'

Yesterday almost sobbed with relief. She had nearly given up hope. Soon enough, Yesterday could see a stone tomb emerging from the undergrowth, crawling with roots and vines. Even she could feel the energy and magic pulsing from its earthen door.

Miss Dumpling flung the kitchen window open.

'*Katabasis,*' she called.

There was the sound of scraping earth and the stone door slowly opened, revealing a dismal-looking grey chamber, littered with dust and cobwebs.

'*This* is the entrance to the Land of the Dead?' said Yesterday.

'Indeed,' said Madrigal, swooping up on to the kitchen table. 'It is known as an Evanescent Elevator, and it goes all the way down.'

Yesterday swallowed, looking at the cramped, dark space. 'How is Dwimmerly End supposed to fit in there?'

Grinning, Jack said, 'Wait and see.'

Miss Dumpling muttered something, and a few moments later, the whole place began to creak and crunch. The kitchen seemed to be getting *smaller*, the walls and ceiling closing in. She poked her head out of the window to see that Dwimmerly End was indeed shrinking, its flamingo legs shortening as the rest of the shop curled into itself.

'Think of it as the teashop shutting up like a telescope,' Jack told her. Yesterday felt certain she had read that turn of phrase somewhere or other.

Dwimmerly End, now in miniature, waddled into the mausoleum. Miss Dumpling reached out of the window and pressed a button on the stone wall. It said, simply, *Down*.

'Hold on to your teapots, darlings!' said Miss Dumpling, and the teashop plummeted into the Land of the Dead.

*

Yesterday let out a small yelp of surprise, her stomach dropping as the Elevator plunged into the belly of the world. She clung on to the kitchen counter for dear life, while Miss Dumpling casually started doing the dishes.

Eventually, the Evanescent Elevator came to a halt, and the door opened up. Dwimmerly End stepped out and grew back to its ordinary size. Outside the window was darkness so impossibly black it made Yesterday dizzy.

The air was cold and carried the odour of rotten meat. Yesterday could hear growls and howls, screeches and squawks. And there was quite a bit of wailing too.

Even the fiercest monsters can be slain, she thought, as Dwimmerly End took careful steps into the inky blackness. *I'm Essie the Dragonheart, after all.*

The teashop soon arrived at a great, black wall, illuminated by torches with icy blue flames. Through the window, Yesterday could see a sea of silver shapes drifting towards it. She leaned in and gasped they were all *people*. People whose bodies were faint and flickering, with sad faces, who seemed more like motes of dust floating in the air than anything that had ever been alive.

'Ghosts,' she guessed out loud. 'What are they all doing here? What *is* this place?'

'Customs,' replied Jack. 'You know, like how humans in the Land of the Living need to show their passports at the border whenever they go to a new country? Well, if *The Pocket Book of Demons* is right,' he continued, and Yesterday made a mental note to find a copy, 'this is the place where they process the newly dead and decide which region of the Underneath they should be sent to. They call it the Afterlife's Immigration Bureau.'

Dwimmerly End followed the small procession of ghosts. Yesterday shook her head. 'You might have thought they'd try to make people feel more welcome after they've been through the trauma of *dying*.'

'Indeed,' said Miss Dumpling, folding her arms. 'They could stand to learn a thing or two about hospitality, that's for certain.'

'Well, luckily we're not here for a holiday,' said Madrigal, flapping on to his podium. 'All we need are our visas, and we can be on our way. Ready?'

Yesterday nodded. She, Jack, Widdershins, and

Madrigal stepped out of the teashop, leaving the comfort and warmth behind for cold and shadows.

Not a moment after they had left Dwimmerly End, a voice growled at them from above. 'Back of the line!'

Yesterday looked up and saw a huge bat with a snarling face and membranous wings. The creature's body was deep black, and its eyes were a cold blue. Huge juts of bone sprouted from its spine in a spiked ridge.

It pointed with a claw to a long queue of ghosts at the bottom of the wall. As Yesterday looked harder, she realised that the faerie ghosts in the queue were changing. With every moment that passed, any wings or horns or beastly ears were quickly evaporating into nothingness, scudding away with the air like smoke from candlelight.

'The faerie ghosts,' whispered Yesterday. 'They're losing the parts that make them look like faeries.'

'Indeed,' commented Madrigal from Jack's shoulder. 'You have Mr Weep's "leave your magic at the door" policy to thank for that. Bit by bit, everything that made you special in the world above – your face, your name, your memories, your magic – all trickles away.'

'But where does all that magic go?' said Yesterday. 'It must end up *somewhere*.'

Before Madrigal could answer, something squawked at them from above. Yesterday looked up and saw that more giant bat creatures were hanging from various perches along the wall.

'Those must be luna-gheists,' Jack said. 'They're in *The Pocket Book of Demons*, too.'

'Keep in order! No queue hopping!' the luna-gheists would cry at the ghosts, though no one showed any signs of disobedience.

Yesterday did not like being bossed about at the best of times, but she utterly despised being bossed about by beasts with such superior attitudes. Even worse, the queue seemed to be barely moving at all, and when it did, it was by an inch at most. Widdershins occupied himself by producing a feather duster from somewhere or other, and giving everyone a quick dusting. Madrigal squawked angrily at the automaton, making Jack giggle hysterically – which had Yesterday laughing in turn.

Then, the laughter was sharply interrupted. *You're very late!* Jack's bossy-watch shrieked at him from his pocket. *Two hours to go! Two hours until sunset!*

They looked at each other and grimaced. At last, they reached the front of the queue. Above a bronze door was a luna-gheist. 'Next!' it would shriek every so often, and the subsequent ghost in the queue would drift over and head into the office beyond, walking right through the bronze door as if it wasn't there.

Over the door, a message was etched in serious handwriting. *Abandon all magic, ye who enter here! And please have your documents available for inspection.*

The luna-gheist bellowed, 'Next!' and Yesterday proceeded to pass through, feeling the heavy weight of the demon's glower as she went.

On the other side was a small chamber and a high desk. The place stank of brimstone and paperwork. Behind the desk, peering down at them, was a gnarled demon with shadowy skin and wings. Her long, glinting claws seemed to be made of ice, not nail. Thin strips of ink-black hair cascaded down from her scalp, and her eyes were the colour of frost. There were two gigantic luna-gheists squatting either side of her like guard dogs.

'A fury! In the flesh!' whispered Jack. 'They're the first entry in *The Pocket Book of Demons*. Used to be sirens, until—'

'Death certificates!' the fury spat at them, extending a clawed hand.

Yesterday's mind went blank. 'Oh, um, we . . .' she began.

'We're not dead,' Madrigal cut in. He hopped on top of Yesterday's head, so he could be at the fury's eyeline.

His claws dug in a little, but she held her tongue. 'Just visiting, thank you very much.'

The fury stared, and spat out her request again. '*Death certificates*! All mortals receive one upon termination and are expected to present documents to the authorities. I am such an authority and you are, or were, such a mortal, so I must ask, *madam*, where are your death certificates?'

'As I was trying to explain . . .' said Madrigal primly.

'I wasn't talking to you,' snapped the fury. Madrigal looked utterly indignant as he flapped down to Yesterday's shoulder.

Yesterday looked up at the demon behind the desk and shrugged. 'We don't have death certificates.'

'Don't have death certificates?'

'No. You see, I'm not dead. None of us are.'

The fury looked Yesterday up and down and sneered. 'What did you say?'

'I said, *I am not dead.*'

'Whether I was ever alive at all is up for debate!' chimed in Widdershins cheerfully.

'Not dead?' said the fury, scandalised. 'You are *not dead*?'

Yesterday thought about the best answer to that question. 'Yes.'

'Wait, so . . . you *are* dead?'

'What? No! I said *yes*, as in yes, I am not dead. Not yet, at least.'

The fury considered this. 'But if you are in the Afterlife's Immigration Bureau, you must be on your way to the Underneath, so you must be dead. Or perhaps you are a witch with tremendous magical power, here in the Underneath to learn necromancy and other secret sorceries. *Are* you a witch?'

Yesterday stood up straight. 'Yes, actually, I am,' she said, feeling very proper.

'Hm,' sniffed the fury. 'Do you have your authorised witch's licence from the Royal College of Witches?'

Yesterday's shoulders slumped down again. 'No, I don't.'

The fury studied her with her fearsome, frosty eyes. 'No licence, no witch, as far as I'm concerned! Are you a Hound of Heaven, here to free souls and duel with demons?'

'A hound of what?'

Jack whispered in her ear. 'She's asking if you're a werewolf.'

'Oh,' said Yesterday. She paused. 'No, I'm not a werewolf,' she admitted.

'I have a wolf snout, if that counts?' Jack said.

'No, it does not,' snapped the fury. 'Logically speaking, if you aren't any of those things, then you must be dead.'

'I am *not* dead!' Yesterday cried.

The fury looked down at her stack of papers. 'I am afraid it's all here on the forms. There are three boxes you can tick.' She waved a sheet at Yesterday. 'See? Dead, witch, or werewolf. No other options.'

'Madam,' said Madrigal, 'I understand the Afterlife's Immigration Bureau often gives out visas to the living. If you could just arrange us a few, we would be out of your hair in an instant.'

'You want *visas*?' the fury said in a hushed voice, as though the word were not something one used in polite company. 'You think we issue visas to just anyone? According to the Dante Concordat, Article Twenty-Four, all mortals in a state of living are required to have a visa before entering the Underneath. But, unfortunately for you, they are reserved for witches and werewolves.' She thought about it for a moment. 'And, provisionally, dentists.'

One of the luna-gheists had risen up on its haunches and was studying Yesterday carefully. 'Dentists?' she said, trying to ignore the bat demon.

'Their profession is in short supply in the Underneath.

Mr Weep relaxed his immigration policy to attract skilled labour to the realm. Since you aren't any of the above, you leave me no choice but to mark you down as –' She looked from right to left – '*not applicable.*'

At that moment, the luna-gheist that had been staring at Yesterday rose up and garbled something in the fury's ears. Her expression slowly changed from outrage to some kind of glee. 'I see,' she murmured. 'I see.' The luna-gheist returned to its position. 'Well, it appears I have been rather careless.'

'Careless?' Madrigal repeated.

'Yes,' said the fury. 'Careless. Imprudent. *Unprepared.*'

Jack raised an eyebrow. 'Um, what is she talking about?'

'It seems I missed a very obvious exception in the handbook,' said the fury. 'Am I right in thinking that you are –' the fury thought for a moment – 'on a quest?'

Yesterday didn't reply. There was something in the fury's smile that she did not like.

'Yep, that's us!' said Jack proudly. 'It's a really good one, too.'

'Oh! Well, then, I have made a terrible mistake,' said the fury. She scribbled on a document and handed it to Madrigal, who took it in his beak. 'Questing individuals are exempt from ordinary immigration requirements. You may come and go from the Land of the Dead at your pleasure. Now, please return to your teashop and continue onwards. Have a nice quest!'

'Hmph,' said Madrigal, as Widdershins took the document from his beak. 'That's more like it.'

Yesterday felt strangely reluctant to leave. *Surely this is too easy?* As she turned to follow her friends out, her stomach crawled with worry.

If Yesterday had learned anything, it was that Mr Weep was not the kind who liked to make things easy.

*

'I never thought I'd be so delighted to see a piece of paperwork!' said Miss Dumpling, once they were back in the tearoom and had shown her their visa. 'Something the matter, Yesterday?'

Yesterday sat down at the kitchen table, still troubled by doubtful thoughts. 'It's nothing,' she said. 'I guess . . . I guess I just can't believe we're here. In the Land of the Dead. And that we need to go to *his* house. Miss Dumpling,' she said, looking up at the tea witch, 'I think I'm scared.'

Miss Dumpling smiled at her and joined her at the table, and Jack came as well, with Madrigal perched on his shoulder. 'Can I let you into a secret?' said the tea witch, her eyes bright and warm. 'I'm a little scared too.'

Yesterday smiled sadly back at her teacher. She tried to think of three wondrous thoughts, just like Miss Dumpling had taught her.

One: how lovely the tearoom looks when golden light shines through the windows in the morning.

Two: I might be in the Land of the Dead, but I'm with my friends, and I'm in a walking teashop, and I'm home. I actually have a home.

Three: even the fiercest monsters can be slain.

Widdershins said, 'Miss Yesterday, shall I ask Pascal to put the kettle on?'

Yesterday beamed at the automaton. 'That would be a great idea, Widdershins,' she said. She glanced around the table at Miss Dumpling, at Jack, at Madrigal. 'After all,' she continued, 'there's nothing that can't be solved with a pot of tea, a slice of cake, and some *very* dear friends.'

And so, Dwimmerly End walked through the opening gates of the Afterlife's Immigration Bureau and into the Land of the Dead.

Chapter Nineteen

Pandemonium

Beyond the gates of the Afterlife's Immigration Bureau, Dwimmerly End found a path meandering between grey hills blanketed with ghostly mist. The path was festooned at the edges with forget-me-nots, and as Dwimmerly End's flamingo legs trod upon them, they filled the air with a melancholy sweetness.

Here and there were grey, leafless trees. Shadowy demons like monkeys with the wings of crows were perched on their branches and cawed menacingly at the teashop as it passed.

It was so cold that Yesterday shivered furiously, and the splinter in her heart began to ache and ache. She wrapped her arms around herself, though it was no use. Miss Dumpling tried to get a fire going in the tearoom's fireplace, but it quivered and soon dimmed into nothing but gently glowing coals.

As Dwimmerly End marched onwards, the silhouette of a city rose up out of the mist like a waking beast. Black spires with pale silver light glowing from their windows speared up into the bleak clouds of the Underneath's sky. As they drew closer, Yesterday could see that around the city was a great wall, its stone battlements studded with spikes.

'The city of Pandemonium, surrounded by the great River of Teardrops,' said Madrigal from Widdershins' shoulder. The automaton was sweeping the floor with a broom, whistling a cheerful tune.

'We came here once,' the not-raven explained, 'before Mr Weep introduced his immigration policy. Delivered a birthday cake to a demon, isn't that right, Miss Dumpling?' He nodded ahead. 'That is our destination, Miss Crumb. Mr Weep's home, Thistle Hall, lies at its heart.'

Yesterday frowned at the grey skies above. 'If we are in the *Underneath*, why is there a sky? And clouds?'

'We are not really underground, Miss Crumb,' said Madrigal. 'Calling this place the Underneath is simply a metaphor. What you see above you is the Veil, the curtain between the Land of the Living and this one. I once read a ridiculous story about a ghost who built a hot air balloon out of the skins of demons. He flew it up to the sky and out of the Underneath and was back home in Paris by day's end.'

The city grew closer and closer and closer, until they reached the bank of the river, over which arched a bridge. The black towers loomed high and bleak above them. 'So, the mournful roses are somewhere in there,' said Yesterday, shuddering.

'Indeed, but we must not count our phoenixes before they've hatched,' said Madrigal, hopping off the automaton and on to the table. 'I fear that the most difficult part is just about to begin.'

Miss Dumpling chuckled breezily. 'Oh, Madrigal, darling, aren't you ever the beacon of hope?' She gave Yesterday a look full of devilish promises and dastardly plans. 'I thought it would be a good idea if the two of us prepared some witch-brews before you set off. A new tea, with which we shall get our hands on those roses without a hitch.'

Yesterday followed Miss Dumpling into the kitchen. 'What's the brew?' she asked curiously.

'Verdant Vanilla,' Miss Dumpling said. 'It lets one bewitch plants, as a dryad might. If you are going to break into a garden, it would be sensible to have a way of getting that garden on your side.'

Miss Dumpling clapped her hands and her copy of *The Tome of Terrific Tea Witchery* shot out of its cupboard, opening to the right page.

Verdant Vanilla
Difficulty Level: Considerably Tricky

Ingredients

One vanilla pod
A dash of will-o'-the-wisp sugar
A leaf plucked from a dryad's head
A teapot's worth of water (boiled, preferably by
tea spirit, salamander, or dragon)

The tricky part with this brew, Miss Dumpling informed Yesterday, was casting the spell. As she said the words, Yesterday had to imagine that she was a tree (or a flower, or a bush, or any kind of plant, really).

First though, Yesterday gathered the ingredients. She sliced open the vanilla pod with a knife, then pressed the seeds into a paste. She added them to a teapot and sprinkled in some sugar, hearing every single little granule tinkling against the sides. Finally, Mr Wormwood (reluctantly) donated a leaf from his hair. Verdant Vanilla would never give her quite as much power over plant magic as a dryad had naturally, but it would bring her somewhat close, for a short time.

'Picture yourself soaking up the sun's rays,' Miss Dumpling told her. 'Imagine your roots sinking deep into the earth. Feel the wind brushing through your branches, the rain tip-tapping upon your leaves. You and a tree are not so different, you know.'

Yesterday wasn't totally convinced, but she tried anyway. She put her hands around the teapot. Instead of imagining she was a tree, she imagined she was a rose. She heard the flutter of her delicate petals ruffling in the wind. She heard the wings of a bumblebee dancing carefully around her dangerous thorns. She heard the pitter-patter of nourishing rain on her leaves. As usual, she had no idea where the sounds came from. But her fox ears twitched merrily as they attuned to the magic of the spell, and Yesterday said the words.

'Trees and flowers, high and low, thrive and flourish and gleam and grow.'

The mixture simmered gently in the pot between her hands. She lifted the lid and took a peek. The liquid inside had turned into a pale green tea marbled with veins of liquorice-black. The air swirled with the scents of vanilla, of freshly cut grass, of springtime meadows.

Miss Dumpling leaned over and took in a whiff. 'Smells divine,' she said. 'Let's give it a try, shall we?'

Yesterday poured herself a small cup. She took a sip, her mouth filling with the tastes of vanilla and morning dew. It was a little soapy, she had to admit, but probably wasn't bad for a first attempt.

The magic sprouted within her. The veins on her arms became a spiderweb of deep forest green, the skin around them like cracked bark. She looked up and noticed a pot of herbs hanging from the kitchen ceiling. Exhaling gently, she blew the energy inside her up through the air towards the plant. It responded with glee, and immediately began growing faster and faster, curling out from its pot, blooming pretty white flowers. It felt like her heart and the flowers were tethered together, and the more she grew in confidence, the more the petals blossomed.

And then, she released the bond between them. The magic faded. Her veins turned back from green to blue. 'Perfection,' whispered Miss Dumpling, her hands pressed together with delight.

Yesterday breathed deeply, exhausted after feeding the plant so much magic.

They made one more witch-brew – another Storm in a Teacup – and stored it and the Verdant Vanilla in flasks in Yesterday's satchel, along with the Quirky Quill from the Goblin Market.

Mr Wormwood turned all the flowers outside grey and grew them to cover the whole exterior of Dwimmerly End, so it would blend in with the moorland. Then Yesterday, Widdershins, Jack, and Madrigal headed out of the teashop.

Miss Dumpling and Mr Wormwood came to the door to wave them off. *You're very late! You're very late!* Jack's bossy-watch was bleating. *Almost sunset! Almost sunset on the solstice! Forty-five minutes, maybe less!*

Yesterday tried to shut her ears to it; if she started panicking about the time, she wouldn't be able to do a thing. *Tea brews best when brought to a boil,* she reminded herself.

She felt something heavy drop into her satchel. 'Oh, I'm sorry, Pascal,' she said. The tea spirit had nestled himself happily in her bag. 'You can't come with me, I'm afraid.'

With a whimper, he floated back to Miss Dumpling. 'Victory is so very nearly in your hands, my dear apprentice,' said the tea witch from the doorstep. She blew them all a kiss. 'Remember, darling. Boil like a kettle and sting like a will-o'-the-wisp!'

Yesterday wanted to say something warm and clever and heroic, but she couldn't find the words. So instead, she went and threw her arms around Miss Dumpling in the second hug of her entire life.

Then she turned away from the teashop and, with her friends, began her march towards the gates of Pandemonium, towards the city of ghosts and demons, towards Mr Weep's garden, towards the mournful roses.

*

Pandemonium lived up to its name.

They had crossed the great bridge over the River of Teardrops and passed under the towering Gates of Ivory (as Madrigal called them). Now, they were surrounded by looming buildings made of rough, black stone. Light came from only a few windows here and there.

Demons strolled and gossiped, their claws glittering with jewel-encrusted rings, their hooves protruding from the ruffles of trousers and dresses sewn from shadows. Some had tentacles instead of arms, while others had a multitude of eyes or hair made of wriggling serpents. All seemed to be composed of darkness and ice. Some, Yesterday noticed, stole furtive glances at their group of outsiders, but then quickly hurried away and pretended not to see.

A train labelled *The Elysium Line* rattled overhead, carrying ghosts and demons. There were coffee-houses, pubs, and more lawyers' offices than Yesterday could count, promising to resolve disputes over soul contracts and summonings.

The ghosts, she noticed, moved slower than the demons, and did not speak to one another. Back in the Afterlife's Immigration Bureau, she had seen how the faerie ghosts lost their antlers and ears and claws, but they still had features and facial expressions. The ghosts she saw on the city streets must have been in the Land of the Dead for much longer, for their faces had grown fuzzy and indistinct.

'What's down there?' said Jack, pointing down a crowded street, his wolfish nose sniffing away curiously. He kept spinning around as they walked, trying to take everything in at once.

'That,' said Madrigal, their resident Pandemonium expert, 'is the Byleth District, where banshees shriek their melodies and phantoms sing the blues. And down there,' he continued, gesturing with his wing to a largely empty street on the other side, 'must be the workshops of the Ten Thousand Sages, who study all the ways to die.'

Then they turned a corner and saw it.

Crouching over the city, casting the place in its mournful shadow, was a mansion. Its slender towers and spires shone silver, as if made of moonlight. A flag flew atop it, a pale mare astride a field of black.

'I-is that frightful-looking place Mr Weep's house?' asked Widdershins, his cogs rattling.

'Yes,' said Madrigal stiffly, adjusting his position on Yesterday's shoulder. 'Thistle Hall.'

They followed a procession of finely dressed demon-ladies and gentleman who were making their way up a long, sweeping road, which curled up a hill and finished at the entrance to the silver mansion.

'Why do you think everyone's heading up there?' asked Yesterday.

Madrigal gave his feathers an anxious preen. 'Must be one of Mr Weep's famous parties,' he said.

'Maybe we can sneak in with them if we keep our heads down?' Jack suggested.

'I haven't been to a party before,' said Widdershins, curiously studying the fancy clothes of the guests. 'What do you suppose is the occasion?'

'Who knows?' said Madrigal. 'The demons of the Underneath love to throw parties, and the ghosts love to attend. I imagine it's the only way to break up the monotony.'

They soon arrived at the top of the slope. Guests were milling around in front of the entrance to the mansion – a pair of huge bronze doors. A demon footman stood before them, checking everyone's invitations on the way in. From the top of his head curled bison horns of ice, and between them sat a powdered white wig. He wore smart livery, with buttons carved from polished sapphires. When he smiled at a guest, he displayed a mouth full of fangs.

Yesterday and the others shuffled along with the crowd towards the doors, hoping they might slip through somehow.

'Invitations?' the demon-footman demanded.

Yesterday patted her apron theatrically. 'Ah! We seem to have forgotten our invitations back home. Don't you just hate it when that happens?'

The footman did not look even remotely convinced. 'If you don't have invitations, then you can get out of my sight,' he said pompously. 'Only *somebodies* are allowed into Mr Weep's party. And you are clearly not *somebodies*. Next!'

But Yesterday was not going anywhere.

Her ears pricked, she was listening carefully. She noticed, then, how he kept fiddling with his sapphire buttons, how his claws kept tapping as he played with the gemstones. She heard how his breathing was light and quick. She heard his heartbeat, knocking away in his chest.

He's hiding something, she thought. *He's nervous about those buttons of his. I wonder why . . .*

'Must I call the guards?' snarled the footman.

'That won't be necessary,' said Yesterday primly. 'You see, if you call the guards, I'll be forced to tell them that the buttons you're wearing are *stolen.*'

Her guess was confirmed when she saw the footman's eyes widening with terror. 'How did you know that?'

'Perhaps I'm more of a *somebody* than you realise,' said Yesterday smugly.

The footman was about to say something when he caught himself. 'Wait a moment. You're . . . *alive*, aren't you? Not a demon, or a ghost.' The footman stretched a fanged smile at Yesterday. 'Perhaps you are a somebody, indeed. Please do forgive me, and go ahead into the party.'

'That's better,' muttered Yesterday, and they marched past him and into Thistle Hall.

'Wow, that was much easier than I was expecting,'

said Jack. But with each step she took, Yesterday's worries that things were going too smoothly were getting stronger.

'Very well done, Miss Crumb,' said Madrigal from Yesterday's shoulder. 'Your powers are increasing with every passing day.'

Yesterday shook her head. 'I don't think they've improved *that* much,' she murmured. 'Madrigal, I think something might be wrong . . .'

But they couldn't turn back now; they were already inside the mansion. The bronze doors opened out into a vast ballroom. The centre of the ballroom was teeming with ghosts, paired up and swaying to some music. The edges, the walls, and the corners were lined with deep, dark shadows. Banquet tables brimmed with platters of strange dishes: fried wyvern haunches, grilled unicorn tongues, battered dragon livers. Horned creatures played eerie melodies upon poorly tuned pipes, while almost faceless ghosts danced along in a strange and dreamy rhythm.

'Goodness,' said Widdershins brightly. 'Isn't this grand!'

Indeed, it was a marvel to behold, but Yesterday would not for a second let herself forget where she was and what she was here to do.

'We need to move quickly,' she said. 'Something isn't right here. First the Immigration Bureau, now that footman – they've let us in here for a reason. Where do we start looking for the rose?'

'In my experience,' said Madrigal. 'Roses tend to be found in gardens, not ballrooms.'

'I know *that*,' retorted Yesterday. 'I meant, where do you suppose the garden actually is?'

Just then, at the edge of her vision, she saw something move in the shadows. Then, she realised the walls were not shrouded in shadows at all.

Rather, the shadows were *demons*, watching the ghostly dance from the side-lines. Some had antlers and pointed ears, like elves, though their antlers were now ice and their ears were wispy, like smoke. Others were small and fluttering like pixies, their wings glassy and delicate as frozen pond water. Others still were towering and round as trolls, composed not of stone but of darkness.

And it occurred to Yesterday that these demons might not be so different from the faeries who dwelt upon the surface. Maybe they once were faeries, somehow swallowed up by their shadows and Mr Weep's frost . . .

Yesterday's ears prickled as she became aware that the demons weren't watching the dance any more. They were all watching *her*.

She should have trusted her instincts. She should have run while she still had the chance. Something was deeply, deeply wrong about all this. 'Madrigal,' she said. 'Madrigal, we have to get out of here. We—'

The music suddenly stopped, and a new melody took its place. It was not the screeching tunes of the pipers. It came from very far away: the delicate tune of a violin.

It was a tune that Yesterday recognised.

The ghostly dancers locked in position. Yesterday looked at their frozen, featureless faces in terror. The demons around the edges of the room began to chuckle.

'How wonderful,' said a voice from across the room. Yesterday turned and faced Mr Weep, who was walking in, playing his white violin with its purple-black strings, followed by his gaggle of imps. 'The guest of honour has finally arrived.'

He stopped and lowered the violin. The ghosts parted from one another, bowed, then filtered out of the ballroom, leaving only Yesterday and her friends, Mr Weep, his imps, and the horde of demons at the room's edges.

'You knew we were coming, didn't you?' said Yesterday. Widdershins rattled with terror beside her. 'That's why we got in so easily.'

'Of course I did, Yesterday,' said Mr Weep. 'I've known for a long time, longer than you. I knew you'd work out that the only cure for my curse lay in my very own garden. I've been waiting for you to work it out and come to me. If anything, I was starting to wonder if you weren't quite as clever as I'd hoped! Still, you made it in the end – with time to spare!'

'We're getting out of here,' said Jack, reaching for Yesterday's hand.

'My thoughts exactly,' agreed Madrigal, flexing his wings, ready for flight.

But when they looked for the door, they found that demons had swarmed around it, cutting off their escape.

'I understand my footman didn't recognise you at first and tried to stop you from coming in,' Mr Weep went on. 'I do apologise. He'll be executed, of course. At least Immigration got the message. After all, we threw this whole party just for you.'

Yesterday's stomach twisted. She had played right into Mr Weep's hands. 'For me?' she said, and in a flash she understood the game. 'I may be here, Mr Weep, but that doesn't mean I'm going to do a single thing you tell me to.'

'I know you're not interested in my gifts, little cub,'

said Mr Weep. 'But this is an occasion for celebration, all the same. You were promised to me a long time ago. And now you're finally here, in Thistle Hall, where you belong. Not that boring old teashop.'

'*Promised* to you?' said Yesterday. 'By who? I'm sick of being left in the dark. Tell me exactly what you want with me, right now!'

Mr Weep tapped his chin thoughtfully. 'Very well,' he said, much to Yesterday's surprise. 'You've proved yourself worthy of the truth. Let's take a walk, Yesterday. I'm sure you'd like to see the mournful roses, now you've come this far.'

Yesterday glanced at the others. Jack took a step closer to her.

'Fine,' she said, fixing Mr Weep with a defiant look. 'But my friends have to come too.'

'Of course, of course,' said Mr Weep, spreading his arms in a welcoming gesture. 'There's room for everyone.'

OK, thought Yesterday. *I can play this game too. And, if he wants to lead us straight to the mournful roses at the same time, he can be my guest.*

She gulped down her fear. 'Very well, then. Lead the way.'

Mr Weep smiled and escorted them out of the ballroom, his imps scampering after him. They passed through the corridors of the mansion, past dining rooms and drawing rooms and libraries and kitchens, past grand staircases that no doubt led up to grand bedrooms, past rooms full of treasure: jewels, coins, antique clocks, priceless silverware, sumptuous robes, all strewn about without a thought, as though they were as valuable as rags.

Almost sunset! Jack's bossy-watch was snapping, muffled in his pocket. Mr Weep's imps cackled. *Twenty-five minutes! Twenty-five minutes left!*

Yesterday's breathing quickened as panic threatened to take over. Madrigal must have sensed it, for from her shoulder he murmured in her ear, 'Do not be afraid, Miss Crumb. You are not alone. Your friends are here with you, and we will never leave your side.'

A hint of hope grew in her heart. She nodded back at him, and pressed forward.

On and on Mr Weep led them, until at last they reached the end of a hallway. A set of grand glass doors opened to the outdoors – to Mr Weep's garden.

It was a serene place, the grass neatly trimmed, the bushes well-manicured, the trees straight and uniform. But for all its beauty, nothing was moving – nothing was *alive*.

Yesterday reached out to touch some ivy growing

on the wall. 'It's ice,' she whispered under her breath. She glanced around the garden. The grasses were twinkling blades of crystal, and the trees were frozen eternally in place. 'It's all ice.'

'Come along, Yesterday,' said Mr Weep, beckoning her to follow him along a cobbled path through the middle of the garden. 'There is ever so much more to see.'

Again, the muffled sound of Jack's bossy-watch came from his pocket. *Twenty minutes till sunset! Twenty minutes till sunset!* Jack winced at Yesterday, and she glanced back at him.

'There's still a chance,' she promised him under her breath as she followed Mr Weep and his imps. 'We can figure this out. Just trust me.'

Mr Weep was waiting by a raised plinth where two statues stood over a waterless fountain. One was of a woman. She had no head, as if it had been knocked off in a fit of rage. The other was of Mr Weep.

Around the fountain was a small patch of soil. Growing from it were the most beautiful flowers Yesterday had ever seen – roses with delicate petals of pure silver.

Mournful roses.

'That's them, Miss Yesterday,' said Widdershins. 'Just like in Mr Rottenpockets' pantry!'

'Don't do anything yet,' Yesterday whispered to her companions. Madrigal stiffened. 'Wait for the right moment.'

Mr Weep turned to her, his silver eyes twinkling. 'Welcome to my garden of tranquillity,' he said. He approached Yesterday, boots crunching upon the crystal grass.

Yesterday reached into her satchel and found one of her flasks of tea. 'Don't come any closer.'

This only made his smile grow. 'Very well. How shall we begin proceedings?' he said. 'I know! Regrettably, we down here in the Underneath do not get much by way of sunsets – the sun is so very far away, after all. But I have arranged something special. Just to remind us all of the *severity* of the situation.'

He pointed his finger towards the grey, featureless sky. A great orb of orange and pink and scarlet coalesced in the distance, dipping towards the grey hills on the horizon. Its light sparkled across the garden of ice, glimmering upon Widdershins' brass body.

'Is that . . . the sunset?' said Jack, jaw hanging open as Mr Weep's imps clapped and cheered. 'Did he *steal* the sunset?'

'A mere illusion,' Madrigal snapped. 'Do not give this demon any more credit.'

Mr Weep laughed. 'An illusion, yes, but an accurate one,' said the Demon King. 'A reflection of the sunset above, captured through a prism of ice. When it sets, so too will the sun in the Land of the Living.'

Yesterday swallowed hard, eyes locked on the sinking false sun. Time was trickling away. She slipped the flask from her satchel.

'Since we have no time to waste,' said Mr Weep, 'we must get started with your welcome gift, as a show of my immeasurable generosity! How about I reveal your real name? The one your parents gave you.'

For a moment, Yesterday forgot the sunset. She froze, consumed with curiosity, the flask left unopened in her hand.

'Bless my frozen heart, you don't even know who your own parents are!' Mr Weep shook his head in mock disbelief. 'I could tell you, if you want. Everyone knows I'm a showman, and I've been waiting for the perfect moment.'

'Don't lie to me, Mr Weep,' Yesterday said, trembling with rage. Mr Weep's imps hissed at her insolence. 'You're just trying to trick me, like you always do.'

'Would I lie to you, Yesterday?' he said. 'When you were left at that circus, your mother concealed it under a powerful magical shroud, hiding you from me until you were old enough to escape and look after yourself – a considerable trick, given that it was a *travelling* circus, but then she was a considerable witch. Once your little familiar friend here set you free, finally I could find you.'

'How preposterous,' squawked Madrigal from Yesterday's shoulder. 'You're not actually trying to tell me . . .'

'That's right, familiar,' said Mr Weep, as his imps cackled triumphantly around his legs. 'It was *your* fault. You allowed me to find her! All it took was a drop of her father's blood.' He rubbed his hands together, relishing the irony as if it were a delicious treat. 'That circus was hardly your mother's first choice, but I was giving chase, and she picked the best hiding place for you that she could, I suppose.'

Yesterday stared at him, scarcely blinking. 'Did you say you were . . . giving chase? After my mother?'

Mr Weep looked up at the statues, at the mournful roses. 'She loved this garden, you know,' he said. He glanced back at her, cocking his head.

'How do you know what my mother loved?' asked Yesterday. Her eyes went to the dipping sunset illusion. *We have maybe fifteen minutes left and he's trying to stall me.*

And it was working.

'Do you mean you *still* haven't worked it out yet? You may have heard that I once had a bride . . .'

And, in that moment, Yesterday knew.

She did not know everything, but she knew enough, and it filled her with horror. 'I've heard about *The Ballad of the Nameless Queen*, yes,' she said, shivering as the ice in her heart swelled. 'What's that got to do with me? Who was she, Mr Weep?'

'Oh, she was many things,' Mr Weep assured her. 'But most importantly for us, she was your mother.'

Chapter Twenty

The Goddess of Tea

Yesterday stared at him. It made sense. It made *too* much sense. And that's what terrified her.

Because if the Nameless Queen was her mother, then . . .

'That's right, Yesterday,' Mr Weep said. 'You are my sweet, precious daughter! And all of this –' he gave a grand, sweeping gesture to indicate not just the garden, but the castle, the city, the entire kingdom – 'all of it shall be yours someday. Now you see why I was so keen to bring you here! I hope you'll forgive my trials and games, little cub. All will be explained if only you'll give me a chance. What do you say?'

Yesterday couldn't speak. Could this creature, this hateful demon of ice and shadow and death, really be her father? And if so, what did that make her? Who was she, if not simply Yesterday Crumb, if not simply a tea witch's apprentice?

She heard Jack saying her name, reaching for her hand to give her comfort.

'What lies!' squawked Madrigal. 'I demand you supply some proof of these outrageous claims. The idea that Miss Crumb is your daughter? It is . . . well, it is simply ridiculous, sir!'

Mr Weep arched an eyebrow. 'Yesterday knows I am not lying. It may seem remarkable that a gentleman of my power and prominence would become entangled in matters of the heart. But I have not always been so sensible as I am now. I once spent my days watching the living, watching them fall in love and raise families. I wanted it so dearly for myself – not so different from you in your cage, Yesterday. Then I met your mother and – *oh* – I was in love from the moment I saw her. Next thing you know, we did what people in love do. We had a daughter. We had you.'

Yesterday's ears twitched. Looking into his cold eyes, it seemed impossible that there was any kindness, any love in him at all. But you did not need a Clairvoyant Coffee to hear the heartache that lay buried in Mr Weep's words. The wounds in his soul were still fresh. 'He's not lying,' she said, and her words came out as a whisper.

Mr Weep was looking off into the distance, as though he had been ferried away somewhere by his memories. 'The mournful roses were her favourites. I should have destroyed them long ago. But I could never bring myself to.'

Yesterday glanced down at the mournful roses. The path to them was unobstructed. And she had almost no time left. The false sun in the Underneath's sky was close to setting.

Now that she had seen the Land of the Dead up close, she certainly did not want to die. She could worry about her parentage later.

'Your mother loved me,' Mr Weep went on, 'until she decided that I was a monster who could never be loved. She took you and ran away – and then left you at the circus, with nothing but a book of faeries, thinking that would be enough to stop you from forgetting magic. She knew I would tear the realms of faeries apart to find you, that you'd be safer with the humans.

'I cannot have her, but I will have you, my daughter. And then ... oh, the things we will do together, Yesterday! The plans I have put in motion – you cannot even begin to imagine!'

'You're out of your mind,' Yesterday murmured. Again, she glanced at the roses.

'You fear me, and I understand that,' said Mr Weep. 'My office is Death, yes; but I have not always been so cruel as the gentleman you see before you. Many years ago, I rather admired the living. But no longer do I labour under any illusions. You have no idea how delightful being a demon can be, how blissful it is to give in to temptation. To let yourself *destroy*. You have anger in you, too, don't you, Yesterday?'

Yesterday had to admit, there *was* anger inside her. She imagined turning her magic on those who had wronged her, choosing hatred instead of the love and compassion Miss Dumpling taught. It would be a glorious thing, even if it were also terrible.

'But that's not who I am,' Yesterday said fiercely. 'Tell me who my mother was, Mr Weep. Tell me *now*.'

'Call me "Father" – I must insist,' said Mr Weep.

'Never!' shouted Yesterday.

Mr Weep smirked. She hated that she was giving in to his bait. 'I can tell you all about her, if you wish. Why don't we start with her note, the one she left you in your *Pocket Book of Faeries*?'

He produced a torn piece of paper from his pocket, full of looping writing. 'That can't be . . .' Yesterday said, groaning as the ice in her heart dug in deeper. She pulled out her copy of *The Pocket Book of Faeries* from her satchel and opened it to the front page, where there was only a corner of paper left, bearing the word *Yesterday*.

Ten minutes left, Jack's bossy-watch grumbled. *Ten minutes till sunset!*

'I never knew what the first word was, until now – nor how it was that you got your name,' Mr Weep went on. 'Shall we put the pieces together? *Yesterday*,' he began, filling in the missing piece, '*was a day I never saw coming, a day I realised I had to take you from your world and hide you in another* ... Shall I go on? Wouldn't you like to find out your *real* name? It says it right here, in black ink!'

'How did you get that note?' Yesterday demanded.

'I found that wretched book with its wretched note in the front and tore it out, brought it to her, and demanded answers. She fled, and I sent my demons after her. I suppose she never had time to write a replacement. Here, see for yourself.'

He let a breeze snatch the paper from his clutches, and it blew towards Yesterday, who snatched it hungrily from the air. She thrust it into her book – no more distractions.

'So, it's your fault, then?' she said. 'It's your fault

I grew up without parents – in a cold iron cage, put on display for people to laugh at and call names?'

'*My* fault?' snarled Mr Weep. 'I am not the one who stole you away from Thistle Hall, who left you with *humans*!' He spat out the word like it was poisonous. 'You have your wicked mother to thank for that.'

Yesterday scowled. 'You don't want to tell me who she is. You just want to make me feel stupid.'

Mr Weep looked wounded. 'Not at all. I will tell you everything. Utterly everything. But first, you will hear my offer in full. I sought you out because I need an heir. I need a *princess*. Someone who will rule the Land of the Dead for me, while I—oops! Almost gave away the *big* secret there, didn't I?'

He let out a snicker.

'But when I found you – at long, long last,' he continued, 'you refused me. I knew then that you had spent too long around humans. That you had become a strangeling. That you had become too fearful and weak to accept the gift I was offering. I had to give you a test. I had to ensure that you were worthy. I placed a curse on you that could only be broken using roses grown in my garden. I figured that if you could find your way here, you would truly be my heir. If you failed, so be it; you would become a ghost, and at least I would have a new pet to keep around the castle.'

'Why does everyone keep trying to test me all the time?' Yesterday burst out. She didn't care how little time she had left. She needed to speak her mind. 'Why can't people just let me *be*? The College won't accept me unless I pass their silly test. You put ice in my heart to figure out if I'm *worthy*. At least Miss Dumpling never did that. She accepts me as I am and helps bring out what I'm best at. She doesn't ask me to be anyone other than Yesterday!'

Mr Weep threw his head back in laughter. He turned to his imps, who roared along with him.

Eight minutes till sunset, Jack's bossy-watch bellowed. Yesterday shot Jack a look. Her eyes went from him to the mournful roses. Jack nodded, getting her message, and began to inch slowly towards them.

I have to keep Mr Weep distracted, Yesterday thought. 'But Mr Weep,' she said. 'You overlooked a key piece of the puzzle.'

'And what's that?'

'You forgot that I have no interest in being your heir,' she said. 'You can test me all you want. But I don't want your crown in the first place. I want to be a tea witch. I *am* a tea witch. And you can't change that.'

'Come now, Yesterday. You can't be satisfied with tea witchery,' he said. 'Something so ridiculous and unimportant! Besides, your world up there, the Land of the Living, is no place for neither-nors. That world hates you.'

'That isn't true,' said Yesterday. 'There are people like Miss Dumpling. There are places like Dwimmerly End. I'm going to be a tea witch, Mr Weep, whether you like it or not.'

'You are no mere witch.' Mr Weep scowled. 'You have my blood in your veins. You should be a *god*. The goddess of death!'

'Keep your ice and shadows, "Father",' Yesterday announced. 'I'd much rather be the goddess of tea.'

Before Mr Weep could reply, Pyewacket shrieked. 'Master! He's going for the roses!'

Mr Weep snapped his head around. Jack stared back at him, fingers still outstretched towards the flowers.

'Just ignore me,' Jack said. 'You were having a very important conversation just then. Wouldn't want to interrupt . . .'

'Pesky troublemaker,' snarled Mr Weep, and he reached inside his jacket.

In a quick motion, Yesterday lifted her flask to her lips. She drained it down in one gulp.

It tasted like vanilla and grass watered by the rain. *Verdant Vanilla*. Her veins turned a deep green as before, and her skin around them went hard and brown like bark.

She directed a blast of energy into the ground, guiding it towards Mr Weep. An enormous vine ripped out from the soil, leaving the earth cracked and riven. It coiled around the King of the Dead, hoisting him into the air.

'Well,' croaked Mr Weep, straining against the vine. 'My little cub has claws after all.'

Mr Weep's imps surged towards her, knives drawn. Yesterday concentrated hard and sent orders to the soil beneath them.

More thorny vines erupted from the ground, shattering the trees of ice. Yesterday directed them with her fingertips, astonished by how closely they followed her directions, by how much control the tea gave her over them. Knitting together, the vines formed a wall, barring the imps' path.

'The roses, Miss Crumb!' Madrigal cried, flapping into the air. 'You need to get one of the roses!'

'Jack, grab one!' she cried, bolting across the garden. Falling to his knees, Jack uprooted a rose and handed it to Yesterday, who stowed it in her satchel. Then, she noticed the Quirky Quill lying at the bottom of her bag. *Now, there's an idea,* she thought.

She plucked it out and dashed over to the statues of Mr Weep and the headless woman. And on the headless statue's foot she wrote: *breathe*.

The statue glittered green and shuddered to life. It leapt off its plinth and stamped its feet upon the ground. Meanwhile, the imps had scaled her wall of vines. The statue thundered towards them and kicked each one through the air and into the garden wall.

'Don't waste your time with *them*,' Yesterday commanded the statue. 'Get *him*!'

But when Yesterday turned to point at the Demon King, she saw that Mr Weep was laughing. He flicked his wrist and immediately the vine ensnaring him dried up and withered. He broke free from it and it fell before him, dead and brown.

'I am Death, my dear daughter,' he told her, turning to face the statue. 'You cannot use *life* to fight me.'

The statue raised its fist at the Demon King, but he simply snapped his fingers, and it fractured into shards. Each chunk of stone hit the ground with a *thud*. Yesterday let out a small cry as the Quirky Quill shattered in her hand along with the statue.

Mr Weep advanced on Yesterday. 'What was your

plan, exactly?' he asked, producing his violin. 'You have nowhere to run. That tea witch isn't coming to rescue you. She doesn't have a fraction of the power I command. She can't even leave her teashop! Let me show you what I can do, Yesterday.'

He began to play. Yesterday clapped her hands over her ears to block it out, but if there was one thing Yesterday Crumb could do like no one else, it was listen.

The violin's music seeped into her limbs. Her hands fell to her sides. Her knees lowered to the ground, and she was forced into a bow, as was Jack beside her. Even Madrigal, landing on Jack's shoulder, couldn't help dipping his head.

'Widdershins . . .' Madrigal whispered in Yesterday's ear. 'He's not under Mr Weep's control.'

Madrigal was right. The automaton was still standing tall. Yesterday remembered Jack's words in the Museum of Entirely Unnatural History, what he'd told her of Mr Weep's violin. *No being of flesh and blood can resist it . . .*

But Widdershins was not a being of flesh and blood. He was an automaton, hewn from brass and clockwork.

'What are you doing?' said Mr Weep, glaring at the automaton. Yesterday was sure she sensed a hint of panic in his voice. 'You will obey my music! You will obey my commands!'

Widdershins glanced around – at Yesterday, at Madrigal, at Jack, at the imps. 'Um. No,' he said. 'I don't think I will.' The automaton took a step forward and, with one quick twist of his wrist, seized the violin. 'I won't let you hurt them,' he said. 'I just won't!'

He stomped his clockwork foot on to the instrument. Its wood splintered and its strings snapped. Jack and Yesterday jumped up, their minds clear again.

'You worthless thing,' Mr Weep snarled, eyes wild with fury. 'Do you know what you have done?'

'I am not a *thing*,' said Widdershins fiercely.

'Yesterday! He's got a witching key,' Jack whispered, pointing to the iron key around Mr Weep's neck. 'We can use it to get out of here!'

'Distract him,' she told the others, slipping to one side.

The Demon King was staring at his mangled violin in horror.

'Well, Mr Weep, you tried, and that's what's important,' Jack called out. He reached into his pocket and produced a small yellow piece of candy. Yesterday recognised it from his laboratory – a Shining Sherbet.

'How dare you!' cried Mr Weep furiously. 'Such disrespect – from *children*!'

Jack tossed the candy in the air and caught it in his mouth and swallowed. 'Know what this does?'

He opened his mouth again and there was an almighty flash of light. Mr Weep recoiled in shock, staggering backwards, holding his hands over his eyes. Jack cackled like a maniac as Yesterday dashed forward and yanked the witching key off Mr Weep's neck.

'I've got it!' said Yesterday, as Mr Weep roared with fury, still shielding his eyes. 'Time to go!'

'Yesterday ...' Mr Weep moaned, stumbling towards her, half-dazed from Jack's blinding flash. 'I am going to count to three ...'

'How do I use it?' Yesterday asked, holding up the key.

'Just twist it in the air and say "Dwimmerly End",' said Madrigal, hopping on to her shoulder. 'Quickly now! The sun is almost set!'

Yesterday did just that. At once, a pumpkin-coloured door appeared before them and swung open. They could see Dwimmerly End on the other side of it.

'You did it!' Jack announced excitedly. 'Let's go!'

'Yesterday, you do not understand,' Mr Weep cried. 'The Land of the Living will never accept you!'

Jack, Madrigal, and Widdershins raced through the hovering door, calling for Yesterday to follow. Yesterday hesitated in the doorway a moment and looked back. 'It's over, Mr Weep.' She walked through the witching door and slammed it shut behind her, the key in its lock crumbling into dust.

A heartbeat later, the door vanished, and became nothing more than a swirl of dust on the wind.

Chapter Twenty-One

Break their Eggs and Spoil their Milk

Yesterday tore through the witching door, bounding breathlessly across the grey grass and into Dwimmerly End, still in the shadow of Pandemonium. Jack threw one fist wildly into the air in celebration as he draped his other arm around Widdershins' shoulders.

'Three cheers for Widdershins!' he bellowed. The automaton chuckled, casting his eyes to the floor bashfully. 'Noble destroyer of violins!' Jack grinned at Yesterday. 'How many people can say they travelled to the Land of the Dead, looked Mr Weep in the face, and lived to tell the tale? We're going to be *legends*.'

Almost out of time! Almost out of time! the bossy-watch yapped from Jack's pocket, breaking the moment. *Almost sunset! Almost sunset!*

The illusory sun in the distance was turning a

bruised purplish colour as it plunged beneath the horizon.

Miss Dumpling burst into the tearoom, drawn by the commotion. Pascal floated after her, steam puffing from his spout. 'Darlings!' she cried. 'Bless my crumpets, you're OK! Now, we have a Perfect Panacea to brew.'

She flung open *The Tome of Terrific Tea Witchery* and clapped her hands. All the teapots on the shelf behind the cake-counter flickered to life. They glided over the tables and chairs, and Yesterday reached for the nearest one – a lemon-yellow teapot decorated with painted sunflowers, lively and bright against the grey outside.

Yesterday studied the recipe, even though she had been memorising it for the past few weeks.

Perfect Panacea
Difficulty Level: Considerably Tricky

Ingredients

*One handful of petals pruned from a
mournful rose
One teapot's worth of unicorn milk (boiled, preferably
by tea spirit, salamander, or dragon)*

Just then, the whole teashop juddered. Everyone stumbled. Yesterday lost her footing, clutching on to the table for support. Her stomach dropped as the teashop plunged to the earth. 'What was *that*?' Yesterday asked as Widdershins helped her to her feet.

'Felt like Dwimmerly End sitting down,' said Miss Dumpling, a look of concern flickering across her face. 'Its legs sometimes seize up when it's too cold. I'll pop out and check everything's OK. You just worry about brewing your tea.'

'But – but what if I make a mistake?' Yesterday asked.

'Couldn't if you tried, my apprentice,' said Miss Dumpling lightly, gesturing for Pascal to pour unicorn milk into the lemon-yellow teapot. 'You've managed far trickier than this, darling, I assure you.'

Yesterday nodded and Miss Dumpling went out of the front door. Carefully, Yesterday took the rose out of her satchel and set it on the table. What little light remained from the sun was dimming. The ice in her heart would take her life in minutes, and she would become a ghost, without fox ears, without her face, without her name, without her memories. She would be trapped in the Underneath, Mr Weep's pet phantom, forever more.

She had to act now. But she only had one rose . . .

'Hurry!' Madrigal squawked, flapping on to the table beside the lemon-yellow teapot. 'If you want to break that curse, Miss Crumb, you have to do it now!'

Yesterday wiped her clammy palms on her apron. 'OK, OK. I'll do it.'

She reached for the flower. She pinched each petal and plucked it free, the rose offering little resistance. Then, delicately, she placed them in the pot of warmed milk, one by one.

She thought about how deeply she cared for Dwimmerly End and Miss Dumpling and the others, and how deeply they cared for her. She ignited that love and sent it flowing through her veins, all the way to her palms. Her whole body resonated with power. She reached her hands around the warm teapot.

She closed her eyes. The incantation had been burned into her mind for weeks, and the words came easily to her now.

'*In this pot, I brew life and give my breath. With this pot, I become the enemy of death.*'

Almost immediately, the petals wilted and released their aroma, filling the air with the sweetness of roses, along with other scents: forget-me-nots, willow bark, the soil of a graveyard.

Yesterday opened her eyes and looked down into the pot. The tea inside glowed the colour of moonlight.

'You did it, Essie,' Jack burst out. 'You brewed a Perfect Panacea!'

Yesterday poured the tea. There were only a few drops of very concentrated liquid in the pot, just enough for one tiny cup. 'Miss Dumpling, I think I did it!' she called through the tearoom window. 'Come see!'

There was no reply.

Yesterday looked at Madrigal, her stomach tensing.

'Miss Dumpling?' she repeated.

The front door swung open.

'I'm afraid Miss Dumpling is rather indisposed,' said Mr Weep, stepping into the tearoom. His imps followed, snickering. They were dragging something that looked like a statue.

It was Miss Dumpling.

Her body was locked and stiff, her skin cold and blue.

Frozen solid.

'What have you done to her?' Yesterday gasped.

Jack sprang forward. 'You're not supposed to be in here!' he protested. 'You can't come in without being invited. The teashop's protected . . .'

Mr Weep looked all around. 'Odd, isn't it?' he said

with a shrug. 'With your teacher incapacitated, it seems the teashop's magic must be starting to fail.'

Madrigal flew straight at him, his beak and claws outstretched, shrieking and squawking furiously, 'Turn her back! Turn her back!' He scratched and pecked but never made a mark on the Demon King. Mr Weep seized him from the air and flung him across the room. Madrigal crashed into the cake-counter. Widdershins dashed over to check he was OK.

'Do as he says!' said Yesterday. 'Turn Miss Dumpling back to normal right this second or I'll . . . I'll . . .'

'Or *what*, Yesterday?' said Mr Weep, brushing one of Madrigal's fallen feathers from his shoulder. 'You'll forget to put sugar in my tea?'

There was a smash as an orange, hovering teapot dropped to the ground. The wintry scene on the tearoom's wallpaper was turning colourless, lifeless: the trees were losing their rich, green pine needles; the ice-skaters were fading from view. The flowers on the tables were wilting, their petals turning dry and shrivelled.

Jack whispered, 'Dwimmerly End is . . . is *dying*.'

Yesterday could not believe what was happening. Dwimmerly End was the first place she had ever felt like she might belong, like she might have a purpose.

And now, she had destroyed the teashop by bringing Mr Weep's anger down upon it. She was going to lose Miss Dumpling. She was going to lose Dwimmerly End. The *world* was going to lose Dwimmerly End. She couldn't let it happen.

Mr Weep nodded at the cup in front of her – the cup containing the Perfect Panacea. 'Only enough in that teacup for one dose, isn't there?' he said.

Yesterday said nothing.

'It seems you have three options,' Mr Weep continued, as his imps pulled out an armchair for him to sit upon. 'Drink that tea and break your own curse. You have only a minute or two until the splinter freezes your heart, and you die, so no one would blame you. Or you could give it to your dear, beloved Miss Dumpling. Save her from her icy fate, and the teashop, as well.'

He gestured to Miss Dumpling's frozen form. The imps dragged her over to their master's side, her frozen heels scraping across the floor.

'Why would you do this?' Jack demanded, his voice breaking. 'Why would you want to ruin a place that means so much to so many people?'

Mr Weep raised a wicked eyebrow. 'You didn't let me get to option three,' he said. 'Once again, little cub, I offer you a humble gift. Take up your birth-right as my heir. Renounce this petty teashop and become a princess, surrounded by treasures and banquets and servants. I will lift both of my curses in a heartbeat. I will save you from death, and I will save your teacher and her teashop. But you must choose now. Soon your heart will become ice. Soon the teashop will die.'

Silent tears streamed down Yesterday's face. No matter what she did, she would lose. There was no way for her to keep what she loved.

Madrigal hopped over and flapped on to her shoulder. Widdershins joined them too, weeping small tears of oil. 'We will respect whichever choice you make,' said the familiar.

Jack took her hand. He opened his mouth to say something, but could not find any words.

Yesterday looked around at her friends, at the sad, frozen eyes of the woman who had saved her life.

How could I ever live with myself, she thought, *if I deprived the world of Miss Dumpling and Dwimmerly End?*

'There was never a choice,' said Yesterday. She picked up the teacup and walked over to Miss Dumpling.

Mr Weep leapt to his feet. 'You foolish, foolish girl,' he hissed. 'You think you are going to call my bluff, do you? You think that I will save you from my curse? Well, you are wrong. I shan't stand for any daughter of mine becoming a tragic little tea witch.'

Yesterday glanced at him. 'You could offer me all the gold in the world,' she said quietly, bringing the teacup to Miss Dumpling's frozen lips and pouring in its contents. 'I'd still sooner be a ghost than be your princess.'

She placed the empty cup on the table next to her, then took a few steps back, and watched.

Nothing happened.

Yesterday stared. Miss Dumpling was still ice, still cold and blue. 'Did I brew it wrong?' she murmured in disbelief. 'But I *can't* have done.'

Mr Weep cocked his head, a smirk twisting his lips as he studied the frozen tea witch. 'How terribly tragic,' he said, shaking his head in mock sympathy. 'And she had such faith in you, as well!'

The imps erupted with laughter. 'Silly girl, trying to mess with the Demon King,' snickered Pyewacket. 'See what it gets you!'

Yesterday was barely listening. She felt broken, shattered, splintered into ten thousand pieces. She had failed. She had failed Miss Dumpling, Jack, Madrigal, the teashop – everyone. They would all be at Mr Weep's mercy now and there was nothing more she could do.

She hung her head and let the tears fall. The room was silent, for a few seconds, but for her low sobs.

Then, there was a cough.

Yesterday looked up.

Her heart sang.

Miss Dumpling's blue skin was slowly turning pink. Her hair turned back to butterscotch-gold. She coughed a second time and her eyes fluttered open.

The pine trees and the snow on the wallpaper filled with colour again. The embers in the fireplace glittered once more. The flowers on the tables bloomed, and the cakes in the counter stood up, fresh and proud.

'Goodness, that was chilly!' the tea witch said, with a light shiver.

'Oh, Miss Dumpling,' was all Yesterday could say, and she threw her arms around her teacher.

'Darling?' said Miss Dumpling, her eyes brimming with worry.

Mr Weep let out a low chuckle. 'There wasn't enough Panacea for both of you,' he told Miss Dumpling. He gestured to the gradually dipping sun in the Underneath's grey sky. 'Clock's ticking, Yesterday Crumb, and I'm your only hope now.'

Miss Dumpling blinked rapidly, eyes going from Mr Weep to her apprentice. 'Yesterday! You ought to have put yourself first!'

Yesterday smiled sadly, shutting her eyes against the tears.

Then, the light paled. All became grey and still in the Land of the Dead as the sun finally set.

It happened immediately. Yesterday doubled over as pain shredded through her. It struck her in the chest, as if someone had stabbed her through the heart with a long, sharp icicle.

'Leave us, Mr Weep!' said Madrigal, as everyone else hurried to Yesterday's side. 'Won't you at least give us this moment to ourselves?'

'No,' said Yesterday fiercely, clutching her chest and brushing the others out of her way. 'I want him to watch. I want him to see the pain he causes and maybe once – just *once* – he'll see himself for what he is: the kind of monster that would rather I turned into some hollow husk, trapped in his miserable kingdom without any thoughts or dreams, than let me live my life the way I choose.'

Mr Weep did not smile. 'What good have dreams ever done anyone?' he said. 'You have seconds left, little cub.' She could hear the urgency in his voice. He pulled out a piece of paper from his pocket – it was the contract, the one she'd signed back in the woods. 'My contract has its escape clause. You can still pledge yourself to me and *live*.'

'No,' she said. 'If I'm going to live, it's going to be on my own terms.'

'Fabulously dramatic right until the end,' said Miss Dumpling, smiling through her tears. 'You truly are my apprentice.'

'Then you will die,' snapped Mr Weep. 'If that's what you choose.'

Another wave of pain travelled through her. Yesterday looked distantly at the contract in Mr Weep's hand. She thought back to that night in the woods, to that poor, lonely girl she had been only a few weeks ago. It was almost as if that girl, the one who had signed the contract, were someone entirely different to who she was today.

She caught a glimpse of her reflection in the teashop window. The proud outline of her fox ears looked rather like a crown.

'The funny thing is,' she said, gasping through flashes of pain, 'here I am, my heart about to freeze, and for the first time in my life . . . I can honestly say . . . I . . . quite like my ears. In fact, since I'd never have been half the tea witch's apprentice that I am ... since I never would have known Dwimmerly End if it weren't for my ears ... I would go so far as to say ... I actually *love* them.'

There was a sudden crackle of smoke.

The contract in Mr Weep's hand had caught fire and was burning at the edges.

'*What's happening?*' said Mr Weep, his face contorted with panic as he tried to put the fire out with his icy fingers. 'What did you *do*?'

Madrigal flapped up and read the contract. He squawked with laughter. 'Look, right there,' said the not-raven, gesturing with his wing. 'Second line. *I, Yesterday Crumb, do hereby grant Mr Weep permission to remove the fox ears I find so very loathsome ...*'

'What are you saying, darling?' asked Miss Dumpling, dashing to Madrigal's side.

'You don't see? The contract is only valid if she finds her fox ears *loathsome*. Since Miss Crumb just declared sincerely that she does not hate her ears any more, the contract is null and void.'

'But ... what does that mean?' said Yesterday. Warmth was flooding back into her chest.

'It means the contract is broken,' said Madrigal. And as he said it, the parchment burned up entirely, becoming ash and cinders. 'The ice in your heart has thawed!'

'No!' shrieked Mr Weep. 'She was just about to give in . . . She was going to pledge herself as my heir!'

Yesterday turned and faced him. 'I will never be your heir,' she growled. She reached into her satchel and pulled out her second flask of tea – the Storm in a Teacup.

'What shall we do, boss?' said Pyewacket, pulling out a knife. 'You want us to trash the place?'

'You want us to break their eggs and spoil their milk?' asked Lachrimus.

'You want us to burn their cakes and scorch their scones?' asked Bread-and-Slug.

But Mr Weep paid them no attention. He was advancing on Miss Dumpling, who stood tall and valiant against him. 'You shall pay a hefty price for this, tea witch,' he said, looming over her. 'If it weren't for you and this ridiculous teashop, the girl would have claimed her birth-right and—'

'Hey, Mr Weep!' said Yesterday, draining the flask of tea. 'I'm sorry to tell you that Dwimmerly End is closed, and I'm going to have to ask you to *leave*.'

The electric-blue light of the magic surged through her body, through her muscles, through her veins, down the length of her arms. Lightning crackled from her fingertips as she held up her hands.

She pointed at Mr Weep and bellowed, 'GO!' and electricity blasted out of her.

For a moment, the whole place lit up with the brilliant blue glow. The lightning arced across the tearoom, forking and flashing. It struck Mr Weep squarely in the chest. His face was a mix of fury and wonder as the blast sent him hurtling backwards through a window, smashing the glass into countless shards. His imps leapt through the window and scurried after him.

Yesterday lowered her hands, her fingers zapping with electricity.

For a moment, everyone was speechless.

Then Miss Dumpling said, 'I think we had better get out of here, don't you, darling? Dwimmerly End, onwards!'

The teashop jumped to attention and began to run, as a furious-looking Mr Weep scrambled to his feet. His silver hair was standing up on end. His suit was tattered and trailing plumes of smoke.

'You shall regret this, Yesterday Crumb!' he roared. 'See, now, the full glory of the King of the Dead! See, now, the power of the Underneath!'

With his words, ice began to spread across the

ground all around him. It grew up into great towering icicles. Then, at a motion from Mr Weep, they flew towards Dwimmerly End, a barrage of deadly arrows.

The teashop sprinted faster, dodging the icy spears.

'But what if the Demon King closes the border and blocks our escape?' cried Widdershins. 'I fear we're trapped!'

Yesterday looked back through the window to see Mr Weep's ice taking the form of different beasts: ice bears, ice wolves, ice spiders as big as horses. 'Destroy that teashop!' Mr Weep barked, and the horde of ice creatures came to life, racing after Dwimmerly End.

Something jolted through Yesterday's mind – an idea, wondrous and wild. 'Madrigal,' she said, 'you once told me that the sky of the Underneath is the Veil between here and the Land of the Living, right?'

Madrigal looked up at her. 'Yes. But what good does that do us?'

Yesterday smiled. 'Let's see.'

She dashed to the teashop's front door and flung it open. Channelling the power of the tea, she reached out her arms and felt a surge of energy run through them. The wind began to pick up at once, whipping up her hair.

A powerful gale swirled around and around

Dwimmerly End, awaiting her command. 'Take us up,' she asked it, splaying her fingers and pushing out all the power she could muster from them. 'Take us higher and higher until we scratch the sky!'

The wind obeyed. It picked up into a mighty, rumbling tornado. Thunder boomed from the clouds that had gathered around Dwimmerly End, and slowly, gradually, the teashop began to lift. Then, with a blinding flash of lightning, the teashop lurched upwards.

And with that, for the first time in its long history, Dwimmerly End flew.

Chapter Twenty-Two

It's Raining Teashops

'I can't believe it,' said Jack, laughing as Dwimmerly End took flight over the Land of the Dead. 'We're flying! We're really flying!'

'Anyone who sees us going by will think it's raining teashops!' Widdershins remarked, as the land below grew more and more distant.

'Just a month of magical education,' Madrigal said to Yesterday, hopping on to his podium, 'and look what you have accomplished. You must be a prodigy, Miss Crumb.'

'A magical *maestro*, I dare say!' Miss Dumpling added, and Yesterday went bright crimson.

Maybe it's in my blood, she thought with a chill, the revelation of her parentage flashing in her mind. *Or maybe it's like Miss Dumpling said: tea brews best when brought to the boil.*

For a while, Mr Weep's ice creatures gave chase. They sprouted wings and swooped after the teashop, talons outstretched, teeth glinting. But their frozen feathers were no match for Yesterday's storm, for a tea witch in full flight.

Yesterday beamed, revelling in her magic, adrenaline firing through her. She spread out her arms and let the magic swell. Blue light shot along her veins as she held the weather in her hands. She could mould it in any way she liked; she was limited only by the bounds of her imagination.

She cracked the lightning like a whip and lashed it outwards.

She struck one, two, three of the ice monsters out of the sky. They exploded like smashed glass, scattering shards of frost all over the teashop. Next, guided by her instincts, she ushered in powerful gusts to buffet the ice creatures and hurl them towards the ground, spiralling out of control.

She was riding on a zephyr of magic, and the power poured out of her with every flick of her wrist.

The last of the ice monsters soon gave up. They shrieked and screeched and fled back to the Underneath, defeated.

Meanwhile, up Dwimmerly End went, up and up

and up, gliding ever closer to the grey unknown that stretched above them.

'We're nearing the Veil!' squawked Madrigal, and a moment later the great misty border between the worlds enveloped the teashop completely.

Standing in the doorway, Yesterday closed her eyes and let the Veil roll over her, enjoying the feeling of it whipping through her hair, sifting over her face.

Everything went very still and quiet for a moment.

Then, there was a *thud*.

When Yesterday opened her eyes again, she saw that they had landed in the middle of a snow-laden field under a sky glittering with stars. A nearby road sign was written in Welsh.

She released her concentration, and the clouds around the teashop dissipated, allowing Dwimmerly End's legs to slump gratefully to the ground. Yesterday stumbled in the doorway, gasping with relief as the magic of the Steeped Storm left her.

'Yesterday Crumb,' said Miss Dumpling, joining her at the teashop's entrance, 'you fabulous little teacup. You broke your own curse and flew out of the Land of the Dead, all in an evening's work. If only the Royal College of Witches could see you now.'

Yesterday was speechless. It wasn't a dream. They really were back in the Land of the Living.

'What about Mr Weep?' she said. 'Do you think he'll come after us?'

'Mr Weep can send all the demons he likes,' said Miss Dumpling with a light yawn, 'but we shall fend them off every time.'

Yesterday hesitated for a second. 'When we were in his garden,' she said, 'Mr Weep said something . . . odd to me.' Miss Dumpling arched an inquisitive eyebrow. 'Miss Dumpling, he said the Nameless Queen was my mother.'

The tea witch did not answer. A little unnerved, Yesterday pressed on.

'It sounds completely ridiculous saying it out loud, but . . . I think Mr Weep is my father.'

There was another pause. 'Is that so?' said Miss Dumpling at last, as though it were of only the merest interest.

Yesterday cocked her head, trying to read her teacher's expression. 'You're not afraid of me?' she asked. 'Even though I could be Mr Weep's daughter? He told me it's my destiny to become the goddess of death. Surely that's a cause for some alarm!'

'Why should I be afraid?' asked Miss Dumpling.

'*Destiny* is a lie small-minded people tell themselves to justify avoiding risks. You can be a goddess of death, if that's what you want. But if you ask me, you are enchantment and gingerbread, not shadow and ice.'

Yesterday felt better after that that, and from then on, the night was full of tea, cake, and stories.

Miss Dumpling brought them all some Pearlescent Peppermint and, as they sipped at the frothy, chocolatey drink, they told her and Mr Wormwood the details of their adventure: how Mr Weep had laid his trap and led them straight to his garden; how Widdershins had so heroically seized his violin and shattered it against the ground; and how Yesterday had brought the statue to life and bound Mr Weep in a great, curling vine.

They chatted, they laughed, they even sang a song or two, and everyone agreed that there was no better way to spend an evening.

*

On their way up to bed, Yesterday thought of something.

'Jack?' she said. 'Do you have some glue?'

He went and fetched her a small jar from his laboratory. 'Here you go,' he said brightly.

'Thanks.' Yesterday hesitated. 'And . . . would you mind coming to my room for a minute? There's something I need to do, and I don't want to do it alone.'

Sitting together on the floor of her bedroom, Yesterday brought out the note she had taken from Mr Weep. Carefully, she slotted it into place, fitting it next to the torn front page of *The Pocket Book of Faeries*. With a bit of glue, she stuck the two together.

And then, she read it out loud.

'Yesterday was a day I never saw coming, a day I realised I had to take you from your world and hide you in another. It is my hope that this book will help you remember where you came from, but I am not so naive as to think that it alone will be enough to keep you from becoming a strangeling. If it were my choice, I would never leave you with the humans. But your father is the latest in a long line of powerful enemies, my dear girl, and they would all do terrible things to you if they got the chance.

Yesterday I decided I would run away from him and his kingdom. It is not a place for a child to grow. And I cannot hide from the Land of the Living for ever. I have caused problems, and I must try fix them.

But that is not for you to worry about. I will cast a shroud over wherever I leave you. It will hide you from

Mr Weep and you must never, ever stray from it – he is
bound to you by blood, and by his blood, he can track
you down. I will find you once it is safe. I will find you
and we will be a family.

Farewell, my sweet, dear girl. My sweet, dear Arabella.
With eternal love, your mother.'

The note ended there. Yesterday looked up, her
throat dry.

'Arabella,' said Jack. 'Is that your real name?'

Yesterday thought about it for a while. 'No,' she
said, at last. 'That might be the name my mother gave
me. But it's not my real name. It's not the name you
and Miss Dumpling and Madrigal and everyone else
know me by. My name is Yesterday.' She poked Jack's
arm. 'Or, Essie, to my friends.'

Jack beamed, then his face grew serious. 'Do you
want to go looking for her?'

Yesterday looked away. She didn't know how to
reply to that question yet.

'I want answers,' she said, thinking out loud. 'And
maybe that means looking for my mother. But I'm not
sure how to feel about actually meeting her. She
promised to come back for me. But that was *twelve*
years ago, Jack. She left me for *twelve years*. In a *circus*.
She must have known how they'd treat me.'

'I guess she probably thought Mr Weep and whoever her other enemies were would treat you worse?'

Yesterday nodded slowly. 'Maybe. Whatever her reasons were, I would like to know who she was, and what happened, but I don't need her to be my family.' She glanced up at Jack and smiled. 'I already have one of those.'

Chapter Twenty-Three

Christmas at Dwimmerly End

C hristmas morning came.

It had been a long time since Yesterday had woken up and remembered it was Christmas Day. But her first Christmas at Dwimmerly End easily made up for all those years of missing out.

First up were gifts in the tearoom, under a tree that had seemingly sprouted next to the fireplace overnight. Jack gave Miss Dumpling the Cake-O-Matic, which ended up splattering batter all over the kitchen on first use. 'Maybe I still have some kinks to hammer out,' he admitted, but Miss Dumpling thanked him all the same.

Madrigal gave Yesterday a book of poems by the late Faerie King Oberon (who was, according to the not-raven, an amateur, but nevertheless a good introduction to fey poetry). Jack gave her a little compass. The needle was spinning around wildly, unable to settle upon a direction.

'I've been designing and throwing out potential gift ideas all month,' he said, 'until last night, when this one came to me. I call it the Pocket Polestar. It'll always point the way home – to Dwimmerly End, that is.'

'Thanks, Jack,' said Yesterday breathlessly, marvelling at the glittering compass. 'I'll carry it with me wherever I go.'

Finally, Miss Dumpling gifted her a new teapot, upon which was depicted a rattling train, a roaring dragon, and lots of little painted ghosts.

'To commemorate your first quest!' Miss Dumpling explained. 'Strictly speaking, this is not *your* teapot – as you know, all tea witches make their very own teapot after completing their apprenticeship. But for now, I thought you could make use of this one.'

Yesterday thanked her; she promised to treasure it until she made a teapot of her own.

'And that's not all, darling!' said Miss Dumpling. 'Tomorrow, I shall teach you how to make a new kind of tea, and I'll let you pick which one.'

'Really? You'll let me decide?' said Yesterday, her mind sorting through the recipes in *The Tome of*

Terrific Tea Witchery. Should she learn how to make an Oracular Oolong, to see the future? Or a Neptunian Nettle, perhaps, to manipulate rivers and streams?

Then, she recalled her first night at Dwimmerly End, and the tea that had started it all.

'How about a Dreamer's Dandelion?' she suggested.

'A tremendous option! One of my favourites,' said Miss Dumpling, beaming.

Yesterday handed out her gifts. She hadn't had time to wrap them, but she gave Miss Dumpling a jar of perfume she'd made with Mr Wormwood, using lavender from the tea garden. Widdershins' present was a pink and yellow scarf Yesterday had knitted under Miss Dumpling's watchful eye, and Mr Wormwood's was a candle made from will-o'-the-wisp wax.

Jack received a tray of chocolate chip muffins. 'Essie, you made these?' he said through a mouthful. 'They're *wonderful*.'

And last, she gave Madrigal a tin of rich, brown fudge. 'Is that . . . fudge?' he said with faint surprise. 'It is certainly possible that fudge is my favourite. Miss Crumb, how did you know?'

Christmas lunch was mashed potatoes drizzled with rich gravy, parsnips roasted in will-o'-the-wisp honey, and a buttery pie stuffed with herbs from the tea garden.

Once they'd all eaten their fill, Dwimmerly End walked to a park and they let the unicorns out to pasture. Miss Dumpling made a tea called a Blizzardly Brew. She took a sip, then flung open the window and blew a frosty blue breath out towards the sky.

Moments later, Yesterday watched as snow began to fall, sifting from the sky like sugar.

When a thick blanket of white covered everything, Miss Dumpling clapped her hands together. Snow began to pile up, rolling itself into large spheres before stacking on top of each other. Soon, dozens of snowmen were standing outside.

Next, Miss Dumpling commanded a team of gingerbread men to leap out of the front window of the teashop, and stand against the snowmen. Once they were all in position, the two armies commenced a snowball fight for everyone's entertainment.

It did not take long for Jack and Yesterday to join in, dashing outside to start hurling and dodging snowballs. Miss Dumpling stood and watched from the doorway of the teashop, which Mr Wormwood had decorated with poinsettias, mistletoe, and holly.

All was laughter and fun, until a wayward snowball struck Miss Dumpling. The tea witch's eyes narrowed and for a moment Yesterday was worried they might be in trouble. But she simply put her hat straight, then commanded her snowmen and gingerbread men to set aside their differences and chase Jack and Yesterday instead, pummelling them with a barrage of snow.

The next day, the teashop re-opened, having travelled to Cardiff overnight. In spite of all the chaos and madness of the last few days, everything continued more or less as it had done before.

Their customers were as peculiar as ever. There was a ghoul who lived in the gatehouse of nearby Caerphilly Castle and wanted some last-minute loaves for his mother-in-law. A young wizard requested some Muffins of Merrymaking to be sent to the witch he was courting. An oracle sought a tonic for his overwhelming fear of pigeons (he was convinced that the little birds were conspiring to move against him). Miss Dumpling sent him away with a box of Jack's Caramels for Courage and a flask of Chamomile of Confidence made by Yesterday, with instructions to take a nibble and a sip each time his fears began to arise.

On their way out, each customer was handed a pamphlet for the soon-to-be-reopened Museum of Entirely Unnatural History. Miss Dumpling had made sure to mail the map from the museum's archives back to Pepperprew, along with a contribution towards the renovations and a box of Firepepper Fondants. Nearly all the teashop's customers said it sounded like a fascinating place, assuring Yesterday they would be looking forward to visiting, and meeting its most gentle and learned curator.

Towards the end of the day, Yesterday was walking into the tearoom with a tray of chimera cream vanilla slices for the last table of customers, when she saw a familiar face waiting in the doorway. She was standing impatiently, with her hands held behind her back, and a cross look on her face as if Yesterday had been keeping her waiting.

Yesterday's heart sank. It was Lady Saturnine in her cloak of feathers, her talons curling on the floor.

Yesterday delivered her tray to its table and walked over. She was ready for this.

'Hello,' she said. 'I hope you had a merry Christmas, Lady Saturnine. I suppose you're here to re-examine my magic.'

The Owl Witch ignored her, and instead held up a piece of paper. 'Are the contents of this communication accurate?' she asked, tapping her talons against the floor.

Yesterday bristled. 'I don't know what the contents of that communication are, so I couldn't say.'

'I have received a letter from the most estimable King of the Dead, Mr Weep.' Lady Saturnine clucked. 'It seems you have been rather busy since we last met, Miss Crumb.'

Yesterday's throat went dry.

'Is it true that, contrary to my express wishes, you used magic outside Dwimmerly End, specifically the magic of a Verdant Vanilla, and stole a mournful rose from Mr Weep's garden?'

Yesterday cleared her throat. 'Yes, it's true,' she said quietly. 'But I had to. Mr Weep put a curse on me and—'

'And is it also true that you used a Steeped Storm to defeat Mr Weep's ice monsters and escape the Underneath by breaking through the Veil?'

'Yes, that's true as well. But I would have *died* if I hadn't brewed a Perfect Panacea.' Yesterday was becoming desperate now. Lady Saturnine did not seem to be listening.

The Owl Witch's brow furrowed even deeper. 'Was this Perfect Panacea produced by Miss Dumpling?'

'No,' Yesterday confessed, hanging her head, 'it was brewed by me.'

'So,' said Lady Saturnine, who was now eyeing Yesterday with interest, 'you have now successfully brewed a Verdant Vanilla, a Steeped Storm, and a Perfect Panacea?'

Yesterday nodded.

'And the magic of these teas worked?'

Yesterday nodded again.

'As you know, any violation of College rules carries serious penalties,' said Lady Saturnine. 'Against my orders, and under the tutelage of Miss Dumpling, you – an unlicensed strangeling witch – performed magic outside this teashop.'

'Iris!' gasped Miss Dumpling, stepping into the tearoom just then with Madrigal on her shoulder. 'I didn't know you were here.'

Lady Saturnine gave the tea witch a withering look. 'As I was *about* to say, before I was interrupted ... These are serious crimes and are highly punishable.'

'Lady Saturnine, you cannot be seriously—' interjected Madrigal.

'*However!*' said Lady Saturnine, holding up a hand for silence. 'Any witch who in one month has learnt to make a Verdant Vanilla, a Steeped Storm, and a Perfect Panacea ...'

'And a Clairvoyant Coffee and a Jumbling Jasmine!' shouted Jack proudly, appearing in the doorway.

'Well!' Lady Saturnine blinked quickly. 'You clearly

have more than enough control over your powers. And, judging by this letter, you were able to use magic so proficiently that you gave Mr Weep a run for his money.' The witch raised an eyebrow, and the faintest hint of a smile traced itself across her lips. 'It is clear that Miss Dumpling was quite right – you must be a *wunderkind*, Miss Crumb, and for this reason I am awarding you with your witch's licence.'

Yesterday's jaw fell open. Jack whooped with joy and everyone in the teashop gave cheers and applause (even the customers, who did not know what was going on).

'Do you really mean it?' said Yesterday. 'You aren't even going to test me?'

'I don't think that will be necessary,' said Lady Saturnine. 'As a familiar once told me, when we witches stand together, when we trust each other ... we are inflammable.'

She reached into her sleeve and pulled out a small, pink rectangle of card, then handed it to Yesterday. In silver letters it said, *Miss Yesterday Crumb – Licensed Witch*.

'*Thank you*,' Yesterday breathed. She didn't know what else to say.

'Hmph,' said the witch, as she began to march out

of the teashop. 'See that I do not regret it. Oh, and Victoria,' she said, turning at the doorway, 'since the records will be corrected to state that Miss Crumb has in fact been a licensed witch since my last visit, you will be blamed for no misdemeanours relating to the carrying out of unlicensed magic, and will not be expelled from the Royal College of Witches.'

Miss Dumpling beamed. 'My darling Iris, I cannot thank you enough.'

But Lady Saturnine was already out of the door, her cloak of feathers swishing as she went. Without another word, she mounted her broomstick and she zipped off towards the clouds.

Once she was gone, everyone celebrated with some tea and shortbread in the kitchen. 'To Essie and her witch's licence!' said Miss Dumpling.

'To Essie!' Jack and Widdershins and Madrigal cried, clinking their biscuits together as though they were goblets of wine. Mr Wormwood soon ran in to see what the fuss was all about and joined in the celebrations too.

Yesterday, nestled cosily between Miss Dumpling and Jack, could barely process what was happening. One thought kept echoing through her mind. *I'm here. I'm not going anywhere. I'm really here for good . . .*

The next day, Miss Dumpling announced that they were finished in Cardiff. It was time for the teashop to go elsewhere. And so, Dwimmerly End closed its doors, picked itself up, and plodded out of the city upon its flamingo legs.

Yesterday sat by the window in the tearoom with *The Tome of Terrific Tea Witchery* on her lap, Widdershins on one side and Jack on the other. Miss Dumpling was pottering around, dusting surfaces and singing softly to herself. Yesterday poured a cup of Pearlescent Peppermint and popped a bit of Éclair for Excellence into her mouth, which let her read and remember things ten times faster (and also tasted delicious). Pascal slept on her lap, his shell warm and comforting, and she stroked his porcelain-white scales as he snored.

It had been her intention to read about brewing a Dreamer's Dandelion, but Yesterday was much too excited to concentrate on anything. She watched Widdershins as he helped Jack clean up the tearoom.

'Boys, I think you missed this,' she said, reaching down for a crumpled bit of paper that was lying on the floor. She smoothed it out. Upon it was written, *The Wild Feast returns this springtime! Book your tickets now!*

'What's the Wild Feast?' Yesterday asked, looking up.

'The Wild Feast is famous!' said Jack. 'It's a cooking competition the Faerie Queen hosts. Faeries from all over the *world* come to watch.'

'Really?' said Yesterday, a thought sparking in her mind. She glanced up at him, and then at Miss Dumpling. 'That sounds to me like a good place to make enquiries. About faeries who've disappeared, for instance . . .'

'You want to start looking for your mother there, don't you, Essie?' said Jack.

Yesterday shrugged and looked out of the window. 'It would be nice to finally get some answers.'

Miss Dumpling nodded. 'I think that's a tremendous idea,' said the tea witch. 'But if I am not mistaken, the Wild Feast doesn't happen until spring, March at the earliest. That leaves us two whole months to play with. Any ideas of where you'd like to go in the meantime?'

'Oh, Miss Dumpling!' Jack said. 'Can we go to Leeds next? Widdershins and I have been talking, and we think there'd be an awful lot to learn from a visit to the Automaton Arena Circuit.'

'*Jack*,' said Miss Dumpling, entirely horrified, 'automaton fighting must be one of the most barbaric practices I have ever heard of!'

'We don't want to *watch* the fights,' Jack explained. 'We want to start a rebellion! And learn a bit more about automatons while we're at it – I have some exciting theories I'd like to test out.'

Miss Dumpling shook her head and looked at Yesterday. 'Do you have any suggestions, dear? Somewhere that *doesn't* involve automaton fighting, perhaps?'

Yesterday realised that she didn't really mind. She sat back and listened as Jack and Widdershins and Miss Dumpling argued and chattered across the tearoom, and Madrigal flew in to disagree with them all. Yesterday just smiled to herself, wondering what adventures awaited her.

Though she did not know where the teashop would be heading next, she was reasonably sure the journey would be full of tea and cake and magic, and that was all absolutely fine by her.

Acknowledgements

Much as a cake is comprised of a great many ingredients, so too is this book the result of the support, friendship, and advice of a great many people. I am more than likely forgetting someone, and for that, I am very sorry, so please take this as a blanket thanks to everyone who has ever believed in me and supported my literary dreams (feel free to write your name in the margins, if that helps).

The first set of thanks goes to the various people in publishing who brought this story of mine into the world. Emily Talbot, my agent, who took a chance on a ridiculous tale about faeries and tea witches. Kate Agar and Aliyana Hirji at Hachette Children's Group, along with Lily Morgan and Gen Herr, whose keen editing eyes have a wonderful tendency to make it look like I know what I'm doing. Jane Willis of United Agents and everyone in Hachette's Rights Team, thanks to whom Dwimmerly End may travel around the world via translated editions. And finally, thank you to Samuel Perrett and Marine Gosselin for their incredible work on the front cover – I'm absolutely enchanted every time I see it!

My next thanks goes to my personal coven of witches, the friends who have supported me and my work, and are generally indefatigable sources of light and joy in my life: Steph D'Costa, Michael Maquieira, Hephzibah Adeosun, Uzair Khan, Lauren Beckwith, Sophie Rogers, Caroline Scully, and Sophie Lawrence. Endless thanks to those who read drafts of this story in one form or another, offering feedback and much-needed encouragement: Sarah Collins, incendiary writer of unbelievable talent; Zoe Adams, my friend and PhD supervisor; and Alison Lim, fellow adventurer and long-suffering law student. I will never take for granted how lucky I am to know you all.

Thank you to my partner-in-crime Walinase Chinula, whose friendship is baked into every word, line, and page of this story. Particular thanks to Oliver Hulme, who was this story's first reader, and its tireless champion ever since. Without you, I don't think I would have ever tried to get this book published. You would both make wonderful tea witches, no doubt about it.

I would also like to thank two of my English teachers from school – Mrs Bolton and Miss Hopkins (using teachers' first names still feels weird). I always dreamed of being an author, but they were the teachers who made me feel like I could actually do it.

Thank you to my sister Becky for convincing every human being she possibly could to give this book a read, from her co-workers to her book club to everyone in between. Thank you to my brother, Alex, a chaotic confidante if ever there was one. And thank you to my most wise aunt, Annie Hurley, an unrelenting source of entertainment and encouragement, who let me stay in her home when I was working on the book's final edits.

Thank you to my parents, who read me bedtime stories every night when I was small and never let me forget they believed I could do anything I set my mind to – including writing a preposterous story about a magical, walking teashop. A certain parent character in this book was most emphatically NOT based on either of them, I promise!

And last of all, thank you to you, dear reader, for giving this book a chance. May your days be filled with tea, or cake, or hot chocolate, or whatever it is that brings you comfort and peace: Dwimmerly End will return, and I hope you pay the teashop a second visit when it does.

Also available as an audio book!